Boardwalk in Disrepair:

The Splintering of Miss Patriotic

A novel by
Ami Feller

COMTEQ™
PUBLISHING
MARGATE, NEW JERSEY

Published by:
    ComteQ Publishing
    A division of ComteQ Communications, LLC
    P.O. Box 3046
    Margate, New Jersey 08402
    609-487-9000 • Fax 609-487-9099
    Email: publisher@ComteQcom.com
    Website: www.ComteQpublishing.com

ISBN 978-1-935232-14-8
Library of Congress Control Number: 2009936699

Cover design by babybluedesigner

Printed in the United States of America
10 9 8 7 6 5 4 3 2 1

"She who gives, can also take away."

— 1 —

The little red light flashes from the answering machine after the phone rang a few times. The unexpected caller is Ann Jo Serberus from the: Miss Patriotic Organization, a renowned American institution, situated in the historical boardwalk town of Atlantic City, New Jersey. Her message states, "I want to discuss an opportunity with you Anni that you are not familiar with. I personally held your credentials on file for a number of months here at the company."

After the dramatic pause, Serberus continues, "The Miss Patriotic Organization has undergone some administrative changes," so Serberus opted to hold Anni Seller's information until the appropriate moment. She wanted to explore a different career path, unlike any Anni was aware of. Suddenly, Ann Jo Serberus' voicemail comment triggers a whirlwind recollection for Anni. She remembered sending her resume' to the organization nearly a year ago in response to their need for a public relations coordinator working at their prestigious headquarters.

As Anni hears the voicemail, she instantly gets a chill down her spine. She thinks, this could be my big break! She replays the message to make sure she understood the point of Ann Jo Serberus' call.

Instead of the traditional office position Anni recalled applying for nearly a year ago, Serberus contacted Anni to consider taking over her previous touring responsibilities with Miss Patriotic. Serberus schedules a meeting with Anni at headquarters to discuss the details.

Anni is intrigued by the possibility…she thinks about how this could be a life-altering proposition. She calls Ann Jo Serberus back to confirm the meeting to learn more about this unusual opportunity, not advertised in any newspaper or website. This may be the rewarding professional challenge Anni was hoping to be involved with. Anni is fascinated that she was hand-selected to explore this avenue.

Anni arrives at headquarters for the initial meeting, and introduces herself to the receptionist and asks her, "What is your name?"

"Marissa," the young lady lights-up and is so pleased Anni took the time to meet her. Marissa responded very upbeat and conversationally and tells Anni she will show her to Ann Jo's office immediately.

Since this is the first meeting at the organization, Anni strives to make a refined impression. The thirty-five year old Anni wears a nice silver-gray business suit to this meeting and adds a scarf for a splash of color. She chose this outfit to complement her auburn hair and sparkling green eyes in an effort to make a great impact. Anni prides herself on keeping in fit shape and tries to take good care of herself. Her regiment includes using regular moisturizer with sunscreen to keep her face looking radiant.

Ann Jo Serberus and Anni shake hands and they exchange smiles. As the introduction concludes, Anni looks around her office which is rather plain. She notices one life-sized image of a Miss Patriotic from years gone by, but the rest of her office consists of nondescript file cabinets, cheap looking shelving holding a few binders on the institutional-beige walls in this office. Anni had been in many other offices of companies with lesser known reputations and some of those looked more impressive.

Serberus tells Anni, "I have been with the company for a number of years beginning as a volunteer, then gained employment and started going "on-the-road" for the past six or so years after I became a widow. My husband lived on the West coast for years, so we did not have issues with my travel schedule."

Upon the summary of Ann Jo's past, Anni notices Serberus appearance; she is hard-looking. Anni considers if being a widow caused the tool-chiseling crevices surrounding her features as if they were stone. Serberus mentions her husband died a dozen years ago. The sadness of life reflects on her stoic face. She wears her black-dyed hair in a tightly swept, low ponytail. Her hair is drawn back calling attention to the weathered skin of her forehead. Along, with her dramatic dark ponytail, she appears before Anni wearing an all neutral palate and pointy shoes. Anni observes there is no vividness in her conversation or her wardrobe. Her dental work seems to protrude from her face, making her look frail and sunken in. Serberus' skin looks like it had not been moisturized in years and she is in great need of hydration and air.

Anni contemplates, perhaps too much travel dries you out and her looks were the result of that.

Serberus tells Anni, "I received my doctor's medical orders not to fly, as I sustained two collapsed lungs in the past couple of years." While away during the tour, Serberus had to be rushed to a hospital in an unfamiliar state and then had to be cautiously transported back home to recover. The pressurized cabins infused with recycled air on airplanes, made breathing for Serberus exhausting—by this time in her life, it was not an optimal situation for her.

Serberus proclaims, "I know the tour manager job inside and out!" She affirms she knows it so well, since she was on the road for a number of years. Serberus proclaims how she loved the job, all the glory and distinction. Anni reads between her words to detect, her time has past. It's time to move on and let go…

Serberus briefly attests that the person who knows most about managing the tour, is Sonny Burgone, the one Serberus learned the ropes from. Sonny Burgone; the true knowledge holder of this position, had traveled along side 18 Miss Patriotics and worked first, as an volunteer, and than, as an employee for thirty years cumulatively. Sonny taught Serberus how to operate as a Manager out "in the field."

Additionally, Serberus mentions her own current responsibility for the organization transitioned, she now handes the internal planning and travel arranging of the tour. She confirms the event details with sponsors in her slow paper-centric way. Anni watches Serberus use her desktop computer, and sees how it puts her in a tailspin. While Serberus was looking-up something on her PC, she had trouble carrying-on the conversation simultaneously. "There is too much happening at once," Serberus chides.

In an attempt to keep the meeting progressing, Anni asks, "What about my credentials caused you to hold on to my information and call me nearly a year later?"

Serberus responds, "Over the past year, our needs here were changing. I used to report to a woman who made my life really difficult. Her name was Tina and she was a "power-monger." After some of the executives were gone and she was asked to leave, I was considered to take over her spot as the travel and event contact. I knew it was a matter of timing. So, your experiences working with people and your previous travel history make you a good choice for us."

Strangely, during this first face-to-face meeting with Serberus, Anni considers many of the questions Serberus poses are inappropriate as far as interview protocol:

Much of this interview focuses on Anni's personal life.

"Are you married?"

"How long?"

"Any kids?" Serberus pressed on.

As this line of questioning progresses, even an unethical as it was; Anni replies. She knows these are not standard questions for the interview, but this profession entails a lifestyle change; not a standard nine to five job.

Once Serberus makes the connection that Anni is newly wed, she persists on grilling her even harder; to the point of trying to talk her out of considering the opportunity. Serberus seems to talk Anni away from considering the job, since she anticipates the effects the job may have; to potentially ruin family and personal relationships due to the prolonged separation. Ultimately, she attempts to "unsell" Anni from considering the job proposition.

Anni thinks, perhaps this thought process was a red flare Serberus fires-off to mean something more; yet Anni is willing to move forward and find out what lies ahead with this intriguing position.

Anni considers, how often do companies call and seek out an individual these days? This is a career launch in the direction I was seeking.

Impetuously, Serberus comments to Anni, "Our meeting is progressing well." She likes her overall presentation; in terms of professional attire, articulate conversation and her smiling countenance.

 Serberus indicates in her day everything was done manually. "There were no cell phones or computers." Slowly, she turns around toward the simple, bracketed shelf behind her to show Anni a report. Serberus grabs a three ring binder opening it to display the wording and style. These reports are rather rudimentary, Anni concludes to herself.

 Serberus said she would show Anni another report and it was essentially the same content, just written about other events in different city. As it turns out these manually, templated-reports would become one of Anni's responsibilities, and Serberus preferred it be continued in this same lackluster format.

At the conclusion of the meeting, Anni reaffirms, "I am committed to making this opportunity work out well and am pleased you held on to my information for nearly a year to be considered for this unique endeavor!"

As Anni departs, she analyzes the discussion. She hopes the personality conflicts that Serberus referred to with her former colleague Tina, do not have similar implications with her potential alliance. She finds it strange that Serberus would talk about former colleagues in the organization at their first meeting. Anni trusts this will not taint her interaction with Serberus, since she tends to think the best of people and give them the benefit of the doubt, unless she has reason to believe other things…

— 2 —

It is 12:55pm according to the time stamp on Anni's answering machine, and Ann Jo Serberus calls. "This is to confirm the organization wants you to take over managing my former part of the tour."

Anni swells inside with relief and elation, as she can now realize her dream as a newly, hand-selected, publicity professional, upon receipt this verbal offer!

Back in graduate school, Anni aspired to become a celebrity publicist. Her goal is now certainly coming into view via this current proposition. She realizes from prior professional experiences she could hob-knob with the best of them: from the higher-ups and the in-betweens. She feels comfortable conversing with CEOs, media executives, directors of philanthropic groups and could maneuver with celebrities without being awestruck to impede progress. Anni had worked in environments where she dealt with a variety of people: C-suite executives, high level personalities, blue collar, and lower-class folks. Yet, Anni imagines all that is in store and then some, with this unfolding endeavor!!

After receiving the good news of the job offer that day, Anni hears a song on the radio, "I Believe I Can Fly." She stops and listens to the words:

"I believe I can fly, I believe I can touch the sky, every night and every day I'll spread my wings and fly away, I believe I can soar through the wind of the open door. I believe I can fly."

She wonders, does this song reinforce how excited I am or will my new office literally become a series of airplanes? As she eventually comes to discover, this "evocative" career path would be a life-changing one, not the office job she thought she might have bargained for ten months earlier when sending them her qualifications.

* * * * * *

Walking in her neighborhood with her loyal Shepard Labrador canine in tow, Susan, Anni's local mail lady pulls-up along side of to say hello to Anni and greet her dog, Selina. At the same time, Anni's friendly dog wanted to jump in her truck and check Susan and the mail out more closely. The social mail lady suggests that Anni should become a flight attendant. Susan draws this conclusion as she observes lots of travel-related mail she delivers to Anni's residence. She assumes Anni had an interest in travel.

Susan tells Anni, "It would be perfect for you to go all over the world." The mail lady's instincts were grounded, as travel is an interest and would become a driving force in Anni's career.

Mid October, the official offer letter arrives in the mail! The mail carrier looks very intrigued as she sees the gold crown insignia on the return address. The envelope is placed on the top of the mail pile in Anni's mailbox. When the offer letter arrives, this confirms the job is officially Anni's!

After signing off on the offer, Anni visits headquarters. There Anni meets her direct supervisor Cheryl Pearson. She is a smiley bottled-blond, with black, spidery-looking eyelashes (that remind Anni of Tammy Faye Baker), wearing a vintage-styled necklace and a teal-colored, boiled-wool jacket. Pearson was a former executive, exhausted from the fast-paced casino industry. Her current ambition, she recounts to Anni, "…is to scale-down and have a better quality of life," with her surfer-dude husband Jerri, whom she married late in life and together raise their young elementary-school-aged daughter. Pearson's primary aspiration is sustaining a good family-life; as her Directorship with the Miss Patriotic group is on a part-time capacity including Fridays off.

Anni could not believe the Director of an event-oriented organization is a part-timer! She thinks to herself—don't attempt to have any meetings with Cheryl or ask questions requiring her review on a Friday or on the weekends. She won't make herself available regardless of the fact the tour rolls on every day of the week…

As their first face-to face meeting in her office was unfolding, Anni notices the lack of ambiance here. There are no pictures hung on the walls of Pearson's office, other than a few pieces of refrigerator art probably crafted by her young daughter. Anni sees a magic-marker, highlighter-colored starfish holding her papers down.

The shelving in her new boss' office is empty. There are no nostalgic artifacts relating to the eighty-five year history displayed in this office. Her space looks very unsettled, as if you could not tell which organization she was a part of by viewing these office surroundings.

Anni considers whether Pearson is keeping the décor lackluster purposefully; is this position only temporary for her? This interior is dramatically different than the hall and foyer which reflect the pride and pageantry in the oil portraits, documents and historical items. These artifacts were displayed intentionally.

Anni thinks her new boss, the Director of Communications, should propagate the name brand and image on behalf of the organization. Instead it's as if Pearson does not want to get too settled by personalizing this atmosphere.

Trying to get immersed with the new culture, Anni asks Pearson, "What have your experiences working with Miss Patriotic been like?"

Since she had only been with the organization for roughly a year, Cheryl Pearson admits, "I have not spent an exorbitant amount of time with any of the young ladies." She indicates she had escorted the current Miss Patriotic on a dinner with executives at a restaurant in Caesars resort. Cheryl recounts, "Anni, you need to be prepared for this different world, because sometimes it is isolating."

"What do you mean by that?" Anni wants to clarify.

Cheryl illustrates her point by recalling a time she was walking toward the entrance of the restaurant at Caesars Resort, the clients surrounded Miss Patriotic, held the entrance door and pulled the chair out at the table for Miss Patriotic, but let the door close before Cheryl had a chance to enter. "The bottom line, is sometimes you are invisible to the client, so don't let that affect you," she interjects.

After the talk in Cheryl Pearson's barren office, Anni walks through the archive room which she thinks is an interesting anomaly. Every contestant and winner over the years has some memorabilia stashed there. Passing through this trove of history certainly is meaningful to many people. It an honor to be here in this moment, Anni believes.

She was told during the previous year there were 35 full-time staffers working for headquarters, but the board opted to cut back by two-thirds and scale-down to the current skeleton crew configuration. Also, a few years had past and the board opted not to assign a full-fledged CEO, rather the leader held the distinction of "Acting CEO" for nearly three years. They held him in interim status to see how the organization would evolve, presumably, out of the red.

Back in 2002, the then Interim CEO, "right-sized" the company by eliminating two Vice Presidents of Marketing and Operations as a cost containment and created a committee to save the organization; seeking further ways to cut expenses. Sounds like the ship had be unable to right itself, Anni pontificates. Hopefully the Miss Patriotic Organization will avoid repeating a similar cycle. Anni is counting on there being stability as she now joined the ranks of this American institution.

The current scaled-down workforce in "the organization" consists of half-dozen full-time employees, and a smattering of part-timers; including Anni's new boss, the smiley Director. So there she is: Pearson (looking like the Cheshire cat) happy to have Anni onboard.

During Anni's office visit, a handful of part-timers comment that the organization prides itself of providing good work-life balance. Mary Beth, a part-time employee, comments she is glad they permitted her to adjust her schedule, in order that, she can spend time babysitting her Granddaughter, and still contribute to office duties. After hearing this Anni assumes any relevant work-life balance would apply to her newly ordained responsibilities on the road as the newest Tour Manager as well.

Both Serberus and Pearson pat themselves on the back, by finding someone to fit the Tour Manager bill. They made the selection based upon Anni's level of professionalism, historical frequency of travel and effectiveness as a trouble shooter. For example, Anni had described to Pearson and Serberus that her finely-tuned instincts enabled her to deal with some risky emergency scenarios as a lifeguard in her younger adult life. Anni demonstrated to them she could handle various situations to ensure the well-being of Miss Patriotic while they are on the road.

Anni leaves the Miss Patriotic Headquarters, and as she stands outside waiting for her car to be pulled up by the valet staff; she is drawn to the bronze sculpture ahead of her. The sculpture is the likeness of the Miss Patriotic pageant's patriarch, Burt Wood. Wood had hosted about twenty-five years of the pageant, before being unceremoniously replaced. Anni notices the statue has a speaker next to it. Curious to know what the message was that would resound from the Wood's figure; Anni approaches the button and presses it…nothing, the speaker was silent.

— 3 —

Prior to Anni's addition as the newest manager of the tour, they had relied on the volunteerism of a state-level chaperone from Ohio. The state chaperone volunteer, Donna, knew the current "Miss" from her months chaperoning her in their home state on the state-system level.

Donna is middle-aged with a blond-bob hairstyle and slim figure, flaunting her active lifestyle. She is an "empty- nester," with plenty of disposable income and plenty of time. Those facets come in handy, since she loves to travel, so for her to be in the company of Miss Ohio, whom she was enamored, has been ideal.

Donna has a strong influence on Miss Patriotic. She does not feel the young beauty queen has had an appropriate connection with religion, so she impresses upon Miss Patriotic to become a regular church-goer. In addition, she encourages this young woman to undergo a Baptism. So, not only is Donna her chaperone in the sense of the pageant system, but she rises up as her spiritual guide as well. Donna is inclined to lead Miss Patriotic toward living a more spiritually, purposeful life.

The first time Anni set eyes on Donna was through the power of television. A few months ago, Anni eagerly watched the reality show highlighting some of the events Miss Patriotic 2006 was involved with during her year. Donna was instrumental in working with the producers on some segments of the reality television episode about life on the road with "her" Miss Patriotic. The premise of the segment, that Donna is involved with, deals with Miss Patriotic receiving a proposal for engagement by her boyfriend, Nate.

Nate, a cliche'ishly good-looking man with dark hair and eyes, has a mystique about him that Miss Patriotic noticed as soon as they crossed paths. The pair originally met when he was a judge at the Miss Ohio Pageant where coincidentally, she claimed the state title. Nate and Miss Patriotic's romance did not bloom for some months thereafter, keeping it under wraps for reputations' sake. The public was not made privy to their courtship. Although Anni finds out about this tidbit, she is told to keep her private life private temporarily.

Presently, Nate works in partnership with the 1996 Miss Patriotic's husband. Together they run a successful telecommunications software firm. He is very assertive and a go-getter, owning this business at just thirty-two years old and having an international presence in his industry.

Anni considers how Donna became so instrumental in their engagement process. She was wondering, is Miss Patriotic's biological mother alive? When Anni questions Sonny about it, since she knows all the details about the beauty queens, she informs Anni, "Miss Patriotic is not very close with her own Mother. She has a closer connection with Donna." There is almost a generation gap or disconnect, because her Mother is not connected to the pageant world.

In terms of the proposal, Donna provides Nate with her blessing. The engagement on the television reality show was then staged by the producers, but was to appear impromptu by the viewers. On the documented engagement, Donna is filmed in her hotel room as the happy couple knocks on her door to announce their big news (which she really already knew took place). In that engagement scene, Donna was to have a natural, surprised reaction.

Actually, this reenacted announcement takes place after Nate conspired with management of The Four Seasons resort five-star restaurant to create an exclusive menu for the two of them. With assistance from the restaurant, the couple is presented a menu titled, "Proposal Dinner" with their names emblazoned on the top.

In watching the show, Anni notices Donna has an intertwined relationship with Miss Patriotic. She also has a pretty significant ego to fill; satiable by making many decisions on behalf of "her" Miss Patriotic, who is a very non-decisive person.

It is concerning why she appears on this show in shorts and a worn tee shirt and hair in disarray? Donna is supposed to be representing the Miss Patriotic Organization, yet through this television episode many viewers could see her looking rather unprofessional and unimpressive.

A time later when Anni was at the headquarters, Serberus matter-of-factly asks Anni, "Have you ever met Donna?"

"I have only seen her on the documentary, not in person." Anni mentions to Serberus.

Serberus tone of voice changes to a more severe tone, "Donna was caught off guard, as she ordinarily wears very high-end $800 St. John's Knit suits."

Anni thinks to herself, the production and filming of the show was over the course of three months, should she have been more aptly prepared? Serberus tried to instill the importance of maintaining the image of the organization as a priority. Have the rules of engagement changed since then?

Serberus chimes up in a fury, "You should not follow Donna's example, since she was not working up to national standards. Rather, you should direct all inquires to Sonny Burgone, who is the veteran of the group and knows how to handle all situations."

* * * * * * *

So now Anni is formally on board with the organization for a week, her counterpart, Sonny Burgone, sends her the most congenial welcome card and acknowledges how Anni is now a part of a long-standing American institution. Through her thoughtful note, she singularly makes Anni feel a part of the team. It is a valuable connection, since she is the one Anni would also learn the ropes from. She looks to Sonny as a Sensei or mentor in the field. Sonny is the most tenured person, with nearly thirty years in this organization.

— 4 —

As early November is upon them, Anni receives an invitation to lunch with her Tour Manager counterpart, Sonny Burgone and Ann Jo Seberus, the Travel Planner, who together, want to provide her an overview.

At this informational luncheon, the focus of their discussion consists of some stale stories they tell Anni. Then, Serberus puts Anni on the spot, "Anni ask any questions you have."

-After scratching the surface with a couple of questions that Anni ad libbed to show she is engaged in the lunch conversation, Anni thinks, how am I supposed to know what I need to ask? What questions would be relevant considering how subjective this all is?

Anni interjects, "I am sure I'll have questions as I experience situations on-the-road as they occur."

The alleged overview from Serberus and Burgone, includes facts that most girls do not enjoy the gourmet foods provided at many of the black-tie events. Rather they opt for comfort foods via room service on the road in the hotel like: PB& J, mac & cheese and ice cream.

So much for the perception that pageant girls try hard to sustain their impeccable figures, Anni contemplates.

Also, the two of them tell Anni that she should feel lucky that the current Little Miss is not a minority. She quizzically asks, "What do you mean by that?"

Suddenly, they gossip tales of having to escort African-American titleholders to tons of Baptist church services, minority-run associations and professional groups, where they felt like they stood out as the odd person out. It was unique they were concerned about how they felt, since the appearances were not about them.

In addition, they rattled on about the beauty maintenance of these pageant queens being more challenging. Often times the beauty regiment included a family member of these minority beauties, meeting up with her on the road to braid her hair, do extensions or update a wig. The coordination was intensive and overbearing at times.

The pair commiserates about the two black Erikas, who were former Miss Patriotics. They differentiate between the two mainly by their personality traits. One of them was more of a challenge, since she had her own agenda and took off at night to indulge her own social life. Sonny said there were a few occasions that she was unsure of her whereabouts and it was this Erika who was a diva when it came to having her hair done when she demanded.

Anni inquires, "What are the accommodations like while on the road?"

Sonny recounts that she's slept in four-star resorts and on the floor in a cardboard box as part of a platform-related appearance on homelessness. "So there can be a pretty big difference, mostly the hotels are moderate. It depends on the sponsor's budget."

Sonny pipes in laughingly, "What happens on the road stays on the road." Serberus smirks at the thought of it.

There must have been tons of stories over the years, besides the select few items they tell Anni about. There are reluctant to share.

At this lunch meeting, they mention, "The crown is getting tight." They went on to elaborate this means that the current Miss Patriotic is in a state of mind getting ready to finish her reign, meanwhile the organization is gearing-up to crown her successor. So the focus is toward the crowning of the new girl, as the spotlight is dimming on the current Miss. At this point, she certainly has her mind set on post Miss Patriotic life too.

In their lunch discussion, Anni is told Miss Patriotic can only ride in vehicles covered by a minimum of $1 million liability insurance anywhere in the U.S. and the driver needs to be part of the coverage. Serberus advises Anni, "You are unable to drive her around when you're on tour." Anni asks about the viability of taking taxis and municipal vehicles and Ann Jo said those are acceptable. The assumption is municipal and commercial vehicles are adequately insured.

I had taken some treacherous taxi rides in my own former professional travels…Anni remembers.

Another question Anni posed to Serberus, "How do you both recommend I pack for such extensive travel?"

Serberus states, "Take three to four suits, one or two cocktail dresses at all times, and a half- dozen pair of shoes,"

Sonny adds, "Be sure to have plastic zipper bags and an extra alarm clock--

not to rely on the hotel's stash. The hotel clocks do not always keep good time and you can't afford to run late!"

Serberus then brings up an interesting topic. "Anni, the organization gave a wardrobe allowance to the Tour Managers last year. We have to see what happens with the budget this year. We should hear something around January." The verdict is out whether Anni would be eligible for a wardrobe allowance. Serberus would let her know if the Board will approve this allowance in the budget or not.

What a delectable perk, but I can't bank on it, thinks Anni.

Anni wonders how they do laundry while on the road. The ladies advise, "You send your dry cleaning out at the hotel." Anni considers: this can only happen if we are in one hotel long enough to provide the service, if we are in town for one night, it may be too tricky to get it done. I'll play it by ear.

They continue, "For the delicates and non-dry cleaning items, you need to hand wash. Make sure to bring along some hand-washing detergent. Miss Patriotic has the same system for her clothes."

That seemed so unbelievably domestic for a national beauty queen to do her own wash…

Anni notices while at the restaurant, Serberus is rather negative to their waiter. Anni has some friendly banter with him, trying to uncover the origin of his accent. He is obviously from another country trying to carve out a living in the States. Serberus abruptly interrupts in the small talk to bark out an order to him, "Get me a slice of banana bread immediately and I'll pay extra for it."

She does not seem to tolerate their interesting chatter reflecting Anni's ability to get to know people and treat folks with interest and respect.

After returning to the office following the lunch meeting, Anni meets with the Controller, who doubles as the benefits coordinator to complete HR papers. The Controller mentions, "Last year the organization laid-off 20 employees. I am personally glad that Cheryl was installed a year and a half ago. She seems like a good addition." My advice to you working here is, "Don't take the staff personally, especially during pageant time."

Afterwards, the interim CEO's Assistant comments, "It is better you are not from the pageant world in this organization, yet being on the road will be different." From this cryptic message Anni thinks she is implying Anni is removed from the attitudes that swirl within the office, since she is working beyond the walls.

The staffers affirm they were there to be a support system for Anni, if ever she has a question at anytime. She receives four business cards with cell phones and a couple of home phone numbers scribbled on back. Anni thinks having a decent support system, is important, since anything could happen being on the road 180 days and nights of the year.

— 5 —

Reality is starting to set in. To her delight Anni has the job associated with this organization that advances leadership development of young women providing scholarships to this segment of society. She feels an adrenaline rush, as she knows how hard she had to work to get a college education and even harder to pay for it.

The next few months are filled with a plethora of adventure, historically significant happenings, learning experiences and an immersion into the greater good of people; additionally uncovering the underbelly of a few ego-centric control freaks.

Now Anni needs to prepare. Most of the communication with Serberus consists of e-mails and phone calls to reaffirm information. Initially, the tone of these e-mails, Anni finds seems friendly. Yet, as Anni asks if Serberus could provide her an itinerary, so she has a better idea how to pack based on the places they were heading and to keep her family informed of her whereabouts, then the tides begin to change.

Serberus does not appreciate Anni requesting information. She tells Anni, "We tend to keep the Tour Managers on a "need to know" basis..." Serberus notes the silence after her comment, so she goes on to say, "...that way you don't have to worry about things that happen behind the scenes."

Anni analyzes that comment and figures it can be construed in a few ways. First, she considers how she may avoid stirring the mire in the day-to-day minutiae at the office. On the other hand, Anni thinks Serberus' bluntness may imply, her own need to be the "exclusive" information keeper and her unwillingness to share critical details. All Anni can do is file these thoughts in her mind, while keeping a discerning attena out for these signals.

* * * * * * *

Anni recalls at the meeting Serberus had mentioned to Anni, "There is a possibility you may receive an allowance for clothing, but the Board has not approved anything." In a recent conversation, Sonny tells her, "I don't wear suits to appearances anymore. The majority of my time I spend in slacks and a buttoned-down blouse," she comments. Anni asks Sonny about where she bought most of her wardrobe and Sonny indicated, "I acquired most of it from Chico's."

Anni concludes that makes sense, since that retailer is more appropriate for woman in Sonny's mature-age category. Sonny had told her, she is a grandmother a few times over and those garments tend to be wash and wear (and rather boxy and shapeless.) This enables women whose personal shape may have gravitated southward to hide it appropriately, yet Anni's athletic physique is still readily in tact. Anni recalls visiting a Chico's shop to see what they carry, and she saw the size tags were renumbered to make the clientele feel good about themselves, as a size 2 in Chico-speak, equates to a women's size 10/12 in standard American merchandising sizes.

In the meantime, Anni diligently goes through her own closet and dressers to assess the wardrobe choices with a fine tooth comb, as if she were her own fashion stylist. She carefully inspects her supply of suits, which had not been worn regularly in about a year based on her working in environments where the dress was more casual. Anni considers some of her suits that she could mix and match jackets with pants or a skirt, to get more mileage out of the garments.

She wonders what places and people they encounter along the way. She will find out when Serberus cues her in soon.

Over a few weeks Anni arranges 17 outfits for her month-long trip after she does a preliminary internet scan of the weather in the locations she is heading—realizing she and Miss Patriotic will be in and out of a variety of time zones, climates and day to night events.

Next in her packing process, Anni decides to carefully consolidate her vitamins. She knows she will need to rely on them as her panacea to the usual ills, with all the germs she would encounter, meeting people from all walks of life and being in a ton of airports, vehicles and unfamiliar places. Anni figures she has to keep her immunity and energy level up. There is no time to get sick on the road. She also hopes the same holds true for Miss Patriotic staying well all along the tour.

So, Anni takes an existing vitamin bottle from the basket in her kitchen, and reviews the types of vitamins on her shelf. There is the multi, B complex to avoid aches and pains of the luggage and items she would constantly have in her possession, E, for good skin and hair having to look good for the appearances, Ginseng, to keep her mind clear and continuously keep the two of them on track with all the itinerary components and vitamin D to assist the calcium absorption for strong bones (to avoid proverbial sticks and stones, too bad there are no vitamins to alleviate the words that could eventually hurt ...)

Anni counts out each pill, enough to account for each day of her long journey and then puts them all in the single container. She also tosses in a few lozenges and plenty of hand sanitizer. Anni is trying to keep everything compact, since traveling for a month is still limited to the amount of luggage the airlines regulate; generally two pieces of check-in luggage and one carry-on. Also, Anni knows she has to keep the luggage pieces within certain dimensions and most importantly less than 50 lbs. per case. Being well-organized and traveling simply is the key.

* * * * * * *

So December 1st comes and goes, as the current Miss Patriotic comes off tour to have unexpected surgery for an enlarged cyst on her ovary.

Anni's time on the road is off to a false start. Around Thanksgiving, Miss Patriotic goes to South Carolina visiting her beau when she experiences severe pain, then is rushed to the ER for an ultrasound uncovering the need for surgery. Following the diagnosis, she travels back to her home state of Ohio to take care of herself and recover.

A few weeks later, with her Doctor's nod, she heads back to work the week before Christmas. Anni is to join her with Sonny, the other Tour Manager, to shadow them and experience life on tour.

Beyond what most people believe or realize, Anni finds out, YES, this is a "real" job forMiss Patriotic. She receives a salary for the year of appearances on tour, which equates to about three times the paltry amount Anni was offered for her part managing the tour. Anni's life is dictated by an itinerary-Miss Patriotic's. The schedule is not her own, meaning travel and appearances can run all hours of the day and night. The office discloses to Anni they try to be sensitive to providing Miss Patriotic a reasonable amount of downtime.

She is employed to make appearances based on the parameters of the sponsors. Anni learns quickly that the majority of the appearances, roughly 70% are based in part by the value-based platform of that particular titleholder. Also, in the past few years Miss Patriotic has responsibilities of being the Goodwill Ambassador for one of the largest children's related charities. The remaining appearances are a mixed-bag of pageant related events, media and sponsor driven situations-depending if the price is right and represents the organization appropriately.

Prior to Anni's departure in December, she attempts to pepper Seberus again with more questions regarding: dress code, how-tos and expectations. During this period, she gets the "thumbs-up" on a wardrobe allowance which will be dispensed three times during the year! Anni is pleasantly surprised by this decision; a nice perk to have in lieu of the minimal pay.

There is no handbook for this job. So, off Anni goes on the tour without many rules, guidelines or parameters provided, but with a handful of some nice new articles of clothing that she bought from Liz Claiborne, Nine West and Ann Taylor. She determines the job will be extremely situational and subjective, so being able to deal with travel, people, and various schedule issues and challenges in real-time is critical.

As part of Anni's new duties, she plans to look for more alliances and opportunities for Miss Patriotic to be involved and get more positive exposure. Before leaving for the road, Anni wants to show initiative by mentioning to Serberus that she had a contact for a high-end car dealership who intends to place celebrities in their upcoming regional car show for "meet-and-greet" appearances.

Serberus, does not respond positively to the suggestion, which really is neatly represented as a good show of initiative. Rather curtly Serberus says, "I have already had a relationship with that group and there are more important events coming up the first weekend in February when that auto show is scheduled."

The idea is shot down in flames! Anni tries not take Serberus' abrupt criticism personally.

— 6 —

Anni's first day of touring arrives, and she is waiting at her home base with her luggage neatly positioned by her front door. At nine am, the allotted time, the driver is not in view. Fifteen minutes later her phone rings; it's the driver asking for directions. He says, "....The map I was given is not specific enough." Anni gives him details to find her pick-up location. It is a bit unusual a commercial limousine driver needs to call for directions with all the global positioning and mapping technology available these days.

On Anni's first travel day, she opts for comfortable, casual clothing; wearing a new light-blue velour pant suit with matching jacket. Upon arriving at Anni's house in the chauffer-driven limo, out strolls Sonny in her blue jeans and white top. Sonny, the veteran Tour Manager, runs up to the door with Anni's newly printed business cards emblazoned with a gold-foiled crown, stationary, photos of our celebrity, blank reports, envelopes, etc.

I need to have a large enough handbag with her to double as a "file cabinet" to house the publicity photos, current itineraries, travel information, contact lists, plenty of Sharpies on hand, as well as Serberus' and my own business cards. She mandated I distribute her cards to clients.

Sonny shows Anni her trusted tote bag. It appears it is a Louis Vitton, but it may be one of those knock-offs. Anni has her bag which looks like a stylish doctor's medical bag, stuffed to the gills with all her stuff, including things she needs at hand like her vitamins, she carefully packed, cell phone, charger, sunglasses, passport, airline frequent flier id's, wallet with cash for a month, postage for the various reports, granola bars and her toothbrush to freshen-up along the way.

The driver then safely delivers them to the airport.

While waiting at the airport before it was time to board their plane, Sonny offers Anni a cup of java, so they could chat about the tour and her experiences working along side more than a "Baker's dozen" of Miss Patriotics for nearly twenty years.

After chatting a bit about their own likes and preferences, Anni realizes, "We have similar tastes when it comes to ordering food and beverage." It was an informal affirmation, that they both have similar interests, considering; Sonny is someone Anni plans to emulate.

Sonny and Anni are sitting at their departure gate in the airport getting to know each other. Suddenly, Sonny receives a call on the company cell phone from Serberus. Anni hears Sonny profess they are both sitting at the gate to Serberus. Following the call, Sonny said Ann Jo Serberus is irritated Anni had not called her directly.

Anni is a bit taken back, as she was not told of a protocol to check-in with HQ at each segment of the travel and she was currently running under the guidance of Sonny's watch. Sonny did not indicate at each airport gate, she calls in to say, "I'm at the gate."

She is not yet on her own. So, she asks Sonny, if she should ring Serberus back and Sonny said, "It probably wouldn't be a bad idea."

Anni dials Serberus. Serberus answers sternly and said, "I was so worried whether you were picked-up by the car service or not and ready to head out on the flight."

She replies she did not realize Serberus expected call-ins for things going along "as intended." When Anni had asked for procedures and guidelines in their meetings this was not mentioned.

Serberus proclaims, "I need to have a comfort level all along." So, from then on, Anni planned to call in to Serberus to let her know she is heading on the road or stepping on or off the airplane, etc., etc.

My business philosophy is "Keep it simple." Intuitively, Anni was intending to call with significant updates, not complicate things by merely stating she was sitting at a gate, which would become the first airport gate in the series of many…So erring on the side of "no news is good news," is obviously not what Ann Jo Serberus wants.

When they arrive at the airport for the events in Florida, the women are greeted by Jon, the national contact for the anti-drunk driving organization, sponsoring these related appearances they are in town for. Their group arranged the limo waiting curbside with Miss Patriotic in it. Along the curb was a police trooper escort too. Upon setting her eyes on Miss Patriotic in person for the first time, Anni notices she's wearing black yoga-style pant, a beige sweater with bell sleeves covering her manicured red nails and brown-hiking shoes. Her arms are folded as she seems to be applying pressure on her abdomen.

Waiting in the limo with Miss Patriotic is the eccentric Dora Cost. Anni thinks she seems unconventional from the first glance of her, because she was wearing a black and yellow, geometric, color-block 80's styled suit. Dora is also a volunteer in the Florida chapter for the anti-drunk driving organization. As a double-whammy she was also affiliated with the pageant system in Florida. Her daughter had competed in Miss Florida pageant a few years ago prior to her life being abruptly cut short by a driver under the influence. So, in her honor, Dora became a local advocate.

Dora very amorously grabs and hugs Sonny, "I wasn't sure who is Sonny and who is Anni," as she grabbed any one of them and hugs anyway.

What a bold greeting from a stranger.

After the greetings and hugs, they head on the road and make a pit stop at a local McD's to get Miss Patriotic an ice cream cone and Anni a salad, as she hadn't eaten lunch yet and is ravenous. The stretch limo is too big to make it through the winding drive-through, so Sonny and Anni exit the car and go inside to the counter to order. A bit of commotion goes on outside as the locals are clamoring to know who is in the tinted out limousine at Mc D's. Inside, Anni notices the worker at the counter was a bit confused, as he appeared to be a young-person with Down's syndrome who needs his Supervisor to work the ice cream machine to fill their order.

Miss Patriotic was not at her usual energy level, just coming back to work on tour following the two-week recovery, yet devoured the ice cream cone. Sonny observes how she is generally more vibrant, but needed a lot of breaks and naps throughout her reigning year even before the medical set-back. The flight really made her feel uncomfortable. She is crampy and has a severe migraine headache.

Dora chimes in that she had a remedy available. She detours the driver to head over to her personal herbalist. Using these services, Dora contends, "I have not seen a Western-style medical doctor in twenty-five years and I don't bother with medical insurance."

Anni's intuition of Dora being eccentric is continuing to crystallize.

So, over the bumpy roads and into the tropical, wooded jungle area they go via the limo to a trailer park community in the middle of nowhere. The driver is in search of Dora's herbalist to make Miss Patriotic feel better. Miss Patriotic obliges Dora's idea, since Sonny, who is supposed to be managing the situation does not have any alternative solution to make her feel better. They pull up to see a few folks with dirty wife-beater undershirts roaming around the dust and gravel driveway, certainly not intended for a multi-axel limousine to be trudging through. The car stops near a non-descript shack that Dora indicates is where the herbalist is located. She and Miss Patriotic go in, as Sonny stays behind to finish her ranch chicken wrap and ice cream and Anni her protein-laced salad.

After fifteen minutes, there was no sign of Miss Patriotic or Dora, so Sonny and Anni decide to check out the situation. When they enter, they notice inside the herbalist shack is like a voodoo ceremony, there is a leader like a shaman, waving some sticks around Miss Patriotic's arm and pressing on alleged pressure points while reciting some chant-like mantra. The herbalist and her disciples, offer Miss Patriotic bottles and vials of liquid herbs to ward away the pain and a handful of brochures to read up on these remedies that cure everything from stomach ailments to schizophrenia.

Shortly after the ceremony concludes, they all were back in the limousine. On the road for half an hour, Miss Patriotic pipes-up that she realizes her purse was left behind at the herbalist's place. The limo is too far on the highway to turn back, so Sonny requests the state police troopers make the run. Unwillingly, they do it, reminding them, under their breath, "This task is using taxpayers' money for their time, to rescue Miss Patriotic's purse!"

While chatting during the limo ride with Miss Patriotic, she mentions to Anni, how she has become the best of friends with Chambre, formerly Miss Patriotic in 1996. Chambre's husband is Nate's business partner.

How cozy is that connection? Anni ponders.

It was Chambre's wedding anniversary, so Miss Patriotic dials her up on her hot-pink cell phone and asks Anni and Sonny to sing "Happy Anniversary" in the tune of "Happy Birthday." It goes over well.

Sonny mentions how friendly she became with Chambre' after traveling with her during her year. She recently sent her a designer throw pillow with three little lambs on it to represent her three young boys after giving birth to the most recent one.

As Anni and Miss Patriotic talk along their ride, Anni is relieved to hear how down-to-earth Miss Patriotic is during their conversations. She knows how important it was to have a prestigious outward appearance, so Miss Patriotic places much time obtaining the right style of clothes. Yet, she tells Anni she had no problem picking-up eight or so St. John's knit suits from the local consignment shop near her hometown. It cost her $700 for the group of them. Normally, each is $500.

Anni is impressed with Miss Patriotic that she realizes you don't have to spend a million to look like a million. The irony is that Anni knows that headquarters provides Miss Patriotic a considerable sum of money allocated for her annual wardrobe. Perhaps, Miss Patriotic is trying to maximize her budget.

At the appearance that evening, under Sonny's watch, the limo is filled with many people Dora invited, her friend, her nieces; who had been state pageant girls and now are pursuing careers as lobbyists in N.Y. and D.C., security detail and halfway to the dinner, Dora has the driver stop to pick-up her daughter and granddaughter. She insists Miss Patriotic pose with her granddaughter, who will not sit still in this moving vehicle.

By Dora's urging, this little girl was forced to put on her girliest dress and a tiara to act like a mini "Miss Patriotic." Yet, when Miss Patriotic asks the young girl what she wants to be when she grows up, the girl says, "A cowboy at the rodeo." She talks about roping animals like her brothers.

Anni conjures images in her own mind of this little girl romping around barefoot in the dusty fenced in ranch, with her hair all flyaway-in need of a good bath. Sometimes you can't take the country out of the baby bumpkin.

After what seemed like a never-ending limousine drive from Lakeland to the special restaurant, they pull-up in front of a Swiss chateau-looking building. The welcome dinner was concocted by Dora Cost. She took Miss Patriotic and the assembled entourage across town to be sure to take her to "the best place." Miss Patriotic was reeling from this extremely, long car ride.

The restaurant was set-back off the main road. Dora and Jon mention many celebrities had dined here before. Dora recounted, "Michael Jackson had flown in here on a small private plane on an old landing strip out back." The General Manager nods as he greets the group out by the entrance.

Based on Miss Patriotic's insistence, Anni sits next to her to keep her company at the long, rustic wooden table. She appreciates the gesture. They notice everyone has different dishware at their place setting. Not only is the table unique...

Dora tells them she worked with the Manager to pre-select the menu. To Miss Patriotic's dismay, the food is not her taste. As the appetizer appears, it shocks Miss Patriotic. A half of broiled grapefruit with fried chicken liver is placed in front of each dinner guest; they both looked at each other in horror! Then as the first few courses arrive, Anni watches as she cuts and shifts pieces of food around the plate to look like she was actively eating it.

Miss Patriotic summons the security detail in the room to see if he'd like some food. The guard politely refused stating he is unable to eat while on duty and said in a quieter tone, "I would not enjoy that kind of cuisine even if I was not on duty."

"I hear you." Miss Patriotic agrees.

After the welcome dinner concludes, Miss Patriotic still complains of sinus pain. Apparently, the herbalist remedy of assorted potions did not solve the problem. So, Dora's daughter offers to have her nurse friend call in a prescription under her own name. Miss Patriotic requests a Z-Pac that she knows had provided her relief other times. So, in the Walgreens' parking lot Dora's daughter gets a bogus script from her Nurse Practioner friend and then calls the pharmacy to fill it. Miss Patriotic gives her the money to get the pharmaceuticals. While this transpires, Sonny does not object and the Trooper riding in the car turns a deaf ear on the bait-and-switch activity.

Interesting technique in the world of tour managing, Anni observes.

— 7 —

The first morning during their stay at The Terrace Hotel, Anni calls Sonny to see if either lady would like to join her for a morning workout in the gym. They both declined. Following the workout, each morning, Sonny and Anni take advantage of the hearty breakfast the hotel offer them in the main restaurant.

Meanwhile, Miss Patriotic always skips all unscheduled meals, as she prefers to sleep late and order room service. As opposed to Sonny, who is delighted to see some comfort foods listed on the menu. She tells Anni, "I only eat these foods when traveling to certain parts of the country." This particular morning she sees on the menu they make homemade grits here and asks if Anni has ever tried some. She has not, so Sonny orders it with melted cheddar cheese then mixed in a few pats of creamy butter and a sprinkling of pepper. She gives Anni a taste.

They both enjoy the dish, and concur they should not eat like this most days due to the richness. "It's enjoyable to try new things from time to time." Anni comments jokingly, "It must be a pre-requisite to have a diverse palate and enjoy similar foods that you do to be a successful Tour Manager," and Sonny agrees!

Later that afternoon, a luncheon had been scheduled by Dora Cost with other executives from her anti-drunk driving advocacy group to meet and greet Miss Patriotic. So a stretch limousine arrives to pick-her up with Sonny and Anni only to drive them around the block to a luncheon place called Acquarius. As they get there, it did not even look like the café was opened. Anni checks her watch and notices that it is 11am. She considers they might not typically open for another hour or so. The driver tries the door and it opens, so they make their way inside. The place is vacant.

Anni asks Sonny if this lunch event was confirmed. Sonny says, "I had not heard otherwise." So within five minutes a café worker comes out from the back and tells them to sit anywhere. Sonny and Anni inform the café worker that there was supposed to be a reservation for the group including Miss Patriotic. She does not seem to be aware, but points out a table in the corner facing the front door.

The café looks like the inside of a garage with pieces of corrugated metal on the walls, painted in bright colors and layered with an eclectic group of local artwork all around. This is offset by the bright red flooring. Anni tries to decide whether, the ambiance is reminiscent of the of café's in old San Juan, Puerto Rico or more like a pit stop on Duval Street in Key West, Florida.

After sitting tableside for ten minutes, Dora Cost comes tearing through the door. Anni asks who else is expected to attend; she says she received a few last minute cancellations that she did not know about until getting her messages en route to lunch. It appears she was fluffing-up her story as she hummed and paused a few times while crafting her reply.

Twenty-five minutes pass, then Jon stops in. He mentions, "Dora just called to join you for lunch, so I rearranged my calendar to stop-by."

In the meantime, Miss Patriotic agrees to let Dora flag the limo driver to join them, since there was an empty seat at the table. The young black driver never had been asked to join a meal with a client, but thought this was a chance he could not pass to eat lunch with a reigning beauty queen!

Miss Patriotic is unsure why she is here. "How is this an appearance?" she whispers to Anni.

"It seems Dora put together this get-together to have more face time with her favorite celebrity," Anni whispers back.

Miss Patriotic glances at the café's menu. As Miss Patriotic is finicky about food, she settles for a tossed salad with most of the ingredients left out and she had a bowl of their famous potato soup. She moves the items around to look like she picked through the salad more than she had. Miss Patriotic does not like eating in front of people she does not know. However, she eats the hearty soup savoring the few heaping spoonfuls she allows herself.

The eating deprivation suddenly ends when Dora tells the wait staff to bring a dessert tray and she proclaims, "This is for Miss Patriotic!"

All along, Miss Patriotic, who was hoping to have a quiet, low-profile lunch, which it had been, until Dora turned this into a production! So, the restaurant crew puts together the most elaborate tray of berry-swirled cheesecake, pecan pie, lemon tarts and more. Uncontrollably, Miss Patriotic digs in. She is a big fan of dessert.

Of course, Dora tells the staff to get their cameras ready to take pictures with her. Most did not have any, but used their cell phones to take advantage of the impromptu situation. Some of the staff clearly did not know who she is, or what Miss Patriotic represents; they were just following along with the excitement Dora created on-the-spot.

* * * * * * *

At the end of the week, the women wake-up for a 6am departure to another part of Florida, so Miss Patriotic can do a series of radio interviews for ten national stations. Sonny has the itinerary and Anni attempts to get some coffee and food for the road. The hotel is not equipped for serving coffee until 6:30am. Since Anni is assertive, she tells them, "We have to hit the road earlier, so can you make a special dispensation for a few cups of coffee and something portable to eat." He obliges and hands Anni a bunch of bananas along with a few cups of coffee.

They assumed by leaving early they can zip past the craziness of Florida's rush hour traffic. Sonny climbs into the sedan in her blue jeans and Keds, as she gulped down the caffeine to start the day. So across the state they ride. Miss Patriotic still is feeling lousy and exhausted on top of it. She is clearly not an early riser and could not get a restful sleep. Sonny tells the driver the address and the scheduled time of arrival for the media event.

Well, wouldn't you know, it is rush hour and their car got stuck in severe interstate traffic. Sonny reaches in her tote for some contact numbers and begins dialing. The numbers are not local to the state. Rather, Anni determines the numbers belong to some coordinators in Tennessee, based on the area code. The phone rings, but no one answers. Sonny leaves a series of voicemails, alerting them, "Miss Patriotic will be arriving late based on the traffic situation." The stress level in the car is rising, since there are not many alternatives other than get there when they can, especially as they are unable to reach a live person to immediately respond to this situation.

The sun is rising as they enter the industrial office complex, after the driver had difficulty finding the specific address. When they turn into the parking lot, there are no other vehicles there. It looks rather desolate. Sonny starts to get increasingly nervous. Anni asks to look at the itinerary and notices the start time is noted in Central Time Zone! They are on Eastern Time. The time zone is listed based on where the contact coordinators phone number is from! The contact was in Tennesee.

Sonny is anxious about holding the driver beyond the allotted drop-off time.

Anni says to her, "There is no place for Miss Patriotic to relax for the next hour as the studio building is locked and we are not close to anything else." So, Anni makes an executive decision to have the driver wait, therefore, Miss Patriotic can continue her nap in the backseat, while Anni grabs a daily newspaper strewn on the front lawn of the building to best utilize the time.

Nearly an hour later, Anni flags some workers in the building to let them into the studio, along with their month's worth of luggage. They had to cram it all aboard an elevator the size of an old telephone booth. The driver was dismissed from his duty at that point.

In the studio, the crew obviously is not adequately prepared for the various interviews. The radio engineers are finagling with the lines and switchboards to be in synch with the central transmission being broadcast from Nashville.

In the meantime, Miss Patriotic is still tired, achy and hungry. The bananas Anni procured from the hotel come in handy, as the volume of stomach growling increases. They thought the studio may provide some snacks for Miss Patriotic, but as it turns out, they are left to their own devices, meaning visiting the vending machine down the hall to supplement the bananas all day.

When the engineers and sound mixers manage to get things underway, it becomes an intense frenzy of interviews, morning show gags and voiceovers for stations across country. Miss Patriotic is performing well, sounding very professional and articulate. At least a half-dozen questions she fielded, target the recent drunken escapades of another high-profile pageant titleholder from a different national organization. Miss Patriotic is not pleased that many of the conversations dwell on that subject instead of focusing on her mission and accomplishments over the past year. Fortunately, she is well-versed at speaking on the topic that she believes that Frump's organization has to do what is right for them and then transitioned back to the work she recently completed.

During the studio gig, the local engineer offers Anni a pair of headphones to listen to all the dialog of the interviews. While waiting for one of the ten radio stations to call-in and get set for their on-air interview with Miss Patriotic, Anni hears background conversations. A particular discussion strikes Anni as out of the ordinary: a South Dakota on-air personality's cell phone rang and he comments aloud that he needed to take the call. He mentions he saw the number on his phone was his teenage daughter's who he indicates is recovering from a recent sexual assault. Anni is amazed he is so open about a taboo subject by making such a statement across radio signals. The show was not yet "on air," but the engineers have the capacity to record any portion of his soliloquy.

To Anni, his comments signal a plea for help. Curiously, Jon, the executive they were just working with in Lakeland, Florida earlier in the week, told Anni he had been instrumental in setting up counseling initiatives for at-risk teenagers years ago. So, a few days later Anni instinctively places a private call to Jon and tells him about the comment she heard from the radio personality from South Dakota. She questions whether he would be open to taking a call or calling this guy to offer any counseling or guidance to assist his family with that challenging circumstance. Jon said, "I'll do anything needed to help." Since he agreed, Anni later called the radio personality to provide him Jon's credentials and number. Hopefully, the contact was made and Jon could provide some professional support.

After a week's worth of appearances in Florida they all head to the airport, and wait patiently while people-watching and making themselves laugh. Anni invents a game where they create stories about why the people they see are at the airport and where they are going. It is very silly and helps make time pass quickly. Especially, a tale she invents about the obese, 40-something-year-old living with his Mommy and Daddy, who still dress him, because he can't manage things himself. Their story dictates this family is flying together to take him to Disney.

Miss Patriotic gives Anni the biggest hug when it is time for her to head through the gate and she proclaims that she wanted to see Anni in her home state as one of her wedding guests this April. Sonny mentions she would definitely attend the wedding since that month was part of her travel time and she said Serberus would come out too for the event.

It touches Anni's heart that Miss Patriotic feels so connected with her, in a short amount of time. She is thinking how she can maneuver in such a way to be able to be in the Ohio region to attend the wedding. Anni says jokingly, "The next Miss Patriotic will have to be from your home state and then we can schedule an appearance near the capital, so we can work your wedding into the itinerary. I can escort the new girl to your wedding as an appearance!" Miss Patriotic thought that sounded like a great idea!

Anni is glad Miss Patriotic could be herself and feel lighthearted. It was time to see Miss Patriotic onto her flight back home for the holidays. Sonny walks on the other plane donning her jeans and white-buttoned blouse and sneakers and Anni in her business attire, since Serberus had told her never wear jeans while traveling.

Sonny and Anni fly back to their home-based airport. When they arrive, Sonny does not see their limousine driver in the designated area to pick them up.

They wait a few moments and then wait some more. Forty minutes later, Sonny calls the limo company to see what their status is. The dispatcher indicates the driver is in the area. So, nearly an hour later Anni flags a limo that appears to be from the service they were waiting for. Sonny says to Anni, "That can't be him, since we are waiting for a sedan," but it turns out they did indeed have a stretch limo. The driver seems ill prepared and didn't know what terminal to arrive or time he was expected. He blames his cell phone receiving poor service causing him to miss his dispatcher's messages.

After the delay they settle in the limo, Sonny pops open some chips the driver had stashed in the car. These chips serve as her dinner. When they are off the road, after plenty of lavish meals on tour, Sonny attests often she just grazes on snacks instead of cooking for herself at home.

Five minutes from her home, Anni phones her husband to ask to come outside to "help with my bags." She doesn't tell him the kind of transportation she is arriving, so he assumes she was coming from the airport via a typical shuttle van. He is surprised to see the white stretch limo pull-up in the darkness, especially as he stands outside their front door in his PJ's thinking this is different. He is intensely happy to have his wife arrive home.

— 8 —

Mid December Anni is back at the airport to meet-up with Sonny and Miss Patriotic en route to Louisiana. The weather back east is chilly, so Anni is sure to have layers of clothing that she could easily pear down as they get to the warmer climate.

When they arrive at New Orleans airport, Anni feels the heaviness of the humid air. She ties her jacket around her waist, while schlepping her personal airplane pillow she brought from home. She attempts to tie it to her carry-on case, but it keeps flopping around and flipping off the case and onto the floor. Life on the road is not completely glamorous.

Their ride arrives and they travel downtown to the hotel. Miss Patriotic had not been to New Orleans and the driver really honed in on that fact. Edward, their driver is a New Orleans native and is so proud of his birthright. He asks, "It is OK to take a quick detour to the Cemetery Number One to provide some history of the prestigious citizenry of the region?" Miss Patriotic was tired, but nodded in acceptance, following Edward's persistence.

He drives them through the narrow, winding alleyways in the car, telling tales of infidelity, politics, blue blood family lines and eccentrism. He shows them Voodoo Queen Marie Leveau's cript. Anni is enthralled by Edward's stories, as is Sonny, who had plenty of anecdotes to add too. Miss Patriotic, however, was fading away. Her interest in the history lesson was overshadowed by her dwindling energy level. She is yawning and looking forward to her next nap.

After the cemetery Edward, detours to the Garden District to point out celebrity homes. Miss Patriotic perks-up a bit when he shows them some homes of contemporary actors that were relevant to Miss Patriotic's generation like Nicholas Cage and Helen Mirren. Anni asks Edward if he could point out the house used in the New Orleans edition of the Real World show on MTV. Miss Patriotic enjoys seeing that landmark.

36

After the drive around town, Anni asks if Edward could head to the W Hotel. The car pulls into the U-shaped, busy, downtown driveway and Edward comes around to get their car door. Sonny and Anni make their way to the reception desk to check-in. The guest services representative greets them politely. Sonny asks about the reservation and the hotel staff scurries to find the three rooms. Sonny had to mention, "Miss Patriotic" is in their party and needs to get to her suite right away. The representative kept tapping away and said, "I'll get you to your respective rooms shortly."

Two keys are presented to Sonny on the counter. Anni sashays to the end of the same counter where they had a carafe sitting over a lit sterno filled with hot chocolate and a dish of marshmallows and pieces of dark chocolate to welcome the arriving guests. Anni grabs a cup and fills it, as she considers how she doesn't have a steady supply of chocolate during her travels. She cherishes this fleeting moment of delight.

Anni observes the interaction between Sonny with the guest services rep. They had to reenter the room reservation, because they found a "better suite" with an attached junior suite for Sonny. Anni's key is presented shortly after. Unfortunately, Anni is on a different floor, but she is shadowing Sonny, so it is not imperative she was next door, just in the vicinity to see how she handles tour duties.

Anni escorts the ladies to their rooms, so she knows where to find them to meet- up later. The décor is very modern and plush. In Miss Patriotic's room she views the suede eggplant colored settee' and chocolate brown suede headboard with geometric-shaped mirrors and the plasma TV was playing a video loop of the amenities of this boutique hotel chain with Argentine tango music playing behind the images. The bellman places Sonny's luggage in Miss Patriotic's enormous suite and Miss Patriotic's bags in the junior one!

Miss Patriotic is fatigued and could only think about taking a hot bath followed by a nap, so she does not mind keeping the junior suite. Sonny insists they switch, so Sonny lugs the baggage to the proper places, as the bellman was already out of site. Sonny's efforts expedites the time for Miss Patriotic to get in the tub and unwind.

Anni swiftly says her goodbyes and proceeds to her room. Sonny summons her back, to show her something. Inside, there is a large assortment of snack trays in Miss Patriotic's room. On one of the beautifully arranged platters are assorted dried fruits, nuts and a cheese arrangement on the other. Miss Patriotic was not interested in those, but does like the "gumball machines" in the corner filled with Mike and Ike candies. Sonny insists Anni make herself a take-away plate, since the food is going to be tossed, as Miss Patriotic will not indulge in it. Sonny helps herself with a variety of snacks too.

Sonny walks Anni out into the Junior Suite and said she'll call Anni later to coordinate some dinner plans. It is questionable whether Miss Patriotic would wake-up to grab dinner with them. Her preference is just to order room service if she wakes up at all. Also, Sonny mentions she had to call Erika, one of her two former black Miss Patriotic's who is in town, for the appearance with the current Miss Patriotic. It is unusual for that to be the case, but Erika works as a radio correspondent for the country cable station that is hosting the grand re-opening of the Boys and Girls Club in New Orleans. Based on her connection to the host, she is on the bill, as one of the talent being showcased at the rededication segment.

Part of her wants to reach out to say hello, but she prefers if Anni would come along to lessen the awkwardness of their reunion. Sonny admits she is reluctant to contact her. Sonny has mixed feelings about contacting Erika, since she had her hands-full working with her on the road.

She says Erika had a big celebrity ego and would not abide by rules or guidelines to keep her image reputable. Rather Sonny said, "She would hook-up with a party crowd of young musicians and celebrities along the tour and stay-out all night and was not efficient about waking-up on time to make the a.m. schedule."

Erika was the youngest of a large black brood. "She wants to carve out her own identity, sometimes at the cost of good ties with her Mama," Sonny said. The family was not pleased when Erika hooked-up with a white guy named Ryan and moved in with him. Her traditional black family thought Erika is losing her connection to her ethnicity, especially because she was looking to pursue a career in country music-a stereotypically white genre.

"You are lucky to start out with the current Miss Patriotic who has been brought-up with good standards," Sonny tells Anni.

Sonny leaves a voicemail for Erika to contact her to see what hotel she is staying and to coordinate catching-up over a drink while in town. Anni goes to her room. Sonny calls Anni minutes later to see if she is up to meeting for a drink or dinner at 6:30pm with the infamous Erika. Anni agrees. She figures it would be a great opportunity to get a wider perspective of Miss Patriotic-personality types.

Anni asks if Miss Patriotic would be coming along. Sonny replies Miss Patriotic mentioned earlier, if she was still asleep just go without her. So at 25 after the hour, Anni meets Sonny by the elevators and they descend to the hotel lobby bar. There, they see a small crowd of young-well put together looking people. Some sitting at a large, heavy wooden picnic table, positioned catty-cornered to the lobby area. A rectangle glass container the size of two residential mailboxes contains an abundance of ripe, green, shiny Granny Smith apples. The color or the apples pop against the darkness of the shiny black floors, the dark wooden table and the rows of crystal raindrops handing beyond the table.

A few minutes later, a young African-American woman walks around the corner with bright blue eyes, shoulder length, wavy hair and a striped tee shirt and jeans. Sure enough this is Erika. Sonny and Erika embrace and Anni greets her with a hug and says she had heard so much about her. Sonny asks if she was up for a drink. Erika says, "I am more hungry," so they proceed to another floor to determine what food options there were.

After settling on a continental steak restaurant within the hotel, Anni asks Erika about her life and her fiancée. It is so easy to get Erika talking. She does not know why Sonny had previously told her Erika was really quiet and did not say much. Perhaps, she did not try to get to know her or there was awkwardness between them. Erika is cheerful and smiling talking elaborately about her professional endeavors. She was on a seven-year plan to write songs, record and hopefully get signed as a recording artist. She was told by others in the industry the realistic average is seven years, beyond that she will consider another strategy.

She had hooked-up with someone she met at a party that promised to get her country music career underway. Erika said the woman was very eccentric. She wasn't sure what her original motive was, if she really could jumpstart her career, but she knew the woman was moneyed or appeared to be. So she scheduled some meetings where they were to review music and get material recorded for a demo, but the woman turned out to be unreliable and did not follow-through on the meetings. Erika was frustrated admitting how naïve she was in that situation.

Erika responds confidently, "If Charlie Pride could break the barrier line, so can I," following Anni's inquiry why she is so passionate about getting signed as a Country music star. Feeling desperate to make a name for herself in the field, she wants to be a female Charlie Pride.

The dinner is pleasant as they toast their reunion and meeting over ice teas and fruited martinis. Anni orders a butternut squash soup to be served table side. Sonny orders one of the specials: Canjun-prepared oysters and Erika ordered steak. Erika mentions how she is trying to be conscientious about what she consumes since she is getting married in less than a year and wants to look good. She comments her fiancée accepts her for what she is. Her parents are not thrilled with the whole marriage, but she is determined to do what she wants and with the help of her planner and vendors "donating" their goods and services she is creating a spectacle worthy of other Hollywood-type weddings. Anni is shocked to hear Erika is taking vendor donations of a designer wedding cake and couture gown. It's funny how people in the entertainment field get things given to them versus those who truly need hand-outs.

Erika goes on to describe that her wedding color scheme is brown and blue. She said, "My groom will be in a blue, retro tuxedo and that will accentuate the chocolate brown of my skin, wrapped in a blue-tuled gown." There will be white magnolias on the plantation in Florida and the invitations will be very VIP, to avoid party-crashers they invitees will need to bring the ring inside to be checked off the list.

Sonny is looking at Anni rolling her eyes with the over-the-top details. Sonny's signal accentuates Erika's need to be the center of attention and insinuates Erika's logic is not normal.

Anni commends Erika for doing what she believes and making her wedding wishes come true and she offers her the best of luck. After dinner they all go back to their respective rooms. Erika is in the same niche hotel to make it convenient to go the appearance, even though she said the hotel blew her budget.

Early the next morning, Anni starts her day by heading to the hotel gym for an invigorating workout. She wants to get herself moving since a lot of her job is stagnant sitting in cramped planes for hours, standing on the sidelines of appearances and riding in various cars from place to place. Anni gets in a groove by raising her heart rate on the elliptical machine. The gym here is top notch; it is spacious, clean and has a ton of state-of-the-art equipment, Anni notices. She is excited the elliptical machines have radios and flat screen televisions built in, as did the other cardio items.

Anni starts multi-tasking between watching a morning news show, flipping through the newspaper left door side at her room, then taking a moment to call home and check in with her husband and in-laws. During the phone call, Anni enjoys the solitude as she had the gym all to herself.

Midway through the conversation on the phone, she sees a movement out of the corner of her eye and turns to see a young African-American woman doing some stretches at the other end of the room on the rubberized floor. The girl has a short pony tail; natural, dark brown eyes and is donning an old worn t-shirt and shorts. She looks like she needs to work out more regularly, because her shape is somewhat roly-poly.

As it so happens, that girl waves at Anni. After a few seconds, Anni realizes the girl waving to her is Erika. She looks so different without her big wig of hair, blue contact lens-colored eyes and accessories. The persona I dined with the prior night cannot be this same person, Anni thinks as she scans the young lady.

After getting over the shock, Anni asks her about her year as Miss Patriotic. Erika had mixed feelings about it. She confesses, "No one really knows what they are getting themselves into." Anni wants to know about what she enjoyed and things she would have liked to have been different. Erika enjoyed the parties and rubbing elbows with prestigious people in music and other celebrities. She felt very empowered to be a young black woman and having a voice and making a difference.

The things she did not want to relive were the interaction with the staff from the Miss Patriotic office and on the road. She admits, "I am pleased to see they brought you on board, because you are younger and a lot more relatable. The women I dealt with while living on the road were older and too stogy. They were too strict," she indicated, "and did not understand things from my perspective: the need to socialize and network at events and beyond. I wanted to take advantage of every situation-in a good way, but the managers always suspected I was up to no good."

Anni inquires, "Do you think they didn't trust you?" She responds, "They did not want to give up any of their control. They felt they had to manage my every move."

Anni is so fortunate to have this exchange with Erika. She knows she can not duplicate Sonny's long standing reputation among the pageant people, but she wanted to make a fine name for herself. One important attribute that Erika helped her realize is that she is more relatable and easy-going than Sonny and Ann Jo are with the young women. They were not in the loop on current trends, music and culture, but are effective at cracking a whip to keep the ladies in line according to Erika's recounting.

— 9 —

The following day Anni receives a call in her posh W Hotel room. It was the chauffer saying, "Your car is ready." Anni alerted Sonny, so they can all meet in the lobby.

Miss Patriotic comes downstairs with Sonny and Anni to depart for the event. A series of drivers are standing with clipboards that have Anni's name posted on two of them. Anni proceeds to correct the drivers that the car service was really for Miss Patriotic. Internally, she is flattered that they made the mistake. Miss Patriotic is a bit miffed her name was not listed on the clipboard, as she is the celebrity.

The three of them hop in one of the two vehicles marked under Anni's name. Anni has noticed that sometimes the transportation vendors would use the Manager's name to give Miss Patriotic some privacy. In this case they overdid it.

Minutes later Erika appears in the lobby and asks if there is some room for her to come along. Sonny advises the transportation is arranged and sponsored by the host, but since she is also on the program they agree for her to tag along in one of their two delineated vehicles. Within minutes, they arrive at the venue, the renovated Boys and Girls Club that had been adversely impacted by the Hurricane Katrina 18 months before.

Edward, their driver greets them warmly again and proclaims how thankful he is for them doing business here. He said it is such a blessing to have people come back and he asked, "Do me a favor, go back home and tell all your friends, neighbors and business people to travel to New Orleans and spend money here again and help put it back on the map to its prestigious pre-hurricane state of being."

At the children's center the Producer comes by to greet Miss Patriotic and comments, "I'm glad you're on schedule. Many celebrities take their time."

However, off to the side the same Producer informs Anni that the crew is behind schedule due to unexpected changes to today's program and continues to walk away.

Anni taps the Producer on the shoulder and asks "Does this mean Miss Patriotic is not on-duty for 4 more hours based on the revised timing of today's schedule?" The Producer affirms that the TV interviews and filming of the rededication of the club segment is set back by about that amount of time. Anni then inquires if some arrangements can be made to have the driver available during the interim, so Miss Patriotic does not have to sit and wait endlessly in the "Green Room."

Anni looks over and sees Miss Patriotic is getting antsy. She is now sharing the space with newly launched country music artist Kellie Pickler, who is busy promoting her first album following her stint as an American Idol finalist. Kellie is a petite-statured girl, with long locks of blond hair, most likely enhanced with extensions. Anni quickly sees her high-heeled signature red patent-leather pumps elevating her six inches taller. Kellie and Miss Patriotic wave across the room to one another, but are busy among their own people.

After a few minutes of deliberation, the TV Producer summons the driver to take them anywhere Miss Patriotic wants to go, as long as she was back to prep for the TV segment.

Sonny is pleased about the outcome Anni negotiated, as Miss Patriotic was not thrilled with the possibility of sitting there when she could have slept-in longer. Anni asks, "Do you want to go back to the hotel or if you are interested we can all see some of the neighborhood, putting things into perspective by visiting the hardest hit neighborhoods from the hurricane?" She agrees and Erika is interested too, so with Miss Patriotic's OK, an invitation was extended for her to come along.

Edward admires their interest in seeing how extreme the devastation is, not just to stay where life appears to be normal. So, he drives them through the 9th Ward, around 17th Street and near Lake Pontchartrain. He encourages them to get out and look around. They step out of the car and investigate the ghost land for themselves. There are a few FEMA trailers strewn around some of the neighborhoods, but Edward mentions the government has set a deadline to reclaim them, so the residents who want to stand by and keep an eye on their property do not know what is next. Essentially, greater than half the population moved away and most do not intend to come back to New Orleans and resettle. Anni asks Miss Patriotic what this ride through the destruction means to her?

"I am very humbled by this experience." It is certainly a far cry from the lavish hotel she was living in not too far away.

After the seriousness of the hurricane damage, they decide to lighten the mood up a bit by getting something to drink at the famous Café' Du Mond and take a look at Washington Square. There was a mob, as there usually is at the Café'. The two Miss Patriotics stand curbside while Sonny mentions there is a line to get seated. Anni sees a back room with empty tables and realizes they are on a certain schedule to get back to the venue to shoot the TV segments, so she proceeds to get to an empty table inside and flags the girls along. "I'll beg for forgiveness if the staff says something to me." Anni takes the chance as the wait staff say hello and don't give them a hard time for self-seating.

Then Sonny tries to track down a waitress to follow-up on their order of two cups of chicory coffee for her and Anni and the Miss Patriotics enjoy two large hot chocolates with whipped cream with three orders of piping-hot beignets.

Anni does not indulge in the fried treats, as she had tasted them before and tries to avoid fried food to sustain her good shape as long as possible. "Why don't you take a bite?" Miss Patriotic pleads with Anni. The ladies feel bad that they were scarfing the donut-like treats down while trying to tempt her to eat one too.

After snacking at the New Orleans landmark, they leave the café, yet Erika lingers briefly to buy a CD from a street musician. Edward flags them toward the car to pick them up. Miss Patriotic asks that the three of them have their picture taken in front of the café to capture the memory. Anni is touched that Miss Patriotic insists she be in the photo with them.

Arriving again at the Boys and Girls Club they get back in work mode, Anni chats with Lynda, a VP of Production for MTV. Lynda asks her if they have dinner plans. Anni said typically Miss Patriotic enjoys staying in and ordering room service in her hotel room. "Although," she comments, "I may be able to persuade her to dine out and enjoy the city a bit, having never been here before." So, Lynda extends an invitation for them to join her for dinner. Nothing stuffy; just a casual, fun taste of New Orleans.

Anni was able to get an affirmative from Miss Patriotic! Proactively, Anni advises Lynda what kinds of foods she prefers, so Lynda could select a place that would cater to her tastes.

Later in the evening, they pile into one car, as Anni sits on Sonny's lap since there was not enough space. Everyone was jovial and looking forward to a laid back dinner. Lynda tells Edward to take the group to Dick and Jennie's. At the restaurant, they are greeted by the owner, yet it is a busy weekend, so they had to wait a few minutes for a table nearest to the kitchen to become available.

When the table is ready, the executive chef stops by to say hello. The group orders from the menu and enjoys a nice bottle of Tucker's red zinfandel that Lynda selects with pride. The restaurant staff proceeds to bring out special food for Miss Patriotic not listed on the menu. They specially made a dish of her favorites: macaroni and cheese along with fried chicken and potatoes. The potatoes were something novel, they carved them into the shape of a crown! She is so happy about all the fuss they made. The restaurant staff went out of their way, even with the beverages. Their waitress ran across the street to accommodate Miss Patriotic's request for a Diet Dr. Pepper that Dick and Jenny's doesn't serve! She enjoys the acclaim she received from the staff that treats her like royalty.

— 10 —

December 19th Anni's home phone rings and a message is left from the Administrative Assistant for the CEO of the Miss Patriotic Organization. She had been busy coordinating the Christmas lunch and neglected to consider that Anni is the newest member on the staff. In a scurry, she asks Anni to RSVP for the event taking place in three days. Fortunately, Anni could carve out some time to drive down to Atlantic City to attend and get to know the staff in the festive setting.

The printed invitation comes in the mail the next day, even though the RSVP date was due the week earlier.

When Friday arrived Anni had carefully planned her outfit to look stylish and jubilant. She decides to wear a white-buttoned down shirt with a new cashmere red cropped jacket, black slacks, red flats with a black accent and she opted for a red tweed hat, since the weather was inclement. Anni departs for the trip rather early to allow for the treacherous roads. The weather in her county was so miserable she had to pull over and scrape hail that froze to the windshield, so she could regain some visibility.

Prior to her arrival in Atlantic City, Anni stops by a store and buys a box of individually-wrapped chocolates shaped like Gingerbread houses and a few shaped like snowflakes, all of which are the size of grapefruits. She also purchases a nifty, eyeglass holder, special for Ann Jo Serberus. She figures this is an appropriate gift for her, since Serberus had trouble locating her reading glasses when she was searching for some reports during Anni's first meeting with her. Anni suspects if she had a proper place to set them in her office, she'd be less likely to lose them and get frustrated wasting precious time looking for them.

With gifts in hand, Anni merrily visits everyone who was in the office that day. Anni goes to distribute the gifts and wish each person a happy holiday season with their family. Overall they respond well. Except the Operations Manager, who has the nerve to say, "What do I do with this? I'm diabetic."

Anni tells him, "Why not share it with your non-diabetic relatives?"

As Anni stops into Ann Jo's office, she says to her, "I have a special gift for you, for all the hard work you do!" Serberus did not acknowledge her comment, nor look into the gift package. (Fast forward weeks later, Serberus never did acknowledge Anni's gift or the overall gesture.)

So the group was heading to the luncheon, Anni jumps in a colleague's car to get a ride there. At the restaurant, Anni introduces herself to a few people and they respond by saying how nice she looks and is even told by Marybeth a part-time staffer, "You should be Miss Patriotic yourself."

Anni thanks Marybeth for the compliment and retorts, "I don't meet the right age or qualification requirements."

At the luncheon, Anni's boss Cheryl Pearson offers her a drink. They each have a glass of wine and Cheryl picks-up the tab. Anni thanks her and they toast the new job and the holiday season.

As she approaches the table, Anni asks where they want everyone to sit and they said just sit anywhere. Anni sits near the Ops Manager and some other office staffers. Way across the table is Ann Jo, sitting beside Sonny. Sonny catches Anni's attention and interjects a comment about them both ordering similar kinds of foods when they were on the road and at this luncheon. Anni responds amusingly, "You have to have a certain type of palate to be a Tour Manager for the organization."

The conversations are pleasant and she has a good exchange with the interim CEO about travel experiences. His wife is native Arubian and Anni comments how her own husband is vying to travel back to the island. "He enjoyed our stay there a few years ago," Anni mentions. The interim CEO blurted, "We still have a time-share property on the island." Immediately, Anni proposes he consider renting it to her and her husband sometime!

The other part-time office workers seated around Anni, are intrigued how well- traveled she is and what she has accomplished in her life so far.

— 11 —

Anni observes how the Miss Patriotic group is a buzz in conversation. They're excited about heading out West to work on the pageant production and activities as they mention these topics at their quiet, little Christmas luncheon in a restaurant overlooking the A.C. boardwalk. Anni stops momentarily to see the beachfront view from the second story of the banquet room. There she sees the subtle fog outside obscuring the boardwalk below.

Since Anni is the newest member and this being a non-profit crew, she figures they couldn't afford to have her also to attend the big show. Her boss Cheryl Pearson confirms this is indeed the case, "We did not budget for another set of travel expenses, as all the reservations were made before you were on board."

The start of the new year signals the upcoming pageant. The January pageant date is now based on the current circumstances; the TV sponsor's criteria to air the show live. These days the organization is at the mercy of the sponsor's commands. No longer is the pageant held around Labor Day in September, as it had traditionally been during its many glory days strolling upon the sunny boardwalk.

* * * * * * *

A few weeks following their luncheon, it is pageant day! Anni had assembled some people at her house to watch the live show during this chilly January day. Anni figures they can determine how her professional fate would be affected. From the venue out West, Sonny e-mails Anni. The message reads, "Let's keep our eye on the girl from Ohio. There are a lot of stories to tell from backstage!" Anni and Sonny are figuratively keeping their fingers crossed, so their new girl would represent the organization well and not be a high-maintenanced Diva.

After watching the show, Anni concludes she enjoyed the pageant from a production standpoint. She likes the fact that this year her local cable system offered the technology to select individual video profiles of each contestant. Anni is able to pull-up the profiles on the cable system's on-demand feature a month before the big show, to learn about each young lady, where they were from and their personal platform. With this technology, she is able to look at the profile segments and review them with some of her friends. "It's very clever, so by pageant night everyone is familiar with each contestant beyond just a one dimensional pretty photo in the program," one of her friends comments.

Anni decides the pageant is very professional with its lavish stage sets and very popular young Latin host, Mario Lopez. Lopez just came off a successful run on "Dancin' with the Stars," so the audience is still enthralled with his charisma. During the crowning moment as the top two ladies were on stage, near Mario Lopez, awaiting the announcement of the winner, Anni notices Miss Texas look directly into Miss Ohio's eyes. Yet, the gesture is not returned. Miss Ohio zones out looking towards the horizon awaiting the decision.

Seconds later, the 2007 Miss Patriotic is crowned. Anni is pleased to see Miss Ohio has become the new Little Miss, her term of endearment for the new titleholder!

Anni had been told that her travel schedule would mainly be the odd numbered months, but she was told she would skip January being on tour.

So, it is just about time for me to fly solo on my new career, but Ann Jo Serberus has other ideas in mind. Within days, she calls Anni to advise, "Sonny will handle the January travel, since it is a major transition for the new Miss Patriotic. She is equipped to show them the ropes as far as life on the road." That seems reasonable and Anni considers maybe she could shadow her for a few events in the vicinity.

Anni mentions to Serberus, "It may be a good idea for me to meet-up with them on some local events to get more of an inside perspective."

"Sonny will handle it," Serberus responds. Anni was slightly dejected; feeling a bit removed from the excitement surrounding the pageant and the start of the tour.

Also, the first events entail a media tour to introduce the newly crowned Miss Patriotic to the country and Anni figures it might be a prime opportunity to connect with, Kelly Ripa, a high school alumnae who made it big with her own a.m. talk show. About a week into Little Miss' newly earned reign, Ann Jo says, "Anni, you should not count-on escorting Little Miss on tour at appearances just because you have contacts there."

Sonny is slated to take Little Miss on the media tour. While in New York City, Sonny escorts Little Miss to a bunch of interviews on a few of the talk shows. From home, Anni listens intently to the reports and first hears Diane Sawyer question Little Miss about Harold Frump's controversial beauty queen, who was partying wildly and drinking underage. After Little Miss affirms, "He had to do what's right for his organization," then they spoke about her own crowning moment.

When Little Miss has the interview with Kelly Ripa, she also recalls the "hand-holding" story, but Kelly thought it would be fun to reenact it— to vicariously get in the moment and emulate the feeling of being a beauty pageant winner. She shares how her hands were held on top of the other finalist's prior to the announcement and this is symbolic of becoming the winner, so Little Miss believes.

Anni listens to the interview from home and stretches her imagination to consider the possibilities of being a part of this new world. It excites her and she stops to consider how her marriage will fare with her professional endeavors. She is six months into her married life and is taking a different path. She certainly does not want to create a rift in her loving relationship with Brendan, however, she knows relationships go through various stages and feels confident in the strength of hers. Especially, because Brendan is very supportive. He has been there for Anni for a decade of her tribulations and successes over their consequential courtship.

Anni knows this will be one of life's tests. Her husband, Brendan, will be forty-years old this year. She wants to make this milestone memorable with him, but now she cannot commit to hosting a celebration, since his birthday is in May, when she is slated to be on tour. Yet, Anni plans to consider how she can honor his special day whether she can be there or not. Time is something Anni will have much of.

Also, Anni's only sibling, her younger brother Willie, who she had wanted to be a stronger part in her life, since Anni and Willie had a challenging childhood. They were latchkey kids and the backbone of their family was their Mother. Their Dad was oblivious to the reality of parenthood. He did not even know how old his children were or what grades they were attending in school. But, now he's gone...he died a slow and unnerving death, as a result of disconnecting from life more than twenty years earlier. Anni and Willie still have unexpressed angst from those experiences, so it holds them back from the loving ties with each other that Anni feels would be useful.

During an infrequent visit in December, Willie and Anni attempt to summarize their own life's current happenings in a five minute conversation in her kitchen. Anni skims gingerly over her new job opportunity. She doesn't want to come across as a grandstander, since she knows her younger brother and his girlfriend have been sensitive to feeling insignificant at times. Then, when Anni turned the floor over to her brother, Willie, he makes an announcement that they have set a wedding date. Leza, his fiancé stands behind Willie letting him do the talking.

This couple of eight years set a wedding date of September 7th.

Anni whispers reluctantly, "I don't know if I can make it, my job will have me on the road." She did not want him to take offense, but it was too late. They both had a tendency to put their guard up, as a defensive response to dealing with their obnoxious Father as kids. The damage was done.

Willie sarcastically responds, "Well, do what you have to do, just send Brendan to represent you both." Leza stood quietly in confusion, as she doesn't understand what Anni does for a living.

Anni remained silent. She knows, she will have to do what she has to and being brand new in this job, she did not want to rock the boat. She contemplates how things will progress and intends not mention the wedding date with the Miss Patriotic Organization until she can identify an appropriate moment, so they may be agreeable to her coming back home. From here on, Anni would cautiously wait and see how she can fit her own life's moments in with her uncommon professional world.

— 12 —

Ann Jo summons Anni to attend a meeting at the HQ, where the newly crowned Little Miss would be in town to review "paperwork" and meet the staff. Since Anni was told the group was assembling for a business meeting, she is in professional dress-winter white wool trousers and a Burberry-looking jacket with black velvet collar and trimmed-cuffs. Anni had arranged to get her hair done before this meeting to look crisp and professional. She wants to make a great first impression when meeting Little Miss.

Little Miss is involved in reviewing her contract with Ann Jo Serberus when Anni arrives. This would be the first time she gets to meet Little Miss! She sees her through the window of Ann Jo's office. Since she's occupied, Anni wants to make productive use of the time, so she dashes into the board room and plugs in her new laptop to give it a whirl.

The third-party computer technician sits beside her to see that the wireless connection is up and running. As Anni and the computer consultant are working, Anni notices a young lady creep around the boardroom. All of the sudden Anni is tapped on the shoulder. It is Little Miss!

Little Miss observes Anni is engaged in a conversation with the I.T. consultant, so she cautiously says "Hi, I'll come back in a few moments."

Before she does, Anni gets up from her seat, and says, "I am so glad to meet you." Little Miss puts her arms around Anni in a warm embrace. Anni's first impression is that Little Miss has a perky, glow about her, with sandy, blond hair a few inches past her shoulders and flawless make-up, less a few noticeable blemishes on her forehead and neck. Anni notices she is wearing a very Summery sweater set-white with primary-colored flowers and tight blue jeans on this chilly January day.

Little Miss tells Anni, "I am from a very "huggy-family."" Meeting her truly warms Anni's heart. She seems like a really nice, down-to-earth gal!

* * * * * * *

When Anni gets to access the computer network, she takes a look at the master calendar where all the events Serberus had confirmed were listed, on it she notices there were no events scheduled for the February weekend of the regional auto show Anni had proposed as appearance opportunity for Little Miss to Serberus back in December. Is there something really more important or was she purposefully being deceptive as part of a power struggle?

Days later, upon receiving a copy of the newest schedule, Anni notices the header had not been updated to reflect the change in the name of the reigning Miss Patriotic. Instead, Anni sees Little Miss' predecessor's name glaring on each page of this itinerary.

Other glitches show-up as well, with contacts' names spelled incorrectly and some lapses in dates. When Anni asks about some key pieces of information, like the jumbled dates, Ann Jo chalks it up to a formatting problem on her computer. This series of typographical errors, lack of organization and non commitment to the brand name, strike a chord with Anni that this may set tone of things to come.

At the staff meeting, the team assembles in the same board room; Anni had been working with the I.T. consultant to get her newly issued work laptop ready for the road. Today's meeting is a forum for Little Miss to meet everyone on the support team of the headquarters, who will do all the footwork for her year of employment with the Miss Patriotic Organization.

At the meeting, the administrative assistant announces, "Lunch is here." Lunch consists of a few hoagies cut into sections strewn on a few paper plates with a plastic container filled with piles of sliced onions, another with mayo and packets of mustard tossed on the table. The assistant mentions to Little Miss, "I got you something special from The White House; it's our best hoagie shop around." I can't believe that the welcome lunch for Little Miss at the headquarters of this fine American institution would amount to $20 worth of take-out on paper plates!

After Little Miss finishes her frenzy of text messages, she eagerly approaches the food selections on the side table in the Board Room. Oddly, Little Miss enjoys fast-food and it turns out take-out is just her style. She eagerly chomps on lots of cheese and grabs a special cheese steak ordered especially for her and accompanies it with potato chips. The rest of the team could select from the cold sandwiches left on the table.

In getting to know Little Miss, Anni is surprised in talking with her that she is a big fan of junk food. She then hears her proclaim, "I am not into working out." Anni observes she also is a big-time nail biter. Some of Anni's preconceived notions of a beauty pageant winner were starting to shift.

When Anni chats with Little Miss, she finds out that she currently has a boyfriend named Ron, who is studying engineering in college and this opportunity for her as Miss Patriotic will certainly test their relationship, she mentions. Ron told her he feels self-conscious about all these millions of other guys checking her out. Anni confirms, "This will be a true test not only of having a long distance relationship, but one that has the added nuances of you being in the limelight."

Little Miss also tells Anni about her family. She has a younger sister, Morgan, who she is immensely close with and a younger brother, Justin, who she continues to have a sibling rivalry with. Her sister has a small dog, she named Hilton. Anni assumes the girls have some interest in faux celebrity Paris Hilton, rather, the dog was a new addition to the family surrounding a local pageant held in the hotel by that name.

In the meantime, Pearson, the Communications Director, wants Little Miss to view her pageant montage, video clip collection she acquired through TIVO including her "crowning moment" at the pageant and assorted interviews she did with various media within her first week as Miss Patriotic.

Little Miss is excited to see herself in these life-changing moments. She tells everyone, "When I'm looking at the tape, it's a lot different than when I was at those studios in Vegas and New York. I remember having to kiss my parents goodbye, leave my deluxe suite in Vegas early to catch the red eye to New York and I could not sleep with all the excitement. Then we were up and headed to the first studio at 4:30am for the media tour. It was a blur. My favorite morning show I did was "Mark and Juliette." They were so down to earth and easy to talk with."

The video whirs statically through the video clips and a few commercials slipped in, so one of the administrators attempts to fast forward, in order that the group can just view the highlights.

The montage is out of proportion and a bit warped. Why is the video so distorted?

Little Miss gets emotional seeing herself and was so pleased recalling how the other contestants greeted her outside of the back of the pageant auditorium in their pure-white designer gowns to see her off on her exciting, new journey and they rallied together to sing her the Miss Patriotic theme song, the one that Burt Wood made famous. Little Miss asserted, "It touched my heart; they thought to do that… most of them."

Little Miss pointed out the runner-up; Miss Texas reluctantly participated in the impromptu serenade. She said one of her close friends among the contestants told her how it was a challenge to get Miss Texas to come along. Little Miss sensed the tension during the preliminary festivities, Miss Texas was standoffish. It was hard to get to know her. Maybe because she was one of the older contestants and one of the two African American representatives.

Little Miss reflected upon the countdown of the top two finalists, Miss Texas commented to her while on stage, "The $25 grand will be a big help to you for your college future."

Little Miss ignored the comment, as she was thinking Miss Texas arrogantly, assumes Little Miss would not win the overall title, but take second place. Hence, the $25 grand comment.

At the staff lunch meeting, Little Miss clarifies, "There were no "catfights" among the girls. All and all we got along. My class of contestants loved spending time together and now I know I have many women who I will have as bridesmaids. Of course there were some rivalries, but it is a competition, but I was equally friendly to everyone."

— 13 —

In February, Anni receives another itinerary produced by Serberus, still listing the former Miss' name on the header.

In reviewing the schedule, Anni sees an appearance at the Philadelphia Auto Show. Wouldn't you know, Serberus, booked the appearance with the auto group afterall, for Little Miss to attend their opening night gala and do an audience meet-and–greet! This was the suggestion Anni had offered in December and was immediately shot down, as Seberus told her, "…there were other more important events that had a higher price tag." Yet, as it manifested, Serberus did proceed to book the appearance and tried to leverage the opportunity as her own unique idea.

Away, Anni was to go along with her Sensi Sonny and Little Miss. The organization wants her to see more real-world tour managing before setting her on her own devices. The schedule includes a number of days that she was to be the caretaker of Little Miss, so Sonny can have some time off. Basically, that entails Anni jumping into Sonny's already used hotel room under her existing reservation on behalf of the company (there were two double beds in the room, so Anni selected the unused one), then to spend one-on-one time with Little Miss better and just stay around the hotel. Little Miss told Anni, "My experience was a whirlwind so far leaving my home state in the beginning of January for the competition, winning the overall title and hitting the road ever since."

Anni asked Sonny what plans she has, since they had her come in during Sonny's scheduled month on the road. Sonny replies, "I have no plans really. I may take my shoes to the shoemaker for repair and see about upgrading the company cell phone."

She assumes Sonny has some place to go or a commitment to take care of and is surprised by her response. It appears the organization wants Anni to be around to get to know Little Miss. Regularly, the two tour managers are slated for travel nearly every other month at a time. It depends how convenient "the switch" can take place in terms of time and logistics, ultimately those details lie in Serberus' realm. So Sonny has no plans other than running errands.

In the meantime, the company makes an overwhelming assumption that just because Anni has a personal cell phone, she will use that for her calls, while Sonny takes the work phone for an upgrade. The company does not mention compensating Anni for using her own phone in the interim. Meanwhile, Sonny uses the company cell to keep in touch with family, as her primary means of communication, since she does not have the intention to acquire a separate phone for her personal calls and no questions were asked about it.

* * * * * * *

While in town, Cheryl wants to keep Little Miss feeling well-pampered and stress-free, so she schedules her a complementary pedicure and manicure, at a spa in Caesar's Atlantic City resort, to get her nails sculptured to hide the aggressively bitten fingernails, Cheryl calls in favors from some of her casino contacts to get Little Miss an immediate appointment and instructs Anni that Little Miss should take care of the gratuity.

Anni thinks it's ironic, Cheryl who sets-up the appointment and gives Little Miss the exciting news about the spa treatment, does not want to be the bearer of the reality Little Miss needs to spot the tip on her own dime. Anni has to play the heavy and relay the message while accompanying her on the excursion. And so, she does. Little Miss gets a bit flustered about having to put the tip down, because she was not told that upfront by Cheryl.

During the appointment, Anni tries to provide Little Miss some down time, so she sits and reads magazines in a separate part of the salon. After finishing a series of magazines, Anni makes her way to the pedicure spa area where Little Miss is receiving her treatments. Anni asks, "Is it OK I join you both by sitting here for conversation?

"Sure!" Little Miss responds.

At times, Anni noticed hours go by where she could go without talking, because she was on her own and did not want to be perceived as imposing to Little Miss. She was happy to have the camaraderie and conversation. Also the time was just right to sit in closer proximity to Little Miss.

Anni has to put her "security guard hat" on momentarily when another spa attendant wanted to take Little Miss' picture. Anni speaks to the zealous admirer and mentions, Little Miss is trying to relax and needs to unwind, but may be willing to get a photo taken when she is finished. The admirer is disappointed she did not get instantly gratified, but understood and is happy to say hello. The well-wisher got tired of waiting for Little Miss' multi-treatment session to end, so she leaves without getting the photo.

At the conclusion of the appointment, Little Miss feels a bit concerned how much she needs to tip, since she does not know how much the services cost. Anni guides her though her concern and Little Miss puts the gratuity on her credit card, which she said her Father has been keeping close tabs on.

Little Miss goes on to tell Anni, "I love to shop. My Dad called me recently, because he was questioning a few hundred dollars in charges that I racked-up in clothes purchases. He paid it off, but he does not like when I go shopping. I told him I got the shopping gene from my Mom. You should see her…I'm sure you will one of these days. She and her girlfriends take road trips to Dallas to go to the great shops there and come home with carloads of stuff."

It sounds to Anni that Little Miss comes from good, solid parents, at least as far as her Father is concerned. He monitors her spending, so she does not max out the credit cards. There does seem to be a twinge of Little Miss' ability to push her Dad's buttons and get her way, especially since she has an ally with her Mother, her shopping compatriot.

Following the salon treatments, Little Miss is famished and ready to grab a bite to eat. In getting to know Little Miss from her few days at the hotel so far, Anni discovered her favorite food is Mexican. Since Anni is familiar with the area, she knew of a well-respected Mexican food place in town and arranges to take Little Miss to have a nice meal there after her spa services. This is Anni's show of concern for Little Miss that she is responsive to her likes and wants to provide her some enjoyable downtime. Anni thinks by stopping at the Mexican restaurant, this may be a change of pace from all the room service.

The spa was a few blocks from the restaurant, so Anni asks Little Miss if she is OK taking a walk there. Little Miss agrees, although the wind off the Atlantic was whipping and extremely brisk. If they opt for a taxi, they would have to pick-up the tab as it is considered this a non-appearance related-event. Little Miss says emphatically, "Let's walk!" She just paid a lot in gratuity at the spa she thought.

They arrive at the well-known Atlantic City Mexican cantina. Little Miss is excited about ordering a hot bowl of queso dip. "Queso dip is one of my major cravings."

Anni jokes to Little Miss, "On the road we can stop-by various Mexican restaurants, so you could rate the queso dip." Anni wants to place her needs before her own, as Mexican food was not Anni's favorite.

Unfortunately, when the waiter approaches their table to take their order, she says, "We don't serve queso dip here." Anni could see Little Miss was clearly disappointed...... Little Miss likes the diversion of getting Mexican food, and mentions to Anni, she still loves her hometown Mexican restaurant the best. "It's the place my family goes to eat for lunch after church every Sunday," she adds.

During this stay in Atlantic City, Little Miss has mostly been eating room service and renting a ton of movies from the hotel pay-per-view system. The organization is concerned about continuing to accept those movie expenses on the road for that she's been acruing. Serberus tells Anni they may need to bill Little Miss for all that entertainment, since no other Miss Patriotic has ever charged the company like she has that way before. Anni was waiting for the verdict, since she figures they'll have her relay the bad news to Little Miss if that ax falls in that direction. No directive was given so far.

While at their hotel in Atlantic City, Little Miss comments how unhappy she is with the dullness of her hair. Apparently she has been texting and calling home recently, as she mentions to Anni the organization did not have a stylist for her. It is cost prohibitive for her to fly her hometown hair guru in for a touch-up. The Miss Patriotic girls do their own hair and make-up most of the time, as the budget does not allow for them to have people on staff to do it week-to-week. For special occasions a stylist and designer may be available depending on the circumstance and the pockets of the sponsors.

Little Miss contemplates flying her own hair stylist guy from home to give her a hair update on her own dime. In reviewing the expenses with her generous parents, that wasn't an option, Dad set some limits of his generosity for his daughter. Alternatively, Lenny, her hometown stylist sends her a package with the color products she needed to brighten up her hair. The only other item she needs is bleach, which wasn't shippable.

So, the eternally smiley Cheryl Pearson, who lives near the hotel, stops at a local beauty supply to get her a bottle. Little Miss' next concern is how to apply product correctly on her own hair. Anni offers to help; she believes it is part of her duties while wearing her "personal assistant hat".

Little Miss is tremendously nervous about her hair color looking uneven for her photo shoot the following day. Anni asks her, "What do you think is the worst that could happen?" Little Miss worries about uneven coloring and how that will affect her portfolio from the fashion shoot to be used for her promotional materials. At this point she is shaking like a leaf in the midst of autumn. Anni attempts to quell her fears.

Anni knows there is the possibility Little Miss' hair could turn green or fall out, which would be far worse outcomes. Those ideas she keeps to herself, not to exacerbate Little Miss' concerns. Instead, Anni assures Little Miss regarding her own worst fear, that if the color is not even they had enough time to reapply it in some areas. Little Miss accepted that retort. The two of them proceed to do the hair color process in Little Miss' hotel bathroom.

This hair process certainly gives the women a reason to bond. This proves to Anni they're developing a level of trust as Little Miss allows Anni to touch her head and to put bleach all through her locks, especially since she is an up and coming celebrity. After the hair processing saga, they joke around, that Little Miss should fire Lenny, her personal hometown hairstylist, now that Anni has proved herself to be so competent in that area of hair color.

Little Miss is pleased with the outcome and she invites Anni to watch a movie that she orders by pay-per-view in her room. "The Good Year," glistens from the TV screen as Little Miss ate a bowl of $12 ice cream from room service, while Anni chows on take-out Chinese food. They both got food they enjoy, as Little Miss tells Anni, "I don't like Chinese food," it's obviously not her taste. It is a good plan that Anni orders take-out while she has the opportunity to get something she wants, lately Anni has been running across the street to grab Little Miss burgers and fries from McDonald's.

In watching a bit of this movie, they both agree it was dull, even though the title had sounded captivating. Anni suggests perhaps the selection of this movie is symbolic of their having a "good year" professionally. Since the movie is not holding their interest, they have a chance to chat a bit about TV shows they enjoy and Little Miss confides in Anni about her boyfriend who is away at college. Then, Little Miss listens attentively as Anni tells her about her husband.

The women also find the common ground in the fact that they both enjoy Propel energy water. So, when Anni went home for a few weeks and came back on the tour she brought Little Miss some Propel to enjoy. Anni tells Little Miss her philosophy regarding the Miss Patriotic trend of two back-to-back Miss Patriotic winners of the same state, "It must be the Propel, that's in the water." Little Miss giggled at the thought.

At the end of the conversation, Anni invites her to come to the gym with her at the hotel, but Little Miss declines. Little Miss comments, "You are so motivated to go workout nearly every day during our stay here." Anni prides herself on Little Miss' observation.

* * * * * * *

A few weeks after using the existing company laptop, Anni receives word from the headquarters that the newer laptop has arrived for her to utilize on the road. This portal would become her connection to the rest of the world as she knows it. The organization does not have an I.T. department, so she attempts to coordinate a brief meeting with their consultant. Serberus is sure to advise her the consultant's time "costs the organization a lot of money per hour."

He confirms the network is loaded on her brand new laptop computer, but when Anni asks what files she needs to access, as well as, documents and calendars, the response if left essentially unanswered.

Anni asks Cheryl, the Director, how she recommends Anni should set-up the organization of her new laptop with folders and documents. Pearson does not offer any suggestions and deflects the question toward a subordinate in the organization. Ultimately, the formatting of Anni's files, documents and electronic signature, etc. was based on her own intuitive protocol.

The original laptop that Anni had been assigned was a leftover from the stash they had when more people worked at the company. The technology was slow and the computer was a bit bulky. Fortunately, the CEO had the foresight to give the approval for the new laptop. It was more compact, which makes it more travelable, has a faster operating system and works on a wireless internet network, which is essential to keep in touch with the headquarters.

As Anni tinkers with the new computer, she determines the ease in the connection to the internet and she discovers she can directly download the photo card through this new laptop onto the file server. This eliminates the delays and lengthy process, in which Sonny was literally handing in the image card to the Public Relations coordinator a month after the events took place for her to sort, organize, match with content, publish in publicity materials and to update the travel log. Anni finds a much improved way to directly handle this key responsibility in an immediate manner. This enables the world to keep tuned-in to the great work and travel that Miss Patriotic is involved with as it happens, up-to-date!

Word spreads about this technological innovation Anni uncovers and Cheryl thinks it certainly can be useful. Sonny says she doesn't know much about using a computer and really only is able to use hers to read e-mails.

Ann Jo still was pushing lots of real paper and even handed a few inches of carbon layered expense reports to Anni to take on all her travels. There is an invisible tug-of-war between wireless activity along with the paper pushing.

— 14 —

It is February 14th, Valentines Day – Jokingly, Anni chides to Little Miss, "Since we are each others' date. Wanna snuggle?"

In reality, Little Miss' family shipped a large heart-shaped box with chocolates to her and her boyfriend Ron made sure she had flowers and balloons to remember him by. Anni notices the next day all the chocolates were gone. Little Miss consumed all the virtual love she received, as quickly as possible. In addition, Little Miss said she was up most of the night electronically conversing with her boyfriend via text message to find out what he's up to and what his social life is like when she's been away. She tells Anni, it's been challenging, since her boyfriend's fraternity brothers all know he is dating Miss Patriotic. He had told her, "Most of them are supportive," but she mentions it's added more stress on them, because she is worried that she'll meet other guys in her travels.

That evening as Anni was heading back from the gym, she brings Little Miss a few heart-shaped cookies back for her that she obtained from the front desk at their hotel. Little Miss appreciates the gesture and quickly eats both cookies.

Ann Jo calls Anni on her cell. When Anni takes Serberus' call, she answers her phone very upbeat and was very pleasant in her tone. When Anni attempts to have a casual conversation to build rapport with Serberus by asking, "How are you?"

She replies, "Just getting by." Anni's second question was, "How are things in the office?" and she said, "I am buried in paperwork." Her comments are curt and the mood is terse. Serberus continues abruptly Little Miss needs to be in the office, as the CEO needs to meet with her. Serberus also wants time to review things with her too.

Anni tries to be helpful and offers Serberus a helping a hand to help her comb through some pending contracts and get more events on appearance calendar. Serbeus does not immediately accept the gesture, as she is not used to delegating anything. Anni mentions, "No big deal, we can figure it out tomorrow." Then asks, "What time would work best for you?"

It is determined they'll come by the office at 10:30am the following day. Ann Jo stresses to Anni to be sure to get Little Miss in the office on time for the meetings. To wrap up the conversation, Anni considers whether she just misheard Serberus say her closing remark... "Talk at you later." Anni hopes she didn't hear her correctly. Why would someone talk at me versus with me? Yikes!

The following day, Anni confirms Little Miss is awake and getting ready for the 10:30 a.m. meeting, as she gently knocks on their adjoining hotel room door and says, "Good morning," through it. Little Miss and her beau sometimes gave each other "wake-up" calls if either had a particularly busy morning. Anni hears Little Miss' phone was buzzing bright-and early.

They scurry into the office as Serberus is busy typing up some e-mails, so Little Miss and Anni casually walk around and chat with the others in the office. Twenty minutes later Serberus greets Little with a big grin, "Hellooo sweetie," Serbeus said as she folded her arms around Little Miss.

She barely acknowledges Anni is standing there with her.

No sooner does Little Miss begin making small talk with one of the coordinators; Anni and Little Miss notice the CEO walking by from the corner of their eyes. The three exchange hellos, but the CEO does not stop to acknowledge the "pressing meeting" Serberus advised Little Miss to be ready for. As the CEO scurried by, Anni steps out into the hallway and shakes his hand congratulating him for being installed as the permanent CEO versus interim status for all those years.

"Thank you for your well-wishes," he acknowledges, "I can exhale now after all that time in a "holding pattern."

Other than that exchange, the CEO makes no mention to meet with Little Miss as he continues to pass-by without a care in the world. Serberus takes five minutes of time to sit with Little Miss and see how things are coming along.

Anni pops into Serberus' office to see how things are progressing in her world. Serberus has nothing to add. Anni optimistically asks if Serberus had any feedback from the clients that she met when she traveled with Sonny in December. Serberus fires back, "I do not get any feedback about you: Good or bad if that is what you are wondering! The only thing I have to tell you is that I got some comments about you wearing a track suit and you should never be wearing jeans on the road."

Anni was taken back. Not until she happens to get an impromptu check on how things are going, does that open a figurative Pandora's box about her manner of dress. Anni takes pride in carefully buying professional work ensembles to round out her existing wardrobe. Anni takes issue that Serberus has nothing positive to report from the travels in Florida.

Anni knows this cannot be all the feedback. As a matter of fact, Jon, the executive director from the anti-drunk driving coalition, had called Anni and sent her correspondence saying how "professional and positive" his experiences had been soon after the appearances in Florida were completed.

This disjointed exchange with Serberus leaves a sour note with Anni.

* * * * * * *

Within twenty more minutes Anni and Little Miss were back on the elevator departing the office toward their respective hotel rooms. Anni asks Little Miss if her meetings were productive. Little Miss responds, "What meetings?"

Little Miss can not understand why she was summoned to get dressed and do her hair and make-up to be in the office just to chat. She said the CEO had nothing prepared for them to discuss.

Anni did not bother to mention the verbal slap in the face she just received from Serberus. She can't concern Little Miss with that "stuff." It definitely does not concern her world.

Even though their worlds are parallel, they don't actually intersect simultaneously.

— 15 —

Cheryl thinks it would be a nice treat to get Little Miss out of the hotel and have a change of scenery, so she invites Little Miss to a Sunday champagne brunch. The brunch is being held at Pearson's old haunt; one of the resort's she used to work as a marketer before it became a Hilton property. Anni asks if she wanted her to tag along, and Cheryl, responds "Absolutely."

Little Miss and Anni dressed very "cas," as it is a Sunday without any scheduled appearances. Anni confirms with her boss if their outfits are acceptable and she said they are. Cheryl intends to pick the women up at their hotel at 11:30am. At the designated time, they were in the lobby waiting with no sign of her, so Anni dials her up on the cell phone.

She answers but is unrecognizable. At first, Anni thinks she hit the wrong button on the phone and dialed someone else. Anni asks, "Is this you Cheryl?" She confirms it is. She is completely hysterical. Anni softly asks, "What is going on?" She assumes Cheryl was involved in a car accident or something along those lines.

Cheryl is too choked–up to say anything for a full minute. Then in monosyllabic, childlike speech, she describes seeing a cat in the street near her house that just got hit by a car. The driver did not stop and she happened to be in the street when this occurred. "I can't move," and is just completely inconsolable, weeping over this cat, while no one came to help. Anni then asks if the cat had a collar and tags and she says it does not. Cheryl is a self-proclaimed animal-lover.

She is trying to regain her composure, but is still hyperventilating through her words. "I feel terrible no one is here to help me. A car just drove-by and nearly hit me as he could she I was trying to rescue the hurt cat." Anni is amazed how she sounded like a wounded child. She tells her to take as much time as she needed to collect herself and resolve the issue and come by when she is ready.

To Anni, this ackward scenario seems like a subliminal test to see how she handles situations when presented with something thrown her way. Is this meant to be initiation?

With that in mind, Anni makes a concerted effort to be sympathetic of Cheryl, her boss; to be a good listener and to help her to regain composure.

Twenty minutes later Cheryl arrives as Little Miss and Anni get into the cluttery Jaguar. Cheryl shows up at the hotel driveway, smiling like all is right with the world! Anni wonders why Cheryl can drive Little Miss around in her personal car on a whim, when Serberus and Sonny indicated the policy was for Miss Patriotic to ride in vehicles with $1 million dollars in liability insurance. It seems that rule did not apply to the executives in the organization... I suppose Cheryl's vehicle was an exception to the policy.

On the drive Cheryl, Anni's typically smiling boss, put her "game face on" and chats with Little Miss about how exciting things are and how she is looking forward to seeing her old colleagues at the property they are headed for brunch. In the meantime Anni is sitting in the trashed back seat, among child safety seat, caked with food crumbs, toys and broken door-latch on this luxury car.

Anni realizes, she is merely a passenger, this outing is really a treat meant for Little Miss' enjoyment. Upon nearing the resort, Cheryl could not determine where to park. Anni immediately offers her VIP parking card she had which was valid for a few casino properties to park at no charge. Cheryl obliges to accept the offer.

At the restaurant in the resort where Pearson used to work, the three women have to wait in the hall for twenty minutes. Anni thought Pearson had reservations. She asks her, "Did they take reservations?"

Cheryl, responds, "I did not think to make any."

Rather, she thinks, since she is connected, they would not even need to wait. In the meantime, Cheryl is telling strangers who are also waiting to be seated in the restaurant, who Little Miss is. Therefore, all of the sudden on this particular quiet Sunday, Little Miss has to be "on," as if this inadvertently becomes an unscheduled appearance. The crowd thickens a bit and a large guy from Brooklyn peppers Little Miss with questions, photo requests and has her talk to his "boyz" on his cell phone.

Way to go Cheryl! Anni is thinking this is rather inconsiderate. On a day off, Little Miss has to get on point and meet and greet people, while they were delayed and starving. It certainly puts Little Miss in an ackward position, but there is nothing she can do about it. This is now her life for the year.

After the forty-five minute commotion, Cheryl points to the restaurant Manager, who quickly seats them at a non-private table and proceeds to cover their table with flutes of champagne. This is their way of honoring Little Miss. Little did the restaurant staff, nor Cheryl stop to consider Little Miss is under the legal drinking age. Anni, however keeps moving the glasses away, since she does not want the glasses to be a prop in any onlooker's photos, which in turn, could appear on the internet and be construed that Little Miss has an underage drinking issue.

In the meantime, smiling Cheryl is having the time of her life, reminiscing with her former resort counterparts from the hospitality industry, while imbibing her share of champagne and desserts soaked with specialty liquors.

Following the champagne brunch, they leave the hotel and notice the weather is lovely that morning at the Jersey shore, so Cheryl continues on the drive with Anni stuffed in back with her kid's junk in the backseat and Little Miss upfront. They take a Sunday morning drive along the shoreline through Atlantic City, Ventnor, Margate and stop briefly in Longport. Cheryl pulls up to a scenic block along a jetty and says, "Let's all get out and look." Immediately, Anni jumps from the car to inspect the shimmer of the sunlight bouncing on the ocean's surface from the jagged rocks.

Little Miss doesn't respond, as she is doing what she normally does in between most other things, sends a flurry of text messages and phone calls. Cheryl struggles catch Little Miss' attention to step outside and enjoy the view.

Anni signals to Little Miss to come out when she is finished with her daily family check-in.

Cheryl mentions, "I wish I had a camera here."

"Consider your wish is answered," Anni replies, as she pulls out the work-issued digital camera out of her large work handbag and they snap a few pictures. A jogger stops and offers to take a photo of all of them on the jetty. But, Little Miss is still involved on the phone, so the jogger takes a picture of Cheryl and Anni and continues on. A few minutes later Little Miss appears from the car and does not have much to say about the glorious weather or the scenery. Anni offers to snap a picture of Cheryl and Little Miss together and a picture of Little Miss standing high above the water's edge with the Atlantic Ocean glimmering behind her on the jetty to capture their Sunday outing in Longport. As Anni snaps the photo, Cheryl kept saying Little Miss looks like a model.

The ladies forge on to Ocean City with boutiques to satisfy Little Miss' need to get some gifts for a friend. Cheryl wants to prove that there is a lot of "good shopping" nearby, so she took them on hours of this shopping excursion. Anni is tired and bored, but more importantly Little Miss likes the shopping part of this trip.

Later Cheryl mentions she'd be glad to have Little Miss to her house for dinner, so her daughter could spend time with her and so Cheryl could prepare some Mac & Cheese for them.

Pulling up to Cheryl's home in Ventnor, she sees her neighbor down the block and hollers towards him that there is someone she wants him to meet. So, reluctantly the neighbor walks toward her driveway and she is compelled to "prove" she is having Miss Patriotic over her house for dinner. The neighbor is cordial and tells Little Miss that his family has been active volunteers with the pageant back in the "good old days" when it was indigenous to Atlantic City. Little Miss shook his hand and tells him, "It's nice to meet you."

She has a nicely interior-decorated home which was completely renovated from its original facade. It is obvious Cheryl takes pride in the beauty of her home and Anni thinks this is such a dramatic difference from the lack of ambiance in her workspace at the headquarters. Cheryl's little girl and her playmate apprehensively come up from the basement to meet the special dinner guest. Mom excitedly tries to get them to say hello and welcome Little Miss. It took a few minutes of them warming-up, but fortunately, Little Miss is very good with the girls and speaks to them in terms of their latest gadget—a Barbie Gameboy. "Is that the new Barbie Gamboy?" Cheryl's daughter realizes then, Little Miss is one of them, as she offers to play video games with the pair.

In the meantime, Cheryl's husband Jerri, comes in from another part of their home to say hello. To Anni, Jerri reminds her of a younger Nick Nolte character. Anni shakes his hand and exchanges pleasantries with him, as Little Miss is still engrossed in game playing with the girls. Jerri, recently came back from Costa Rica where he was pursuing his life's passion—surfing. He was trying to live out his fantasy of being pro-surfer Laird Hamilton; to the extent that he implores Anni to watch some of his surfing videos. Cheryl is a bit embarrassed how excited he is that someone will actually indulge him in his interest, as she "poo-poo's" it as less important.

Anni watches a few minutes of the big wave surfing documentary, while Cheryl is in her modern kitchen stirring the mac & cheese. Shortly after viewing a bit of the video, Anni goes upstairs to check-in with her hostess (her boss), and chats her up about cooking. Cheryl admits she not cook regularly. Most of their meals are take-out, but for Little Miss she goes the extra mile by putting together

her own Kraft Mac & Cheese. Cheryl and Anni laugh at the thought of it. Cheryl also presents side dishes of store bought pre-made meatballs, a leftover spiral ham, and eggplant parmesan-for Jerri who tries to keep vegetarian. His diet correlates with his current persona of being a natural surfer, Anni considers.

The girls squirm tableside and attempt to avoid eating dinner. After the meal, Cheryl insists, like an excited child, she gets to view the most recent Miss Patriotic pageant along with Little Miss. Even though they were there at the pageant, in the moment, while it unfolded, it is different to see the show through the TV.

Anni sits on a small loveseat, while the two fidgety, little girls plunk down on both sides of Little Miss. They were more engrossed in the Barbie video game and did not realize the magnitude Mom felt about having Little Miss in her own home to view the tape. The copy of the tape looks poor: not very clear and a bit distracting with lots of static. Anni craws-up to the video machine, since their remote is dead, to fast-forward through the advertisements, so they can get the gist of the show.

Anni tells Little Miss how she had a gathering at her home the night of the live pageant. Anni had viewed all the contestants' video profiles beforehand and was familiar with the participants. Anni then took copious notes prior to the pageant. "So I could consider who I may be heading on the road with." Then she and her guests shared commentary and narrowed down their selections. Little Miss was in Anni's top three picks! She also indicated that she contacted Sonny who was in Vegas behind the scenes at pageant, and tells her that Little Miss was the girl we wanted. "As it turns out, our mutual hunch came to fruition!"

The little girls playing the Barbie game were really antsy. Jerri drove his daughter's playmate home. It was getting late, so they wrapped-up the pageant recap, as Cheryl opts to drive Little Miss and Anni back to their hotel.

— 16 —

"Are you ready for the photos? Anni asks.

"Well, I hope they come out, but if they don't, I'll get my own photographer to take other pictures for the program cover," Little Miss responds.

They head back on the road for local duties in Linwood, as they hop in the limousine service to head out to the suburbs for a photo shoot. Little Miss has her collection of gowns and designer outfits piled and ready and she was told the jewelry sponsor shipped a package of numerous accessories for Little Miss to don in the pictorial spread. When they were approaching the location with the Public Relations coordinator in tow, who set-up the logistics, she was not certain where the precise address was located. "I believe it's toward the back of the square," Anni surmises. Fortunately, Anni glances past the steeple towards the back of the plaza and finds the studio tucked in the corner.

The PR coordinator is sure to name drop that "Miss Patriotic" has plenty to do when the driver lets them off. Suddenly, her comment triggers a flurry of autograph and picture requests that Little Miss graciously obliges for the driver as she scribbles her name across his clipboard. Anni and Little Miss look at each other, as Anni knows how Little Miss dislikes being announced off guard to do impromptu autographs, especially as they were standing at the curb trying to off load her garments into the studio, but she continues to be a good showman and did her duty.

Each of them grabs a handful of wardrobe bags, which had slithered around in the trunk of the limo. The owners of the photo studio introduce themselves to Little Miss and the others; then their young granddaughter crept out from the rear of the studio holding a bouquet of grocery-store flowers to present to Miss Patriotic. Her Mother, sitting on a small settee in a corner, was too shy to request a photo of her daughter with Little Miss to capture the floral presentation that just took place. The owners whisked Little Miss, Anni and the PR coordinator upstairs where the hair and make-up artists were sitting waiting for Little Miss's arrival. The photo studio staff is excited to have this opportunity to shoot this footage of a locally-based celebrity, since their primary niche is taking aerial shots of commercial property along the shoreline. Fashion shoots are not at the top of their primary services. Beside commercial photos, they take kids pictures for holidays. This was evident by the amount of stuffed animals and Easter-related props that surround the backdrop where Little Miss would be getting cover shots taken for her promotional materials and the pageant program.

In the makeshift dressing room generally used to process film, the staff placed the boxes of accessories. The jewelry pieces were displayed along a counter where Little Miss is getting her hair and make-up done. Much of this jewelry collection is more artsy than functional. It is a collection of costume jewelry; many of the items are a mishmash of chunky glass stones in an oddly arranged cluster hanging off cheap wire. Little Miss and the PR coordinator attempt to sort through the clunky pieces to get a handful of promotional shots selecting some of the more simplistic jewels, so that the jewelry designer-sponsor may use them for her own promotional indulgences.

The PR coordinator advises Little Miss that the purpose of the photo shoot is to get the cover shot for the upcoming program. It is evident by Little Miss' face she is not thrilled with the test shots the photographers are taking.

In a side conversation, Little Miss reiterates how pleased she is with Jimmy G, the photographer from her home state, who shot the prints used in her state-level pageant and shots from the national pageant. She is hoping to have a chance to get him to shoot some current pictures when she's back home to use for her headshots…Anni suspects she feels more comfortable working with Jimmy G.

Anni had a chance to see the state-level promotional shots he put together, and she thinks those old pictures did not accentuate Little Miss. She recalls seeing her roots in her hair that were in desperate need of touch-up and the background nearly camouflaged Little Miss' outfit in the photo that she used for her State Title promotional material…

Currently, at the studio, Little Miss attempts to be the professional by complimenting the hair and make-up girls and making them feel like their work is "up-to-par." In reality, she says to Anni privately, "I'm not happy with the results. It does not look like me," she tells Anni.

As the shoot was winding down, the owners indicate they want to have their pictures taken on set with Little Miss and one with her and each of their nephews for their private portfolio.

Afterwards, Little Miss was slated time to cut a demo in a nearby recording studio. Serberus had arranged for Little Miss to work with a local singing coach to produce a CD demo of the "Star Spangled Banner." Some perspective clients wanted to listen to her sing before they book her for an upcoming NASCAR event to perform it.

Anni remembers how peculiar Serberus acted as she tells her about this vocal coach contact she knew from years ago. Anni reads between the lines, as Serberus blushes when she calls him from her office, while Anni was sitting there to make these arrangements. Serberus places the call using her maiden name, Frangellico, as she tries to make the connection with him. She is not sure if he realizes she was ever married.

Serberus avows out loud, "Back in the day, he was hot stuff-very sophisticated, as the lead singer in one of the Philly sound doo-wop groups." She figuratively lets her hair down, as she mentions how he used to chase her around in a flirtatious way and they had good times together.

After the studio time is confirmed, Anni tells her, "I'll take a picture of Vic in his studio with Little Miss, so you can see how he currently looks, since it's been years." In one of the only times Anni saw Serberus' light-up facially; Anni noticed the gleam in her eyes, Serberus could not wait!

From the photoshoot, now they were off to Vic's local sound studio. Anni asks the owners of the photo studio, if they may leave the items behind for a few hours. The women leave the gowns and wardrobe gear at the photo studio, so they wouldn't have to schlep the garments.

As it turns out, Vic, the singing coach, (Serberus' former crush) has his studio in the same plaza at the photo studio. It became evident as they jump in the limo, only to get back out a block further--literally across the parking lot.

They proceed to climb the narrow stairway with the grey-paneled walls, plastered with headshots and photos (mostly of kids Vic must have tutored over his many years). Sprinkled among those shots are Marilyn Monroe collectibles including beach towels and cardboard cutouts. Anni sees the scotch tape is yellowing around some of the items. At the top of the steps, they arrive in a cluttery, waiting area with mismatched chairs and memorabilia so overwhelming it looks like wallpaper. This cavalcade of pictures has notes scrawled to Vic thanking him for his help.

The mysterious Vic is not in sight. Anni hears some noise eminating from a room within the waiting area. Gently, she knocks on the door, as she didn't want to disturb a recording session; if that was what was happening.

A booming, man's voice yells out, "It will be just a few minutes," from the cavern inside. Five minutes later a pre-teen with her Mom struts out of the room, then the booming voice says, "Come on in the studio."

Upon entering Anni does the announcement of who's who. Little Miss is then introduced to Vic. They see seated in the farthest side of the room, an enormous, scraggly man.

Anni professes, "Ann Jo Frangellico is so grateful, you are able to see Little Miss on short notice." Anni purposefully uses Serberus' maiden name, since that is how Serberus brokered the appoinment. Anni also mentions that she said he was a consummate professional that she always admired. Sure, Anni exaggerated a bit.

Based on Anni's first impression, he seems to be a nice man, but also is morbidly, huge-- over 380lbs, wearing big men's polyester pants and orthopedic shoes that were worn out on the sides to hold this teetering, out-of-balance massive man.

Anni could tell he loves his life in entertainment and relishes in the accolades from his glory days: like recording with Elvis at Sun Studios back in the day. He mentions this to Anni after she comments on the Elvis "shrine" he had amassed with all the collectibles in the corner on cheap plastic mismatched shelving.

In the middle of the studio, Vic's microphone, stack of recording and editing devices were weighing down an everyday plastic folding table. Anni is amazed the table had not collapsed from all the weight. The table looks warped, similar to the curve of what were formerly the insoles in his orthopedic shoes sagging from the weight of his body.

Anni couldn't get over that the old flimsy furniture used to support the magnitude of Vic's gigantic body. He was sitting on a meager chair and his tower of equipment sat levels high off the sagging gray folding table. The burden of all the furniture was being maxed out by its current function.

During this brief vocal session, Anni observes the power that emanated the vocal coaching segment Vic gives Little Miss. Little Miss has the natural talent to sing on key and in pitch from the catalog of songs she has stored in her memory. Vic asks her to perform the "Star Spangled Banner." The first rendition gives Anni some goose bumps, as she spectates sitting in a plastic lawn chair in this small wood- paneled room amongst tons of katchtke-Sinatra, Beatles, Marilyn Monrow, Felix the Cat and more lining the walls on cheap plastic bookshelving.

Vic gives Little Miss some sound advice about vocalizing certain sounds differently and breathing in an alternate pattern to extend her notes. He even searches through his paper files to find the words to some patriotic music, so he could verify she was singing the lyrics appropriately. With just some minor correction, she again sang the National Anthem using his recommendations as Vic recorded her this time.

Anni could not get over how mystified this experience became. Little Miss' voice just popped; she took a well-known song to another dimension adding some notes in a higher octave and shrilling a few others in a couple of pivotal areas. Following Vic's guidance, the supercharged demo of "The Star Spangled Banner" was burned on a CD to be sent to prospective clients and they headed back on the road.

— 17 —

Midway through February, Anni sends an email to Serberus to get an idea of the types of events and the relevant details which were placed on the radar for March when Anni is scheduled to meet-up with Little Miss on the road again. Anni wants to be prepared and let her family know her whereabouts when she was on tour. Very curtly, Serberus balks, "I am still working on the itinerary." Yet, she gruffly rattles off a short list that there is a black-tie event planned and two cocktail party events. With that Anni was able to begin to layout her month-long wardrobe.

A week later the itinerary appears in Anni's electronic inbox.

March is underway and they have a lot of travel ahead of them. Anni's touring month of March begins as the hired car service picked her up mid-morning to take her to the hotel that Sonny and Little Miss would be arriving later in the day following their flight back from L.A. They are heading to Washington, DC for a few events. She arrives at the check-in desk of the Marriott and posts the corporate card for the hotel room. There is a bit of maneuvering at the check-in to determine whether she is checking in as herself or getting the key under Sonny's existing reservation, or whether the reservation is billed in part or in its entirety to one or more clients. Anni certainly needs to think quickly on her feet, be flexible and become proficient at uncovering these details effectively.

After check-in, Anni has her luggage dropped off, then quickly determines where the fitness center is, so she could change clothes and do a workout. She completes a decent cardio workout on the elliptical machine, then free weights, followed by yoga stretches, Anni sought out a salad that she retrieved from the hotel's express café'.

Anni realizes early in her travels, she does not have an affinity for hotel room service. First, she is not a fan of sitting in the same four walls that she sleeps and works on her laptop to eat her meals. Secondly, the cost of the service is astronomical with the delivery fee and taxes even if it is not coming from her own pocket. Anni has enough wherewithall to consider it is not cost effective for the organization for her to order food in this way most of the time, if other options are available.

While cutting into her salad, her work cell phone rings. Serberus says sternly there will be a meeting at the office when she's back from D.C. She does not give Anni an indication what the topic of the meeting is about. Anni asks if the meeting is to provide current status of the tour?

Serberus retorts, "You'll find out when you are in the office and be sure to bring all your completed reports." Anni thinks this is rather curt, but Serberus generally seems preoccupied when Anni speaks with her, so she figures she has other things on her mind as she makes those abrupt comments.

A few hours later there is a knock on her hotel room door. When she opens it, Little Miss appears smiling broadly and Sonny standing along side of her. Anni asks how their flight was. Anni came to D.C. to meet-up with Sonny and Little Miss who were flying in from the remaining February events that she executed on the West coast. Little Miss is tired, but glad to settle in and order some room service, as their flight was really LONG…

Little Miss says, "It was very tiring and my back is really aching from sitting so long." She gave Anni a huge, friendly hug, then Anni hands them both their respective room keys. Sonny is holding up fine, but mentions, "I can't wait to get out of these clothes," describing her jeans, white top and keds. Little Miss' plans to get some room service and go off to sleep.

Before calling it a night, Anni checks in with Serberus at the HQ to confirm Little Miss and Sonny have arrived. Serberus tells Anni that Little Miss and Sonny have been placed on a security clearance list to take a tour of a few military hospitals tomorrow: Walter Reed and Bethesda. Little Miss is doing appearances working on behalf of the USO. There are a limited amount of clearances they grant and they are slated for actor Lorenzo Lamas, Wrestling Promoter Jimmy Hart and Little Miss along with Sonny. There is not an additional spot for Anni to attend. She completely understood and tells them, "I will be available upon their return."

Lucky for Anni, this carves out an entire day in a great city with plenty to see and do. Anni takes a refreshing walk and spends a few hours taking advantage of the D.C. sites: inspecting a few very intriguing museums including: Holocaust Memorial Museum, in which Anni feels drawn to the magnitude and isolation within the exhibits and other landmarks including Ford's theatre, which brought back memories of Anni's deceased Father's college buddy who used to be a tour facilitator there.

Anni finds it interesting that Little Miss is doing a tour in the V.A. Hospital System, just as the Washington Post broke the story about the dire conditions of some of the facilities that the wounded soldiers are forced to endure. Anni's sure this does not cross Little Miss' mind though. She is not abreast of the news.

Upon Little Miss and Sonny's return to the hotel around dinner time, they mentioned they did a ton on walking, toured the building and now are tired. Little Miss asks, "So what did you do all day Anni?" Anni responds she had a very enjoyable time, going to a few prestigious museums and learned a great deal about history. Sonny and Anni both suggest Little Miss take advantage of sightseeing in the various stops of the tour when she had enough downtime to take advantage.

Little Miss says her Mom encourages her to do it too, while she has the chance to see the country, but Little Miss opts to sit in her hotel room, listening to music on her ipod, renting movies from pay-per-view, ordering room service and lounging around returning text messages with her friends and family. She knows her possibilities were limited in terms of seeing the sights while she has the chance to be in so many places, but she chooses to hole up at the hotel.

When Anni asked about her day, Little Miss did not have much to say about her tour of the high profile military hospitals in which current war vets injured in Iraq and Afghanistan were rehabilitating. While she and the entourage are on tour with various assorted B-celebrities like Lorenzo Lamas and Jimmy Hart,Little Miss was just overwhelmed how exhausted she felt being "on" all day long, meeting soldiers and seeing them in their wounded state. She had no connection to the squalor being reported about in the hospital system.

The next day, Anni and Sonny assemble, so Little Miss could be a special guest at a Youth Leadership Program on behalf of the National Guard and USO. There she presents awards to at-risk youth, who participate in this service and leadership group to accelerate their ability to flourish in society. Little Miss is one of a handful of notables along with Pat Boone and an unknown county music vocalist, Michael some-thing-or-other. Most of the special USO guests are not the most appealing to today's youth receiving the awards.

The President of the USO, Elaine Rodgers, who emcees the awards is a bombshell. For twenty years, she has been orchestrating large amounts of fundraising and high profile events. At this luncheon, this four-foot woman, blabbers on about the awards in her rhinestone-studded jeans, high heels and brilliant, blond "Peter Pan" hairstyle. In the meanwhile, the youth award recipients are sitting uncomfortably, stiff in their starched uniforms.

Little Miss attends the luncheon wearing a black knit, form-fitting, mini dress and heels. Anni had suggested to her after showing Little Miss' Mother a picture of her in this outfit from another appearance that she should wear a black bra, since her white one shows through in pictures…

Anni makes sure to wear business attire with a red wool jacket and black skirt, which she purchased with her wardrobe allowance.

The emcee relays stories about her friendships with some of the high-ranking generals and celebrity guests and does her share of name dropping. The hard-knock students receiving the awards shake hands with the upper-level military in gratitude of their accomplishments.

One young woman named Nicole, reads her story of being a child from the projects. From spiral notebook paper, she recounts her testimonial, written in a very elementary manner. It's challenging to hear; her voice does not project through the microphone. She clenches her handwritten notepaper and garbles her story with her Black, Southern drawl reading it word-for-word.

Straining to listen and follow along, the audience gets the gist of her struggle to break away from the gang and drug life that engulfed her. She wants to break away, as her Grandmother tells her, "You could have a fighting chance to be somebody." Her story represents the population of the youth guardsmen being honored here. These candidates are overcoming their tumultuous backgrounds to add value to their lives through military service and leadership.

The next evening is a gala to honor the National Guard award recipients, as a fundraiser, with music and other assorted bells and whistles. Anni corroborated with Sonny earlier as to the dress code and tells her she plans to wear a full-length velvet skirt and off white silk Ann Taylor off the shoulder sweater. Sonny arrives wearing her polyester wide-leg pants and sequin- jacket and sandals.

Sonny, Anni and Little Miss arrive early, in order that Little Miss has time to rehearse and do a sound check. Sonny suggests Anni check her coat and the "hat box," which holds Little Miss' crown, in the coat room. The "hat box" is empty as Little Miss is wearing her crown for this appearance. Anni weaves through the throngs of guests circulating around the coat room and the registration table.

In the meantime, Sonny tries to find their table assignments. She tells Anni she couldn't find a place card with her name on it. Anni is concerned whether the USO reserved a seat for her to attend, but no sooner did she start to worry when Elaine, the woman who emceed the awards luncheon earlier in the day,

President of that USO Chapter exclaimed enthusiastically, "No worries, there's definitely a spot saved for you!"

Sonny and Anni go looking for the Audio Director, so Little Miss could rehearse. They notice none of the other performers attend the rehearsal. Little Miss is exasperated she was scheduled to be in full make-up, hair and regalia to arrive at this venue two hours before the event began. For this gala, she has on one of her many designer gowns, but if no one else was coming to rehearsal, she would have bagged it too.

Being the talented vocalist she is, Little Miss' rehearsal took five minutes and the adjustment of the equipment was minimal. Sonny says,"This is a good opportunity to take unobstructed pictures of Little Miss, as we were probably not going to be sitting near her." Sonny found a good purpose to being here two hours early.

Following the rehearsal, Little Miss is slated to attend the VIP reception. She did not know what to expect. Sonny said this is where good social skills are helpful to have a handful of one-on-one conversations. Mostly those attending are high-ranking military and dedicated sponsors of the local USO chapter. Upon entering the door to the reception area, Little Miss was greeted by a series of military Generals including Four-star Marine General Peter Pace, who is the current Chairman of the Joint Chief of Staffs. Sonny whispers to Little Miss and Anni, "Many times the Generals have a tradition of giving special commemorative coin to esteemed people they meet."

No sooner did Sonny tell them about that occurrence when General Pace offers Little Miss his special coin. She appreciated the gesture, but then whispers to Anni, "What do I do with it?"

Anni replies, "It's certainly an honor to be acknowledged by these military powerhouses." Little Miss felt overwhelmed by this situation. She tells Anni how she did not like these receptions where people expect you to carry-on a conversation with them, like you've known them for years.

Anni suggests she make the most of it, as Anni shares with Little Miss how she has attended some events in her life and at that time could not see the purpose and wished she was somewhere else, but down the road she crossed paths with a few of those people she had met at those functions and she was able to make connections. Anni told Little Miss, "You never know what opportunities can come out of times like these."

* * * * * * *

Anni notices her work bag/purse is starting to wear out. Her work bag is like life on the road, sometimes exploding out of control. The main zipper and handles were splitting from the weight of all the essentials Anni needs to have with her to keep Little Miss prepared and all the additional items Anni was collecting along the way. When Little Miss is handed souvenirs and keepsakes from people, Anni holds them for her and gives them to her back at each hotel to arrange in her own suitcase. After awhile this process takes a toll on Anni's Doctor-inspired bag. She knows the bag needs a replacement very soon, but hopes she can get a few more travel days out of this one until there is time to find a replacement. To reinforce the handles, Anni attaches a metal hair clip to the ends.

After the VIP reception, Little Miss is seated at a head table surrounding the stage. Sonny and Anni are at a table at the far rear of the ballroom among 600 attendees. At their table and all the others, bottles of wine were situated. Sonny said she wasn't much for wine as she had given up bread, meat and sweets for Lent, which would normally help her absorb the alcohol. She doesn't want to drink wine at her regular pace without having some carbohydrates to absorb it. So, Sonny has just a bit and she thanks Anni for the offer, as she pours some for the other folks on their side of the ten-person table.

Anni has a glass of wine with her dinner and carries on small-talk with the people assembled among them. One was a 16-year old Detroit guy who was one of the soldiers being recognized in this gala for overcoming their at-risk environments.

As was part of the daytime luncheon program, once again they had Nicole, the black young, soldier read her story. It is the same story she read earlier and she droned on again, but it is even more difficult to hear her in this larger venue. Her message is lost this time, but the audience is compelled to rise and give her a standing ovation.

* * * * * * *

Their host in the D.C. area, Dick Zweber, offered multiple times to give Little Miss a private tour of the region, when she has some free time. She had not spent much time in this region before, so that was a tremendous offer from someone who is like a talking encyclopedia of facts and stories. He is well-connected to many diplomats, politicians, military and celebrities working in the area for more than twenty-years. He is a close personal friend of Elaine, the USO President and together has rubbed elbows with many legends. Little Miss thanks him, but prefers to just hang out in her hotel room when she had any down time, even if it is a few days worth.

Little Miss did confide to Anni, "My Mom told me a few times how she was hoping she I would take advantage of exploring different places when I am not working." Once again, Little Miss knew she just passed on a great opportunity, but chose not to capitalize on it...

— 18 —

The next evening they went to a McCormick & Schmick's, national steak house chain, as Little Miss is craving a desert she had had when she was visiting her boyfriend in their Kansas City location called a "chocolate bag." She describes this decadent concoction as a chocolate sculpture formed with an actual paper bag used to mold the hardened chocolate. Once you break the outer shell, you enjoy the molten chocolate drenched inside.

The three of them anxiously wait for a table. Before they are seated, Little Miss decides what to order. She picks a standard hamburger, Sonny some fried oysters as her entrée and Anni orders an appetizer of dim sum. She does not feel really hungry for a full entrée.

After the wait for a table and for the slow service, the food arrives and Little Miss' burger is scorched like an unrecognizable piece of meat, blackened like a scaley-hockey puck. She does not complain, but munches on the fries. Anni's appetizer is inedible, way over-salted and not even lukewarm. It took 45 minutes to get the food served, so Anni speaks-up to the waitress that the food is unacceptable.

Little Miss passes on the meal, but proceeds to go for the dessert, which is the reason they chose this place anyhow. To her demise, this franchise does not serve the "chocolate bag." So, disappointed and still hungry, Little Miss and Anni share a hot apple pie with caramel sauce and a scoop of vanilla ice cream to serve as their nutritious dinner that evening.

The next day they taxi around town, in order that Little Miss completes some of her goodwill duty on behalf of the Children's charity to visit with patients at the local children's specialty hospital. After hours of visits including one room in which, Little Miss is not told by hospital administration that the patient in this room is taking her last breaths. Little Miss is overwhelmed with despair how badly this girl looked, while she is gasping for each breath; connected to tubes and equipment to keep her going for a few more minutes. This situation drains

Little Miss emotionally. She expects the children to be in better condition than the one who was nearly being given last rites.

In the meanwhile, Sonny has a good 'ole time downstairs, as she buys a handful of children's books and toys on sale in the lobby of the hospital to bring back home to her grandkids. She is already mentally home with her family, whereas Little Miss feels homesick away from her parents and siblings. She continues to phone her Mom about half-dozen times daily.

After the appearance, Little Miss is ready for food. Sonny and Anni offer to take Little Miss for some authentic Mexican food in D.C. at Rosa's Cantina. Sonny takes the liberty of telling the host that "Little Miss" is in their establishment, so suddenly they receive "star treatment," which includes conversation with the Chef's (who is obliged to come out and introduce himself), slower and more thorough food preparation (as they felt they have to impress her), and being offered samples of special delicacies, not on the menu (that she does not appreciate, as her taste is rather simple and not open to new dishes and exotic spices).

While the "festivities" were taking place, Anni excuses herself to wash-up in the ladies room. The temperature change in D.C. is erratic and making Anni feel congested with a sinus cold. She goes to the Ladies' Room to clear her nose, in an effort to try to breathe easier and to check-in with Serberus to give her a status report. Serberus is glad Anni calls-in, but again ends the conversation by stating to Anni again, "Talk at you later!"

As Anni reconvenes at the table, Sonny is munching on table-side prepared guacamole. Little Miss is not thrilled with it, as avocado is not a vegetable she enjoys. Instead she chows on baskets of tortilla chips and salsa. Their artistically designed plates are presented to the table by the Chef and Little Miss eats what she can. It is not a big portion, but the pesto spices in her meal make her not enjoy the dish. Sonny ate a bowl of the guac, as well as her entrée, then felt the indigestion swell even before they left the confines of this well known establishment.

After their early supper they head back to the hotel. Little Miss plans to rest up, as Sonny has to accompany her to CBS studio for a live midnight interview.

From spending a few days in the damp weather, Anni's head was floating in congestion, so she tries to quickly medicate with some sinus pain reliever and forces herself to sleep, as a means to heal her aching body. About 10 p.m. that evening, Anni's phone rings and it is Sonny on the line, "You need to take Little Miss to the studio alone, as the Mexican food has been repeating on me and giving me trouble for hours."

So, Anni, being in training, replies, "of course," and wishes Sonny well that night. After the call, Anni says all kinds of prayers to assist her in getting through the night without getting full-blown sick. It is unusual a Tour Manager has back-up to take their place, but Sonny is lucky Anni is there in D.C. to "fill in" for her that evening. Wouldn't you know, Anni hears the rain coming down in sheets and the windows were fogging up from the differences in temperature from the outside.

Before they leave at 11 p.m., Anni calls Little Miss in her hotel room to alert her it was raining and cool. She does not have an umbrella, "Don't worry, I do, you may want to take a jacket with you," Anni advises.

They jump in a taxi as the city was rather quiet this hour. Anni takes some hot tea with her along for the ride. The driver seems to drive around the block a bit, as the address is not easily discernable, then Anni identifies the sliver of building with the CBS letters on the entrance. They enter the narrow facade, approach a security guard and Anni indicates who they are there to see. Anni provides him the producer's name and the name of the radio host. He calls their office and they sit and wait, then wait some more, quietly on a bench trying to warm up from the damp cold of the night.

After about 20 minutes, Anni rechecks with the security guard. It seems like an eternity, Little Miss and Anni hear the elevator door around a wall grind to a halt and clunk opened. The anticipation is mounting when a creepy looking techie guy comes around, but did not utter a word. He dons a buttoned-down polyester blue shirt with black polyester pants. To Anni, this combination looks like a bad bruise. His hair is black and stragglely from the oils needing to be washed from it. He has outdated black plastic framed eyewear and had pens in his shirt pocket. So, with no words being exchanged Anni rises from the bench, as did Little Miss. Finally, Anni introduces herself and Little Miss and asks, "Are you John?"

He replies, "Who else would I be?" So much for him welcoming them to the studio and letting young ladies traveling at this time of night feel secure they arrived at the right place. The three of them take the elevator up to the studio floor in complete silence. Anni asks what the topic of the discussion will be. John retorts Jim Bo will review the details with Little Miss prior to going "ON AIR."

They make their way up to the studio, a well-worn and outdated looking area. Yellowed papers strewn in every direction. Books about news, history and current events in piles clustered around electronic audio equipment. We could hear a current talk show conversation taking place upon our entry to the studio. The host Jim Bo is speaking with a college professor hawking his most latest title. Jim Bo attempts to stir up the conversational pot by including a few live callers for the author.

What kinds of listeners are involved at the midnight hour to this kind of content?

The answer becomes evident as Jim Bo takes a call from Kim. Her question, "I want to know if someone could use their ATM card to fund a foundation?"

Anni thinks, Are you kidding me? Who are these overnight listeners? If the callers during the show were a reflection of the majority of them, they are a bunch on flaky insomniacs that don't have a grip on reality...

The author politely explains using an anecdote about a transaction from an automatic machine does not constitute the funding in replenishing foundation monies. Jim Bo thinks it is comical to question the author's propriety: using foundation dollars to fund his girlfriend or other assorted hobbies?

Anni is not sure how the conversation deviates in that direction of borderline inappropriateness. With that being the line of questioning from the interviewer about to host a segment with Little Miss, Anni abruptly puts on her censor hat and asks Producer John to have Jim Bo review the content of Little Miss' segment with her prior to her portion of the interview. During commercial, Jim Bo steps out of the booth and mentions the interview will center on her pageant experiences, education, objectives and more about the websites she was plugging for internet safety.

Ultimately during the interview, Jim Bo relies on a handwritten talking point list and asks her silly things like what it felt like wearing a bikini in front of millions of people. The questioning is banal and trite.

While they were in the booth Anni chats with John to try to get him to seem more human and less creepy to her. She asks how he got involved in the industry and if he enjoys working the all night shift, which he does. She is surprised to find out he has been married for years, but he and his spouse are like passing ships in the night as she works days and he works nights. They make sure to have one meal a day together, he interjects.

In the background of their chitchat, he said, "Hang on, I have to adjust some levels on the board," then Jim Bo gears-up to ask Little Miss most of the same questions he had already in their live on-air conversation. Anni considers the time and knows Little Miss is tired, so she asks John, "Why it seems the interview was being repeated?"

"They have to record this portion to do a morning show version of the interview."

Anni responded, "I was just wondering. I assumed he could have recorded the live version for posterity and replay it, but I suppose they did not want to confuse the listeners who think there is a call-in segment in the morning." It seemed awfully redundant especially at the midnight hour.

After the segment, Anni flags Producer John to call a taxi back to their hotel. He responds, "I do not get involved in that!"

"OK, let's get the guard in the lobby to make the arrangements as it now half past midnight in D.C., Anni retorts. John comments the security guard does not provide that service, but indicates, "You can cross the street and get a bellman at the hotel there to hail you a taxi."

I could not believe I am hearing this!

Anni put these observations in her follow-up report to HQ and Serberus railed her for questioning John, the Producer's work. Anni indicates she was not "questioning his work," but wanted to find out for Little Miss' well-being why the interview process was repeated. Serberus said the PR coordinator who booked the interview would follow-up with them directly, as to why they did not assist in appropriate transport back to the hotel. She said they have been working with them and doing this radio show for many years and didn't want to jeopardize the relationship.

— 19 —

The next day, Anni still tries to get over the congestion in her head, vexed by being out in the rain late during the night to escort Little Miss for the midnight radio interviews. Now they are gearing up to take Little Miss to the local speaker's bureau, so the partners there can get to know her and determine her marketability as a speaker to add to their long client lists for speaking engagements beyond her title-holding year.

After a confusing ride with a local car service within Fairfax County, Sonny opts to call ahead, as the driver could not locate the address. Upon their arrival, the speaker's bureau group gathered in a large glass, enclosed conference room reminiscent of a large aquarium from the hallway outside it. The group polls Little Miss with questions mainly about her pageant experience, dealing with celebrity and if she gets along with Harold Frump (someone did not research that she represents a different pageant, not his). Little Miss sits at the head of the table, Anni beside her and Sonny next to her.

While under the line of questioning and scrutiny, Little Miss' internal thermostat begins to rise, then goes on overdrive. She starts to break out in a flushed hive pattern on her neck and chest. Yet, she is still able to maneuver through the questions and discussion about how she came through the pageant system, her experiences with her family and her most rewarding moments working with the children who are patients at various pediatric hospitals in the country.

The bureau executives indicate they can spin a more extensive message for Little Miss to use in her speech delivery and make her into a more marketable spokesperson. From their perspective, they are just glad to have another name to add to their client list, The more people out doing speaking tours, the increased revenue this group makes, so they'll polish her-up and get her on their roster.

After those activities, it's time to head home. On the drive up the turnpike back to New Jersey, Sonny tells their limousine driver to stop en route, since she is hungry.

* * * * * * *

On Anni's answering machine, Serberus leaves her a message to come to the office before she heads out back on tour this time to Tennessee. Anni attends the appointment they set and replenishes plenty of forms and supplies for the road. "While at headquarters," Serberus comments, "you may want to check your mailbox, since it is yours and everyone respects the privacy of everyone else's mail."

That comment as rather peculiar.

Before leaving, Anni proceeds to the very back of the office at headquarters. In the mail room area, there in her mail slot with a single item--the minutes from the last staff meeting dated March 15, 2007. Most of this memo agenda had to do with reinforcing office regulations like designated lunch times and dress codes.

As Anni reads further on, she sees some bullet points screaming out. These mention the need to "lessen expenses," things like: elimination of phone extensions, plans to clean out promotional material from the warehouse and reduction of square footage in the current office space. This could not be a good sign. I hope my job is not in jeopardy since I am the newest addition to this team. I wonder why Serberus had not approached me openly about these changing tides, but subliminally points me in the direction of the agenda and to read between the lines…

* * * * * * *

The next few days Little Miss flies to rendezvous with her college-aged boyfriend in St. Louis. Anni intends to reconnect with her for the next leg of the tour in Nashville. By this time, Anni's meager "carry all" bag reinforcement totally bursts.

Delightedly, Anni scrambles home to celebrate her birthday that weekend, since she will be on the road during her real birthday the following Wednesday. She knows she has to celebrate when she can…and she has to be on the hunt for a new large tote/pocketbook to hold all work her essentials.

The hired car service, whom she had to help navigate to her house, finally makes it safely back to her driveway. As Anni arrives home, a sense of warmth and stability envelope her. Anni's husband was so pleased to spend some time with his recent bride. This was obvious when Anni sees the technocolored Spring floral arrangement he surprises her with. The lovely display is prominently displayed on their kitchen counter. It makes a great focal point, as the center point of their peaceful home.

Anni's husband, Brendan, a quiet and loving man, who is cautiously affectionate, reaches out to give his wife a warm, snuggly hug, and then silently leads her upstairs, where they do not even make it to their bedroom. He had to have her, right then and there. The hallway becomes an impromptu scene for the love they make—not seeing one another for so long...

Their love making reunion is not slow and mechanical; rather it is spontaneous and monumental. They equally miss each other physically and emotionally. Husband and wife long for their counterpart. As they lay on the carpeted floor intertwined, they realize how much they treasure being together again. Anni pauses after their powerful but concise love making ended. Absence makes the heart grow fonder.

Anni has a few days to spend quality time with her precious husband, who she loves and deeply cares for until she's required back on tour.

— 20 —

It is time for Anni to go back on tour and accompany Little Miss on the journey. She was flying out of her home base airport, Philadelphia to meet up with her in Nashville. Anni is excited to meet her again and together experience the country music capital.

Upon her arrival in Nashville, Anni thoughtfully gets a luggage cart from a stand and continues to have it ready at the baggage carousel that Little Miss was to arrive. Little Miss' flight is behind schedule, so Anni grabs her laptop and makes sure all her expense reports and appearance reports are completed with care. She takes pride in writing her reports for corporate and uploading the photos she took from their on-the- road adventure to be used for Little Miss' travel log on the website and in various media clips. Sometimes she stays up late into the night, as she gets an adrenaline rush, excitingly transferring the images of these historical events she's documented for the world to view and enjoy by seeing them on the official website!

The two women hug. Anni asks Little Miss how her visit was in Kansas City. "I had a blast being a regular girl, hanging out with my boyfriend and his buddies. We went to the movies a couple of times, did lots of shopping at the mall and had a ton of great food: "Steaks and Mexican!"" she exclaims.

Anni flags the limo driver after a couple of phone calls of trying to track him down, he arrives and had assembles all of the luggage on the cart. Away they go in the humidity to the hotel. The driver, Curt is very friendly and proud of living in the Nashville area. He asks, "Have either of you been to Nashville before?"

They say in harmony, "No." So, Curt begins gushing with landmarks and trivia to immerse them in the town. Anni looks around and sees many nifty boutiques; café's, grills and live music bars and arenas. Little Miss is excited about the scenery too. She can not wait to dial-up one of her pageant friends to see if she has time to get together and enjoy the town a bit, even though the main reason she is in Nashville to head to a country cable TV studio to tape a show.

On the other hand, besides being pleased to be here in Nashville, a great city, from what Little Miss had heard, Anni notices her body crumple-up a bit next to her in the sedan. Anni asks, "Are you alright?"

Little Miss grabs her belly and mentions, "I have shooting pains in my back. This happens when it's that time of the month for me."

"What do you do to relieve your pain?"

"Usually I take Midol or something like it, but I think I ran out, so I may take a hot bath and try to relax when I get to my room," Little Miss expresses.

At the Marriott, Curt lets them out on the corner near the front door, since there is no real driveway at this hotel. "Let me help you with your bags," as Little Miss and Anni already grabbed for their things, because they were both anxious to make it to the room straight away and get Little Miss settled.

Curt indicates, "I'll see you both on this same corner tomorrow to take you to the studio. See you then! Enjoy yourselves during your first night in Nashville."

"Thank you Curt." Anni responds.

At the check-in, Anni gets the reservations fulfilled and the keys. She also asks the staff, "Where is the closest pharmacy?" Fortunately, they apprise her Walgreens is a short walk around the block.

Anni informs Little Miss, she can get her some items to minimize her aches and pains if she needs some. Little Miss was very comforted by the thought of that.

In her room, Little Miss checks her suitcase, only to find her over-the-counter medicine supply was diminished. Anni confirms, "After you have some time to unwind and relax, call me if you want me to run to Walgreens."

"Sounds good."

Anni gingerly asks, "Have you ever considered some kind of birth control pills? It can provide you considerable peace of mind from eliminating your PMS symptoms, to being able to pinpoint precisely when your period is to begin. This way you have control over it, which is a bonus when you are traveling and living on the road. On its' own, sometimes it comes at unpredictable times when you may not have access to the Ladies' Room or to the supplies you need."

Anni feels like her big sister for the duration of this talk. She did not have these experiences counseling young women about birth control pills any time before, yet she felt implored to share with Little Miss how this may add to her current quality of life.

Little Miss listens intently. "I talked with my younger sister about it once, but I don't want people to think things…" she remarks simply. She appears reluctant to consider the subject, review it all and take action on this possibility, if it may be right for her. It seems to Anni, Little Miss' makes a rash reaction regarding our conversation. Perhaps, Little Miss' younger sister Morgan, did not explain the same benefits.

"It's merely an option, one that can alleviate the worry and pain. Maybe, you can talk with your Doctor about it further to see if it may be right for you." With that comment, Anni walks out. "Goodbye for now, I'll be next door."

A couple of hours later, Little Miss is still achy, but feels slightly more relaxed after soaking in her Jacuzzi tub and lying flat on her bed. "I still can't get comfortable, my back is in knots." She tells Anni when she comes back for the outing to the pharmacy.

"Do you want me to knead it out a little?" Anni asks.

"Sure," Little Miss acknowledges. "Any relief would be great."

"We'll give this a try," as Anni rubs Little Miss' Lower back, "and then I can head to Walgreens."

"Let's go together, I want to see what they have. I need other items too and it'll be nice to go out to a store for a change," Little Miss' eye glimmered. Anni knows shopping is one of Little Miss' number one pastimes.

"I'll knock on your door, when I get some jeans on for our walk," Little Miss indicates.

Anni heads back to her room. "Great, I'll get my jacket, since it's breezy here."

The two ladies walk up the street and around the block. Instantly, Little Miss' outlook is more upbeat. "I love being able to go shopping!"

It isn't Anni's favorite activity. "I don't mind it, as long as I have a purpose. I don't enjoy walking around and looking at everything in a store, if I don't have a reason to buy something for someone or some reason, it's a hassle."

Anni observes the streets in Nashville look like they have a 1950's flair about them, with the storefront architecture and motif-a lot of rounded and ribbed stainless steel designs.

They arrive at the local Walgreens. It looks rather small, than the freestanding Walgreens in my neighborhood in N.J. and even others I had visited in cities like one in Miami. This storefront may have been an old dime store pharmacy or small luncheonette that some developer converted into a modern day Walgreens.

"I need a basket," Little Miss advises. She makes her way through the narrow aisles toward the pain reliever, and there are so many choices. She dials up her Mother on her Blackberry to verify which selection is best. Anni walks away, so

Little Miss can converse with Shannon a bit more privately. Little Miss embraces the "Mother knows best" adage.

After wandering around the cluttered Walgreens with narrow aisles and lots of products, streaming from the end caps, Anni chats up a merchandising associate. The cheerful worker mentions, "Management is in town from corporate. They came in from Chicago."

"What are they here for?" Anni asks.

"They want to see how to make the store more efficient. It's a really old facility-much smaller than many other Walgreens and they aren't getting the level of business they should."

"That makes sense." Anni's suspicion was coincidentally confirmed.

Little Miss makes her way around the corner, towards cosmetics where Anni was chatting with the Walgreens worker. Her arm was getting tired from the weight of the rather full hand basket.

"Here, put your basket on the counter, while you finish-up your shopping, so your arm doesn't ache."

Little Miss notices Easter candy at the end of the aisle. She lets out a high-pitched shriek. "I love Cadbury eggs!!"

Anni is surprised Easter items are out already. "It seems retailers are constantly rushing the holidays to push all the seasonal merchandise."

"I know what you mean," the Walgreens worker retorted.

Little Miss tossed 10 Cadbury eggs in her basket.

"When will you eat all that?"

"Oh, they'll get eaten." She says with a toothy grin.

"I don't think they'll travel well—either melting or getting crushed if you try to pack them somewhere," Anni mentions.

Smiling brightly she says, "I plan to eat these really soon, maybe before we make it all the way back to the hotel... OK, I'm ready to ring-up my order," Little Miss tells the Walgreens associate.

The register is abuzz with the various items besides the pre-menstrual pain medicine that's now buried under all the other miscellaneous nonessentials.

Midway through the transaction, Little Miss exclaims, "I need a nail product, so my nails won't look so bitten and to help them grow."

Anni looks at Little Miss curiously, as she is beginning to consider how her nails look and wants to make them better.

The Walgreens associate leaves the transaction-in-process on her register, while Little Miss goes off to review bottle after bottle of nail hardening products.

In the meanwhile, unsuspecting customers approach the register, where the associate was standing. She appears to be ready for other customers, but really her register is still tied-up with Little Miss' purchases.

The customers start to get anxious and antsy. Anni hears them grumble. The Walgreens associate caves to their anxiety and voids Little Miss' transaction, to make way for other customers. Little Miss approaches but, the register is in mid process for someone else. Anni tells her, "Your things will be rung-up next."

Little Miss pulls out her charge card from her Coach wallet and says defiantly, "My Dad will be calling me soon. He checks the activity on this card everyday."

"Make sure you offer him some of those Cadbury eggs then. It might make him happy and temporarily forget about your credit card balance!"

They both chuckled. "You may be right," she adds.

On their walk back to the Marriott, they comment how clean and nice Nashville is. "It's a city I'd like to spend more time in," Little Miss advises, "Maybe I'll settle here after my year, who knows." My perspective on her life after having the Miss Patriotic crown is evolving. Earlier in the year she indicated she wanted to live and study drama in New York and work on Broadway in a hit musical.

"What about New York City?"

"I don't think I can survive the craziness of such a big place yet. I'm a small town girl. This is more my speed."

Anni agrees how this city has a lot to offer and would make a great place for a short visit. "Someday I'd like to return with my husband. He'd enjoy the nightlife."

"I'd love to go to the piano bars, maybe after my 21st birthday in November I'll look into that, so I can celebrate and not get a hard time about getting in. Although, I have been to some piano bars; early for dinner and then stay to sing along with the musicians later."

At the hotel, Little Miss breaks out the Extra Strength Midol and says a silent prayer to make it work quickly.

* * * * * * *

The day of the taping of at the Television Channel for Country Music, Little Miss contacts one of her pageant hair stylist friends, Morton, to give her a trim and a professional highlight.

She comments to Anni, "I feel like I am two-timing on my "one and only" hairstylist from home, Lenny. Lenny is a queen in his own way. One of the many flamboyant gay men I know who get all wrapped up in the fashion world working to make pageant girls their prettiest, even though he is less than ordinary looking: large boned, crater-faced man with undistinguished features."

Little Miss says laughingly, "Lenny tries to give all his pageant girls the same exact hairstyle. He wants us all to be blond and have a "ledge" of hair in the front. Lenny styled the 2006 Miss Patriotic's hair last year and as you know she is a dark brunette, but he attempted to get her to be one "his blonds" too. She had no part of it!"

Little Miss jokes, "I already "cheated" on Lenny when you did my color touch-up back in Atlantic City." It's just too expensive to fly Lenny on location, so I plan to hook-up with him to work his magic when she appears in her Ohio.

In the meanwhile while in Nashville at least, Morton becomes her man, (or maybe queen), in terms of her hairdo. "I am proud to have had my hands in the hair of many beauty pageant queens from the most prestigious national groups!" He professes.

Morton has his own salon. There is a buzz in Morton's place that Little Miss is on site. She receives the biggest reaction from the other gay stylist, Clay. He breaks out his own feather boa and cheap tiara and says, "This is how I look competing as a queen," prancing between the chairs. Anni was observing the theatrics and had tears running down her cheeks with laughter. Suddenly, he stops and turns towards her, "What are you laughing at?" Clay interrogated her with a serious expression.

"That boa really brings out your eyes." She replies to make him feel comfortable in his own element. Anni's comment resounds with them and they all laugh together!

Alternatively, the female technicians in this salon are a little more subdued in their excitement of Little Miss being here. They are familiar with this drill, as they are used to being the primary salon for the other pageant's state titleholder: Harold Frump's girl. Currently, Rachel is going on to compete at the end of this month to seek her national title. As Morton was relaying their connection with Rachel, would you know who comes walking through the corridor?

"Rachel!" Morton exclaims.

She stops in and Morton is instantly overjoyed, with tears collecting in his eyes. This is a momentous occasion: two of his favorite pageant women are in his salon at the same time! Rachel is in to pick-up the beauty product samples she bought from him to give out as gifts to her fellow contestants in Orlando.

When Rachel leaves the room, Morton softly mentions that during Miss Patriotic's pageant he had an instinct she would take the crown, while his make-up consultant upstairs had "her money" on the Frump's pageant banking on Rachel to earn her way to the top. Ultimately both of them were right! Their catty competition at the salon yielded two winners!

After the trim, Little Miss looks in the mirror and her expression is pure excitement! She is delighted by Morton's work. He took creative liberty by cutting some long bangs into her hair. During the process, Anni sits by flipping through a fashion magazine during the appointment and while Rachel visited to pick-up her give-aways. Anni notices how natural Rachel was, wearing cotton sweat pants, sports bra and flip flops with not a fleck of make-up on or any hairspray. It is refreshing to see a pageant girl by so "unpageanty."

She tells them, "I just came from the gym. My trainer's been working me out extra hard, since these are the last few workouts before Orlando."

"Well you look amazing!" Morton comments as Little Miss sits in the chair in front of him. Little Miss points to Anni on a stool off the side and chimes in, "Anni, who travels with me on the road, goes to the gym all the time too."

Rachel reverts back to her own workout regime. "My trainer really ramped-up the work-out in preparation for her competition." Little Miss retorts, "I can not believe I was the recipient of the most "physically fit" award in my pageant, since I does not workout. And now that I have my title, I have no plans to be in a bikini in public, so I eat what I want."

Rachel replies, "I cannot wait to have that luxury too!"

After the hair appointment and stopping at Panera Bread to grab salads and cookies for Little Miss, Curt zips them past University of Tennessee to point out the perimeter of campus and then back to their hotel downtown. They arrive at the hotel and Curt is still talking about all the places the ladies need to see while they were in town.

"I am an expert, since I have driven plenty of celebrities around town: Reba, Dolly, and many others." he exclaims. Little Miss gently taps Anni's hand and she rolled her eyes at his last statement.

Little Miss' phone suddenly lights up as her friend Kristie, living in Nashville, wants to get together if she had some time to have dinner. She sets the phone down for a few seconds, with her friend hanging on the line to ask Anni, "Would you like to join us for a birthday dinner?" Anni agrees and thanks her for her kind offer, acknowledging her birthday.

Back at the hotel, Little Miss takes some muscle relaxers and takes a rest prior to heading out to the taping of the karaoke show variety contest show at country cable station. Anni wanted her to be prepared, so she researched the details of the show. Little Miss was unfamiliar with the show, and its concept, so Anni fills her in. She tells her the debut episode had a music-related theme consisting of music from Dolly Parton in which contestants try to emulate her. Anni mentions the celebrity, whose music they are using, may also be one of the judges but she was not sure.

Little Miss gets excited thinking she may be meeting Dolly Parton. Per the studio's instructions, Little Miss grabs a couple of designer blouses to bring to the studio, so their stylist can confirm which she should wear, and then off they go. Curt picks them up promptly from the hotel to take them around the block. Anni jokes, "We could have walked." Curt agrees, but mentions, "The account pays "big money" to take good care of their clients."

The staff working the door of the television station acknowledges Little Miss' arrival and whisk both her and Anni to the seventh floor and into a cluttered storage room they affectionately call "The Green Room." The Producers stop in and ask Little Miss, "Do you have an idea about the show?"

She mentions something about Dolly Parton, but the Producer indicates they already taped that episode. This one is homage to The Judds. As the Producer gives Little Miss the overview, a bald-headed, muscular, black man enters the Green Room. He walks-up to Anni and introduces himself, "Hi I'm Eddie George," then proceeds to shake Little Miss' hand too.

Apologetically, he asks her who she was and she tells him. Immediately he pipes-up how excited he is to be working with Miss Patriotic as a judge on the show and asks, "Are you going to wear your tiara?"

Anni replies on her behalf, "Actually it is a crown and it is inside this box. A tiara only covers the front and has no back; a crown is an enclosed headpiece encircling the entire head. Would you like to see it?"

Eddie is interested in checking it out. The big, burly football player thinks it is cool. Little Miss responds, "I have to tell my younger brother and Dad I'm working with a Heisman trophy-winning football player. My brother will think I'm cool now.

The stylist appears in the room and approaches Eddie. "What are you planning to wear?"

He motions to the black-long-sleeved tee and jeans he has on and replies,

"This is it." She responds, "Your assistant did not inform you we suggested you bring a few colorful shirts, so we can see which pops best visually on set?"

Quickly, he punches buttons on his Blackberry, but doesn't get a quick response from his assistant, so a few technicians at the studio mention, "We may have some extra items hanging in wardrobe, maybe a cowboy shirt."

A few minutes later they came up with a country music cable television tee to be layered over a long john shirt adding contrast to his dark complexion and the vividness of the set. Little Miss dashes to hair and make-up and to the set when the director raps on the door. "We're ready to start taping." He announces.

Like being a fly on the wall, Anni observes the episode as she spectated from the bar stool she found in the back of the studio. She sits behind the extras that compose the audience base to add excitement and energy during the takes. The show is a mockery to real music talent. It is really canny, Anni considers.

The hosts pump-up the smiles and "happy factor" during the takes. Between takes, off-camera, the female host growls at the audience members, "Step to the side and get out of my shot," then making sure her make-up was touched up just right.

After all the takes of the contestants and the audience reaction, which are separate segments, the taping is complete.

Afterwards, Little Miss scurries past Anni saying, "I'm headed back to the make-up room to get my clothes and things." While she does, Anni meets some Senior Producers of the TV station.

Anni mentions, "I'll come by in just a moment to help you carry everything." Beside her, Anni indicates to John Volt, a station Producer, 'Little Miss had a great time being a part of this variety show. She really lit-up as a guest judge." She asks him about upcoming projects he was planning. The Producer was aglow and affirms Little Miss may be a great fit for the upcoming County Music awards show he is booking red carpet personalities for. Also, he thinks it may be useful to consider her as correspondent for an entertainment news show, The Insider. Anni asks him for his contact information, so she would put the booking agent from the headquarters in touch, to review dates and details to make things happen!

Anni feels energized to be the rainmaker for Little Miss. Now she can be booked for other exciting appearances and boost her exposure as Miss Patriotic. Anni knows how to make things happen. She intends to listen and observe other situations that may hold possibilities to drum-up even more excitement on Little Miss' tour!

— 21 —

At 8:30 in the evening Kristie pulls-up along side the hotel as Little Miss and Anni jump inside her car. The two friends catch-up about the past couple of years. Kristie has been busy lately with her husband renovating the fixer-upper home they bought ten months ago. They are trying to become DIY's (do-it-yourselfer's) by investing in a saw to cut natural stone for their dining room floor. So in the meantime, she tells them, their washer and dryer are stationed in the living room unhooked, to get access to the washroom area that is being sheet rocked simultaneously.

Kristie notes to Little Miss, "This is a far cry from the glamorous life I had when I was in the state pageant system."

She remembers her day in the sun when she won her big title. Kristie still keeps connected to the pageant system by being a judge on last year's state panel, but has too much going on now. She and her husband are trying to get pregnant. Plus she mentions, "The composition of the candidates isn't as plentiful as it was when I was going through the system."

Little Miss corroborates, "There seems to be a lot more plastic and less real talent."

Kristie states, "I can't believe some of the girls that come out for the initial audition."

Kristie's car pulls-up at the Mediterranean-inspired grille. After a few minutes, the waiter finally seats the three of them. Little Miss is famished, as she devours most of the bread basket while waiting for her entrée.

She tells Kristie she has been speaking to her State Director, May Zander, almost daily and hearing the contestants registering for the Ohio State pageant are really diverse.

"I'd love to be in town to spectate, but since that's not an option, May will try to video the event and send me a copy. That way I can whittle down my own selections to top ten and top three and see if there is any chance for another

Little Miss Patriotic in the near future to represent Ohio."

Their food is served. Little Miss ravishes the steak and potato combination on her plate. Anni ordered an appetizer, since it's after nine, she did not want to sleep on a full stomach for an early rise. After the meal, Anni excuses herself to go to the Ladies' Room. As she was gets up, Little Miss asks, "What kind of dessert do you want us to order for your birthday celebration?"

Anni turns and replies, "Surprise me." When Anni gets back, the waiter returned to the table with a candle lit atop of a crème brule and Happy Birthday written in raspberry sauce on the charger surrounding the soufflé dish. The two ladies sing, "Happy Birthday." Anni is pleased Little Miss acknowledges her birthday in this way.

Then the check came. Anni pays the bill for Little Miss and herself.

Ultimately the birthday dessert was a cute idea, but paid for as a business credit card expense on the next report.

— 22 —

As the next stop of the tour, Anni is headed to Arkansas with Little Miss, where she is slated to model for a high-end gown designer. As Anni and Little Miss check in at the airport, they were pleased to find out they are booked in the first-class cabin. Up until this day Little Miss had never flown first class. Anni points out to Little Miss, "We need to note this on our "list of firsts." These are the things that they experience for the first time together; like when Anni bleached Little Miss' hair at the hotel in AC that made their proverbial list too.

Little Miss excitedly walks aboard the plane. On this flight their designated seats are across the aisle from the other. Anni figures it gives Little Miss some down time to be alone, instead of having to asking to switch seats with someone in first class to sit right next to her.

As it turns out, Anni enjoyed sitting beside her airplane seat mate on this trip. They made friendly conversation and she determines, he is a nice, middle-aged man in his late forties, returning from Switzerland. Anni is fond of Switzerland, as she had traveled there a year ago with her husband.

This man tells her he spends nearly half the year there because he runs an international mining firm that has dual headquarters. Now, he looks forward to reaching his destination back to the U.S. in Pennsylvania. He has another home there, where his wife and three kids live mostly.

"I love my kids dearly and enjoy their company along with our hyper dog," the man tells Anni. Since he doesn't get to see his children all the time, he tries to ramp up the excitement factor to compensate for being away so long. He shares with Anni how he offers each of them one wish for their birthday within reason. Hence, his son got the dog for last year's wish. His middle daughter wanted to go ice skating in Rockefeller Center, so he took her there. Finally, his oldest wanted to go shoe shopping in Paris; he has that trip scheduled and is cashing all the frequent flier miles he accumulated to make it happen!

Anni enjoys his story and asks, "Can I be adopted?"

The man replies laughingly, "I have my hands full granting the wishes of my three existing children."

Anni looks across the aisle and sees Little Miss curled up with her fleece Miss Patriotic blanket listening to her tunes on her ipod. She woke up naturally upon decent of the plane into Little Rock. They collect their bags and Anni locates their driver. A short, statured man named Billy Joe, who looked a bit confused. Anni asks if he was waiting for them. He shuffles through the couple of papers on his clipboard and announces he was waiting for "Arny Keller." Anni and Little Miss laugh since the name on his list is hacked-up to the point he assumed he was expecting a man, but they set him straight.

Billy Joe notices Anni grab for one of the suitcases from the baggage carousel and he states, "Let me do it." Anni rolls a bag towards him, but sees the others approaching so she lunges towards, so they don't miss the chance to get them the first time around from the rolling conveyor. Billie Joe takes the handle of another suitcase, which happened to be Anni's and carries it off the ground. She notices his face turning red and she tells him, it may be easier to reconnect the luggage leash the airline took off for the flight and wheel it."

He responds, "I'm feeling really strong today, because I had lots of collards and fried chicken and macaroni and cheese earlier."

Little Miss quips, "Sounds good to me. Where'd you get all that good food?"

He says, "At the buffet in town. I've been eating a lot more vegetables including greens and spinach."

Anni retorts, "Popeye would be proud!"

They arrive at the new looking SUV. Billy Joe piles the luggage inside and Little Miss and Anni get inside. They can tell Billy Joe has no idea who Little Miss is, but she enjoyed being just a regular girl.

Once they got Billy Joe talking, he would not quit. He asks if it's OK to have some music playing. Little Miss is tired and has a headache, but knew he was only being friendly, so she agrees. Then he asks, "What kind of music do you want to listen to?"

"You choose." Anni confirms on both of their behalf as Little Miss was not in the mood to converse. He mentions he loves music and is excited about heading home that evening to watch "American Idol." He inquires if Little Miss enjoys the show. She said she does, but doesn't get to see it every week, only when her schedule permits. Billy Joe announces, "I can't live without it." Anni asks if he calls in to vote for his favorite singer. "Yes, Blake Lewis 113 times." He responds.

She asks, "How much did those toll calls cost so far?" He isn't sure, but he thinks it put him in the running to win a prize too!

Anni admires the view along the ride. She notices a beautiful sunset as they pass the V.A. Hospital along the highway and she is pleased to see the pear trees in bloom already here.

The weather is cooler in other places. She makes a mental note. It puts her in a good mood.

The SUV rolls-up to the Embassy Suite Hotel in Little Rock. When they arrive at the hotel, they step out of the vehicle and Anni is told by guest services they do not need to check in, as the designer took care of everything. She is immediately handed the keys and they hurry up to their respective rooms.

First is Little Miss', they open her door and her jaw drops. She tells Anni, "Come in here," and immediately they view a large dining room with six impressive chairs surrounding it and a lovely red rose bouquet on the marble counter. The fresh, rose stems were cut short and they were wrapped in a tight cluster to fit snuggly in a square-shaped glass vase with a wire surrounding it. Anni admires how lovely it looks. On the center of the dining room table is a hospitality basket with candies, goodies, and sodas galore.

Little Miss can not believe her eyes; the grandeur of her suite.

Beyond the dining room leads to a small kitchenette, with dramatic drop lights in hand-blown glass tulip-shaped fixtures, stainless steel appliances and marble backsplash. To the left, the power room brilliantly decorated, then the see the living room with puffy couches and silk trees surrounding the massive entertainment center. Passing through the sliding parchment doors, she gasped as she first notices the massive bed in the bedroom area. There are a ton of chocolate and earth-toned throw pillows and a lavish bathroom with sunken tub and double sink with brass fixtures. Little Miss is in heaven!

Anni passes through the connecting door to her Junior Suite. It is charming too and to her surprise and delight the gown designer placed a snack basket, a lovely arrangement of white tulips with an iridescent blue bow and a small package there on the table. What hospitality! Inside the wrapped gift, was a pen encrusted with Barbie pink Swarovski crystals. Later she asks Little Miss if the unique gift was meant for her, but Little Miss shows Anni, she received one as well in a Leopard pattern of amber and brown.

The phone rings minutes later and Tony, the well-known and generous designer calls that he was on his way up. He comes into Little Miss' suite with his make-up artist, Joel, to review the selection of gowns with her. First, he wheels in on a bountiful garment rack filled with ball gowns. Then, Tony asks Little Miss and Anni to share their opinions about the collection. "I am so glad Little Miss is so pretty and slim. It makes the gown fitting easy." Tony comments

Quickly, they narrow down the selection of gowns in preparation for tomorrow's photo shoot. Tony mentions he scouted an unusual location for the shoot. He asks if Little Miss would be OK working in a vacant building that was a YMCA years ago, but over time has been decaying away and it a bit dilapidated.

"I chose it, because there are some fantastic architectural facets about it."

Since this appearance was booked well in advance and Serberus crosses all her T's and dots all her I's, Anni does not concern herself that Little Miss is entering a decaying building. Tony would have had to review all the logistics to get Serberus' blessing to get this off the ground.

Little Miss is intrigued, so the shoot is a go.

After the fitting, Tony insists on hosting a dinner for the group, so they go to an intimate Greek-owned Mediterranean-styled restaurant. He made reservations, yet when they arrive it appears reservations are not necessary. There is only one other table of patrons who look like they were finishing-up. Tony asks if it is OK they stayed for dinner, since the staff are cleaning-up and nearly ready to close, but the restaurant manager obliges, although the group was delayed fifteen minutes later than the said reservation.

They all agree the food is enjoyable and the portions were filling, so Anni skips dessert. Little Miss hedges on ordering dessert, then remembers she had to wake-up early to put on a bunch of fitted gowns, so she passes.

On the drive back, Joel, tells Anni about his extensive doll collection and his obsession with a doll specialty shop near to the hotel. They joke and laugh all the way back. Little Miss and Anni were entertained and enjoyed his exuberant doll tales. Little Miss mentioned, "The gay men in the fashion and pageant industries are surely passionate about their interests."

The next morning they meet with Joel, the doll-loving make-up artist staying down the hall in the hotel, and the three have breakfast together. They were glad to have met the night before, so by breakfast they were fast friends. This morning there is a lot less chatter, since they all not yet awake at this point and are livelier in the evening.

After they finish eating, they pull up in the SUV to downtown Little Rock to the legendary building that Tony told them all about. Anni looks at it as they approach and could tell it had character in its heyday, now it's pretty dilapidated.

Little Miss walks out of the SUV and sees the trailer parked in front of the car. It isn't a 40-foot trailer, but more of a camper a small family might own or rent for a Summer outing. This beat-up rental looks like it had been used on a number of those kinds of trips. Anni notices it was a rental from "Party Time Campers." She says to Little Miss, "If that sign sets the tone for the day, you are going to have a blast!" They all laugh.

Inside, Joel assembles his beauty bags, products and hairpieces.

The commercial realtor, who owns the property, arrives to let them into the property. He also made sure to stop by since he wants to meet Little Miss. "I'm honored my building is being used by you!"

As they enter, they see Tony had moved the garment rack inside. They wander through the room to take a peek at the location he described. They see the plaster strewn all over, as was the paint, tiling and wallpaper. Yet, in looking at the architectural aesthetics, there are interesting columns, antique-titled stairwells, sconces and old fashioned glass on hexagon patterns forming some gothic looking windows surrounding ancient fireplaces around the building.

There certainly was room for artistic images to come out of this place.

Tony, having creative control of the shoot, determines which gowns will be worn in the various rooms to evoke certain moods and feelings. To set the scenes more thoroughly, he also had a friend drop-off some estate furniture to add dimension to the shoot.

In the camper, Joel is filled with excitement to have control over the hair and make-up masterpieces he is about to undertake. Little Miss tells Joel, "I am open to letting you work your magic."

This is the first "high fashion" shoot Little Miss has done. Another first for the proverbial list Anni and Little Miss were crafting.

When arriving on set, Little Miss asks for Tony's guidance and patience, so she can execute the poses and looks up to his expectations. Tony requests input from Anni, Joel and the photography staff to indicate how the shots look.

In the first segment, Tony wants Little Miss seated in an antique chair to formulate a royal look in a big ball gown. Little Miss places her hand down across her lap and Tony comments, "Make less "man hands" in the shot." He refers the overall look of Little Miss' hands since he notices she has bitten all her nails severely short and to her lack of daintiness as she robotically poses. For the rest of the frames she stretches her arms and hands out of obvious view.

To get Little Miss more focused on the shoot and less on worry about her hands, Anni suggests they place the crown in the shot to add to the richness of the campaign.

Little Miss loves the idea and soon finds her groove. She begins to enjoy all the attention and treatment from Tony and the photographers. She is having a ball!

Mid-day Anni calls Serberus to give her an update how things are progressing well, and that Tony is so hospitable. "He sets up the shots, directing which gowns should be worn in each area, and he arranged for antique furniture to be used as props in the shoot."

Out of nowhere, Serberus is angry that Tony makes all the decisions. Anni tells her, "I do not want to overstep my bounds," but Serberus tells her, "If the poses get too provocative, step in!"

Anni is unsure why she even mentions that. Anni responds, "I will ask Little Miss about her comfort level with each part of the shoot. It has not been risqué so far." Anni was not sure why Serberus is trying to micromanage the shoot from long-distance. Does Seberus have some past experience with Bowls pushing the envelope?

Anni informs Serberus that she'll comply with her directive.

After the call, Anni gets Tony's attention and advises him that headquarters wants Little Miss to be represented "appropriately and in a positive light." He surely does not think anything is going too overboard as far as his direction on the set. Anni affirms and reiterates she is relaying the organization's position.

"I understand, you're the messenger," Tony quips.

They progress through the photo shoot; to do other layouts of Little Miss standing along the mosaic stairwell, then lounging on an antique settee' in the corner of a small room with layers of peeling paint and leaning against an old wooden green door. Little Miss is having fun when Anni and Joel propose she wear a headpiece of peacock feathers to accessorize a sequined gown with an ostrich plume pattern.

"Great idea!" Tony collects feathers from one of the centerpieces from his loft to get the perfect shot in the spirit of this project.

After the photo shoot, Anni indicates to Tony, "Before any of these pictures can be used in publication, send the proofs to the headquarters for their review." He agrees and knows Anni is just doing her job.

Afterwards they stop for "authentic Mexican" food. Little Miss salivates as she cannot wait to dive into a good bowl of queso, so they order three for the table.

Anni asks Little Miss, "What is your review of the queso here?" since they were trying different kinds in various states while on tour. Little Miss responds, "This is one of the better ones I've tasted, but not as good as my favorite hometown queso. That's number one!" They finished their Mexi-meal, head back to the Embassy Suite, check-out of the hotel and dash to the airport.

* * * * * * *

From Arkansas, Little Miss is off to Atlantic City to make some regional appearances. Since the women cannot take the flower arrangements along that Tony sent them, they leave the bountiful bouquets and most of the snack baskets for the hotel staff to enjoy. Anni takes a photo of the arrangement she received as a colorful memory of their time in Little Rock.

When they arrive back in Philadelphia, they collect their luggage for the ride back to the Marriott hotel they stay in when they're in the Atlantic City-area.

Serberus imparts to Anni during their last phone call, "There will be a package for you, waiting at the front desk." When Anni arrives, she requests the package that Serberus told her to review and that she would need to turn in reports the next day when the office was open. Anni opens the stipulated package in her room, which contains a large three-ring binder outlining the policies of the organization.

Anni thinks it was peculiar that Serberus opts to leave that for her when she was only in town for one night then flying back out, which means she has to stash the bulky binder in her luggage. Anni scans the policy book in the evening to find that most of the information is relevant to the few folks that work in the office; things like lunch breaks, dress codes for the office and vacation policies. This material is really overkill, as the majority of the policies are not relevant for those whose jobs were 99% travel-focused.

— 23 —

Another local appearance is slated for Little Miss, this time to do a television interview on a live morning show. Little Miss realizes the TV studio was near Anni's hometown, so she asks, "Wouldn't it be great if you could get together with your husband and family for a visit? I always take advantage of having a slice of home by getting together with family or friends wherever I can arrange it!"

Anni admires her suggestion. Little Miss is adept and focused on sustaining her own strong personal contacts, as long as she continues the itinerary to get her work completed. Anni likes how well-connected she remains with her friends and family

So, Anni affirms, "You know, you have a point. The organization has a strong sense of family/work balance."

Anni calls her husband and in-laws, who are retired, to take a short road trip to the TV studio outside of Philadelphia, so they could visit and have a chance to meet Little Miss in person. Anni's Mother is not able to join them, since she is working that day.

Little Miss and Anni go by car service an hour and a half from their hotel to the studio.

Anni tells her the show's format is pretty fun, upbeat and casual. One of the hosts had just become a new father, she mentions. Anxiously, Little Miss sits in the Green Room waiting for her segment. Anni gets a pre-production overview of the interview script. Boy, it took a detour... with ten seconds until live, she sees they are planning to show clips erring on beauty pageant controversy. The show runs B-roll of Little Miss' crowning moment back to back with footage of the drunken and disgraced title-holder from Harold Frump's organization.

Noticeably, the tone spirals downward, as the hosts put Little Miss on the hot seat asking her take on the underage drinking controversy, whether the punishment is suitable and the situation fair. Little Miss feels blind-sighted, since she is hoping to discuss her own objectives, aspirations and responsibilities as ambassador for a national children's organization and working with politicians for a safer virtual environment online.

Anni notices Little Miss looking a bit dejected after the lambasting. Little Miss collects herself and waves to the audience then hustles out. She scurried to the hired car to complete a phone interview for a magazine article in some local publication from her home state. After the commotion, she is so ready to grab a bite to eat, but becomes shaken by the way the TV interview played out. Little Miss did not even know they ran B-roll of the other pageant titleholder which got more air time than her own crowning images.

On the flipside, Anni's family attends the show as part of the studio audience, that's open to the public, where they all enjoy the frivolity of live TV. They had never been to a television studio before, as is evident when they wave to Anni who sits off set, peering through the curtains.

Following the show, based on Little Miss' encouragement, they all stop for lunch nearby before the ladies have to head back on the hour trek to the hotel. Conveniently, there are no other events scheduled today that they have to physically attend, so timing is not an issue.

The group has a pleasant lunch in a restaurant across the street from the studio. Since it is not prime lunch hour yet, the place is a bit secluded, so Little Miss could relax. The only diversion occurs as Anni's Father-in-law barrages Little Miss with lots of stories of how jealous his buddies will be when they hear he lunched with a beauty queen!

After lunch, the two women jump back in the car and head back to Atlantic City. Anni calls Serberus with status to indicate they are on the road. She questions why it took so long to get going. Apparently Little Miss has already tipped off Serberus that Anni had them stop for a luncheon with her family.

Anni clarifies, "We just grabbed a bite to eat." Serberus is angered that the car had to wait while they ate, since he was "on the clock."

Anni tries not arguing with her. With her foresight, Anni realized it would be unrealistic for Little Miss to get-up early and hit the road for an appearance and be expected to wait all day long for a meal. "The girl had to eat and not wait for half the day to pass just so she could get food at the hotel. I was not aware the driver is paid by the hour rather than on a flat rate for the drive."

Also, Anni recalled coming back from Washington, DC during her overlap with her Sensei (trainer) Sonny; during that trip, Sonny instructed the limousine driver to pull into a rest stop area, so they could get a meal. Of course, when Anni observed this as acceptable behavior from her mentor, she concludes it is acceptable.

Now, Serberus still questions Anni's decision-making ability.

* * * * * *

The next day Anni and Little Miss arrive in the office as per Serberus' request after Anni drops-off Little Miss' dry cleaning.

She pulls Anni aside and says, "You will meet in Cheryl's office." Anni was not told the intent of their meeting.

Cheryl begins, "This job you have, is so unusual, but very important, the most important in this organization in fact."

Suddenly the proverbial hot lamps turn on intensely as the probe expands from the prior day. Serberus questions Anni, "Did you take your family in the limousine to go to eat?"

Anni thought this was already addressed yet responds, "No. We met my family for a bite to eat per Little Miss' strong recommendation, since they live so close to the area of the TV appearance. Little Miss told me how important it is to see family and if they were her relatives she would definitely do the same thing." It's a novel idea, and Anni agreed with Little Miss' reasoning, and tells Pearson she called her relatives to come by as members of the studio audience, since it is open to the public. "Little Miss mentioned she was hungry after the interview, so we needed to get her food in any case." Anni's family met them across the street for a quick bite to eat.

Serberus' fury embroils. "Anni, it costs us money to have the driver sit and wait!" she growled. Anni was not aware of that, and reiterates Little Miss had not eaten all morning and afternoon and they had an hour commute ahead of them, so it was only natural to satisfy her need to get something to eat. "There aren't any drive-through restaurants by the studio, so we selected the closest place."

Changing gears, Pearson goes on to mention she thinks Anni has a creative sense of style, but that her outfit is not necessarily an appropriate look for the manager. Anni asks what specifically she is referring to. Cheryl Pearson said Serberus had informed her details, so Anni inquires to Serberus, "Tell me in which place was I not appropriately dressed?!"

Serberus softly replies, "Well, I have seen some pictures."

Anni questions, "Of what?" The conundrum is exasperating.

"When you were at the USO Army Ball!"

"But I was not at any Army Ball," Anni retorts. "If you are referring to the USO National Guard Award Gala, I asked Sonny if my outfit I had planned was acceptable and she said absolutely."

Serberus face contorts as she responds louder, "She did not want to hurt your feelings, plus she is not your boss. I am!"

Anni rapidly answers, "I thought Cheryl is?"

"Well, Ann Jo knows more about what goes on during appearances since she did it for years and I haven't..." Cheryl interjects.

Anni could feel her blood boil. Why am I on trial for inappropriate dress, when time after time I have been complemented on my wardrobe? She even asked Sonny, the veteran Manager her opinions on dress etiquette for particular events.

Anni wants so badly for this opportunity to work, so she tries not to be resistant or push back, rather she just sits there and tries not to retort. She notices Serberus with her arms now folded tightly, giving her the once over while she perches across from her like a bird of prey in Cheryl's office.

Cheryl pipes up, "Ann Jo does not think this outfit you're wearing is really appropriate for today's appearances."

Anni has on her cashmere red suit jacket, with cropped, black pant and a button-down printed blouse with skin-colored fishnet knee highs and matching kitten heels.

Anni believes she looks fashionable and appropriately professional for the appearances on the itinerary. It involves her accompanying Little Miss to Sigma Recording Studio to record a song for use in the upcoming Cherry Blossom Parade, later she will do an interview on a live Sports Talk Show in the area too. Anni considers these stops to be fashion-forward and hip.

Serberus squishes her nose and shakes her head.

Anni attests, "What is the problem you have with my outfit?"

Serberus has to be primed like an oil well for an explanation.

Abruptly, she points and waves her finger in Anni's face, "I would never wear fishnets...EVER!!"

Anni tolerates her opinion, as she says, "No problem, easy fix, I'll run up to my hotel room upstairs and see what options I have."

She can feel her heart racing as the unexpected blow-up transpires. Minutes later Anni appears in the doorway of Serberus' office and asks, "Is this better?"

She now dons regular black trousers and nylon knee highs with red ballet flats. Serberus does not utter a word—just gives a single nod. I'm really taken back by this unforeseen treatment, considering all the compliments I've gotten during my professional career for style, and dress, even by some colleagues at the Miss Patriotic Organization. This must be like part of an initiation more than anything else. How many times have I seen Sonny in jeans and sneakers on the road?

Those staffers, who admire Anni's dress, tended to wear inexpensive-looking stretch pants and polyester shrunken tees and shrugs. Apparently, there are different standards in dress code for her versus for the office staffers.

Anni opts not to linger with Serberus and Cheryl overanalyzing her manner of dress. Fortunately, Marissa mentions a call comes in that the driver is ready for Little Miss and Anni to head out to the recording studio. Anni is relieved and puts that scenario behind her, so she could rev-up back into an excited, upbeat state-of-mind for Little Miss benefit.

Ironically, this scrutinizing meeting in the office ran right through the time for lunch, now they have to make a 50-yard dash to Philadelphia, which doesn't leave time for them to eat a meal. As the car makes its way into the City of Brotherly Love, Little Miss grumbles how she is starving. Their driver, Vladim, has the address of Sigma Studio on a piece of paper but doesn't know how to best access the place from the Vine Street Expressway. Along this drive he was very conversational and tells the ladies one-liner jokes and stories, most of which are indiscernible with his heavy East European accent. Something about a boxer checking out the ladies…Anni attempts to translate to Little Miss.

Since Little Miss is so hungry and they have a bit of time, their driver suggests going to South Philly for an authentic cheese steak. Anni knew better. It would have taken them 15 minutes just to get to that neighborhood, let alone wait for the food, eat and return destined to hit traffic. Instead, Anni suggests that they hop out, as they are approaching Reading Terminal Market, where Anni is sure Little Miss could find something she would like to snack on quickly. The market is known for its diverse variety of ethnic foods to choose from. Little Miss and Anni dash in and then hurry to Ladies' Room. Even with the many choices of food at the Market, Little Miss leaves with just a bag of sour cream and onion potato chips and a Diet Coke!

Fortunately, Anni has some familiarity with Center City, so she guides Vladim, their driver, around the one-way streets and around a few blocks, where she spots the non-descript location. Bernice, their contact at the recording studio for the Cherry Blossom Parade, steps out of the studio's front door and waives when she sees the black tinted sedan pull-up curbside.

Bernice is a friendly, full-figured Ebony woman, wearing a bright orange leather jacket, black slacks and slip on trendy shoes, with her nails done as equally bright to match her jacket.

Was it really necessary to "tone down" my own outfit earlier? Anni wonders.

Inside they walk through the legendary Sigma Recording studio. It feels like a vacant space, but actually is undergoing a facelift; so many rooms were stripped down to the studs. There is no electricity or heat in the front of the building …Anni is astonished.

The two ladies ask to take a restroom break and find the nearest Ladies Room. There the fixtures and plumbing look like they were in place since the 1960's. Little Miss and Anni look at each other and can not believe this is such a legendary place, looking so run-down.

Bernice leads them through the construction maze of dangling wires and plastic tarps into the sarcophagus of this edifice. In the central part, they enter the working recording studio! They climb-up one step to access this inner sanctum. The room is dimly lit room, the size of a freight elevator, with acoustic foam panels encasing it. There is one tiny lamp with a red-beaded lamp shade, adding a boudoir feel to the room. Two cabin-cruiser chairs are behind the large sound editing board providing a hint of Star Trek.

Standing behind the board, is a young, Hippie-looking man named Joe, wearing baggy, ruffed-up, frayed blue jeans, Chuck Taylor sneaks and layered T-shirts, with his goatee and scraggly hair. Anni asks him whose work he's produced. "In my accelerated music production career, I dealt with the likes of Jill Scott, Patty La Belle, Bono and others." He said he worked on Patty La Belle's most recent album that she recorded the majority of the vocals here.

"Do you need time to warm-up?" Joe inquires.

"No, I prefer to record in the beginning when I sound my best before I wear my chords out." So, he points Little Miss into the sound booth.

She is excited to sing again, since this is her passion and she does not get to use her craft regularly. Like a conductor, he begins to infuse the sound booth with the instrumentals behind her. On cue, she sings, in good form, but needs to capture the song to be played at the upcoming parade in about four takes.

In between takes, Anni asks Joe if it is acceptable for her to take an "action shot" of Little Miss singing in the booth, for posterity and as part of her travel log. He gives the nod and Little Miss smiles proudly.

After the recording, Joe works diligently to mix and edit the song and layer the vocals in appropriately. "How did it feel being in the booth?" Anni inquires.

Little Miss' initial reaction to the recording is purely "the joy of singing."

Anni comments, "Do you realize all the musical history that has been created here? Many of the great sounds of Philadelphia recorded here. Now you are contributing to it."

Little Miss is elated to be in the presence of greatness, no matter how perfunctory the facade appears.

As the session wraps-up, Anni dials Vladim to say they are be ready for pick-up in ten minutes.

He replies nervously, "Does it have to be that soon?"

She steps outside the studio, so not to worry anyone and to appear to hear the conversation better. Anni asks why he is questioning the time. He admits, "I drove to South Philly for a cheese steak and the sedan died and now I have to wait for someone to provide a jump."

Anni asks him, "How are you going to remedy the situation?" He said, "Don't worry; I'll pick you both up in twenty minutes."

Anni isn't about to worry, as she knew the TV show is not taping for three hours, yet it is disconcerting the hired car service is not reliable. She asked him if he has had this trouble with the sedan, and he mentions he thinks his company had taken care of it. "The car was serviced recently," Vladim postures.

Following the brief contact with Vladim, she wants to give Serberus an update, so she would be alerted to the situation. Serberus answers and Anni tells her the recording session went well, although the location was hard to find and the building is under reconstruction. She transitions the purpose of her call to the situation with their ride stating, she took the driver's phone number and gave him a notification call a few minutes before they were ready to leave to tell him to bring the car around. Since they are downtown, the driver was intending to circle around, because there is no legal place to leave the car in the meantime.

Anni tells Serberus, "Upon calling him to bring the car around, he immediately got nervous and I questioned his whereabouts. He was in South Philly getting himself food when he noticed the car would not start, and was waiting for a jump. I asked him if he alerted his dispatcher and they told him the car was maintenanced recently and suggested he keep the car idling the rest of the day once it gets restarted."

Serberus barks, "What do you want me to do about this?!"

I am taken back...way back! Anni swallows hard.

Serberus has the nerve to rail into her about knee highs and having her call in to say she was at a boarding gate at an airport, but when there is a real situation that needs resolution, Serberus removes herself from the equation.

She tells Serberus, "I want to keep you informed, since you contract the limo service that they may need to send another car or pay for a taxi if we can't make the itinerary." There is dead silence. Serberus did nothing and said nothing more. Anni takes a deep breath, and then tries to regroup, so Little Miss would not notice the frustration glaring through, when she went into the studio to meet her and provide her the departure update.

Anni tells Little Miss the car would be by in twenty minutes, not troubling her with the car problems. The driver arrives and tells Anni he got a jump to start it up. She asks how they were going to manage the next stop at the TV studio. He decided they'd be alright, since he would idle in the parking lot and not shut off the engine.

Since there are a few hours to go prior to the sports show, Little Miss feverishly sends text messages to her friend that works in the area. To her pleasure, her friend Kristy has a few hours to carve out to grab a snack with her before they both have to head back to work. She relays that to Anni, who in turn requests Vladim take them to Positano Coast, so they could get a quick bite before the television studio stop.

Minutes later Kristy pulls up in her white Mercedes. Little Miss knows Kristy from their district pageant days, before she made it as far as she had on the national level. Kristy is a few years older than Little Miss and held a District pageant title in the late 90's. These days she's focused on being a recently married woman with a successful career for a non-profit health facility. Her husband happens to be the director at the same place, who she met back at their days at Ohio University. Kristy is easy-going and includes Anni in the luncheon chat. She wants to know how Anni got involved with the Miss Patriotic Organization and is excited for her. She comments, "It seems you have a nice rapport with her."

At the end of their visit, Anni offers to take a quick photo of Little Miss and her friend from her home state, Kristy, to capture their pleasant reunion that afternoon.

Afterwards, Vladim pulls the car around and off Little Miss and Anni go to the South Philadelphia studio for the Live Sport talk show. Stepping inside the front door, Little Miss walks into make-up, just for a minor touch-up by Melinda, the on-set make-up artist. She freelances for a number of local media opportunities.

Melinda had just finished powdering the face of Joe Lunardi, known as "The Bracketologist" who selects teams for March Madness. As he leaves the small closet-sized room, he shakes Little Miss' hand and tells her tales of the days when he dealt with the contestants back in the heyday on the Atlantic City boardwalk.

Anni asks Melinda how long she had been a make-up artist. Melinda tells them, she lived on the West Coast in Santa Monica for about seven years to refine her craft, but moved back East and also recalls years of watching the pageant around Labor Day. It was a tradition for her family too. Anni brings her up to speed that the pageant changed location two years ago to Las Vegas and the schedule of the pageant is currently dictated by the television station handling the show, therefore it became a January program.

Joe and Melinda both chimed how they hadn't seen it in years. Part of the challenge is people don't know where to find the show, especially if you're not on a specific cable system, you cannot even get the specialty channel the show appears on now.

"That's too bad," Joe said. It was an American institution.

After make-up, Little Miss goes on set for the Live Sports Show. She was looking forward to it and even attempted to prepare beforehand, by dialing-up her best childhood boy friend Kody, and her brother to ask them their picks for March Madness. He tells her the verdict is OSU and Kansas City. "Any of those teams over Texas."

In the studio, Anni took position on the sidelines with the crown box. The panel of sportscasters asks Anni if Little Miss has the crown with her. "She wears her crown broach on her lapel for interviews." They want to see the actual item, so Anni opens the hat box, zips up to the desk on set and sets the crown on it, since they wanted the dazzling prop in the shot. The segment with Little Miss is less than three minutes, yet she has her name prominently flashing across an electronic billboard overhead along with sports scores. The hosts merely ask her basic questions about her pageant experiences.

As the Director waives his hand to wrap-up, Little Miss proclaims loudly, "Aren't you going to ask for my March Madness picks?" They are fading out in 10 secs and didn't expect her to know about that stuff. She gave the teams that she was advised on, "Any but Texas," Little Miss mentions.

The sportscaster panelist concurs, "She knows her stuff…"

(THE SCREEN FADES TO BLACK)

— 24 —

The following day Little Miss and Anni are driven from their stay in Atlantic City to Philadelphia airport for the moment Little Miss has been looking forward to following her crowning moment…HOMECOMING. It is a pageant tradition, especially in Little Miss' home state of Ohio. The current titleholder does not come home until properly recognized with an official celebration. It is a rite of passage, where her home state constituents can honor and celebrate her.

Little Miss is quite a home town girl; extremely proud of being from Ohio. This is where all her pageant experiences transpired. Not only that, her state plans to celebrate the anniversary of their statehood with an assemblance of pomp and pageantry, so the combination heightens everyone's excitement there.

Even though Little Miss kept telling Anni, "I can't wait to go home for Homecoming," unofficially she had been home in February, but she had to slip in very quietly like being under the radar, so not to destroy the official Homecoming debut. She had come home earlier on, because she appeared on a local edition of "Extreme Home Makeover." They selected a family from her hometown based on the Father being a soldier who faced combat in Iraq and lost both legs serving his country. Then months later his young son was involved in an automobile accident, also severing his legs. They needed a house that would be handicapped accessible for the Father and son amputees.

Little Miss was the pretty face as part of the pep-rally on the project, when the local football team, cheerleaders and band members rallied as the family got to see their newly built home. The episode was slated to air Easter Sunday and Little Miss mentioned, "I'm so glad I could go and help. I felt a part of the team wearing the blue tee shirt. My brother was excited to see the cast and crew in town; he thought it was especially cool. I got to meet the lead designer, you know the one with the sixty's dark frame glasses, but the host, Ty Pennington was not in town the day we shot my segment. He flies in and out to film his parts while going to other sites for projects he is working on."

Anni asked her, "How did you manage to be in town without your neighbors realizing you were there?"

"No one knew ahead of time and security was tight. I was like a hostage in my family's home. I couldn't come and go during the day, but had to basically be undercover, so less people would suspect anything. That way Homecoming would be official."

"I see," Anni replied.

Little Miss and Anni arrive at the airport in Philadelphia to fly to Ohio for Homecoming. Anni was looking forward to flying Delta Airlines, since Anni noticed she had some beverage vouchers for Delta from other trips she had taken recently. They have mainly been flying other airlines like US Airways, which has its hub at this airport. So, they board their plane and Little Miss settles in with her black fleece Miss Patriotic blanket and gets in her zone by listening to her ipod. Anni, sitting across the aisle reads a bit and has one mango vodka drink to unwind, as this was a travel day. There are no events scheduled until dinner that evening.

The excitement factor was mounting as Little Miss is counting the hours down to being back home and reuniting with her peers: the national titleholders from the pageant she won in January.

Little Miss' Executive Director from Ohio, May Zander, was so thorough with all the details of the Homecoming program. Zander is able to connect with the Executive Directors from the "Top 10" titleholders' states. These were the young woman that placed, out of all the 52 contestants. In addition Zander invited the ladies Little Miss became really real friendly with during the competition. Overall, there was an excellent turnout to honor the pageant winner!

Upon arrival to the airport in Ohio, Little Miss is advised that a press conference would ensue at the arrival gate, so state troopers and patrolmen would greet her with Anni and Sonny on the tarmac. Sure enough, there is a pep rally of well-wishers and local newspaper and television reporters. A bevy of activity awaits Little Miss. The rally is complete with fans waiving balloons, streamers and wearing t-shirts emblazoned with their hometown Miss Patriotic on them. It certainly is a well-orchestrated mission.

Zander dashes Little Miss around the terminal to speak with each of the scheduled reporters. They ask, "How does it feel to be home?"

Little Miss exclaims, "It couldn't feel any better with the outpouring of support from everyone. These people are the reason I achieved the title, since 500 of them came out to the pageant to be there for me and last year's Miss Patriotic who is also proud to be from Ohio."

Following the barrage of welcoming, Anni locates their driver and she helps collect the luggage to get to their prestigious accommodations. Anni determines that Little Miss' boyfriend's family is friendly with a niche hotel owner. The Diplomat; the hotel they will stay, is a historical building from the 1920's. It was renovated into an upscale hotel in the downtown area. Apparently, it is booked regularly, so the connection got them the coveted reservation.

When the entourage of limousines and state patrol cars pull up to The Diplomat, the driver receives word that Little Miss is to remain in the vehicle until the "all clear" signal is given. Anni sees a trooper escort a young Golden Labrador into the building. It appears they are sweeping the premises for weapons or explosives. A few minutes later the Trooper approaches the car and waives to let Little Miss know it is safe to enter.

Anni is intrigued by the comprehensiveness of their safety check. She briefly converses with the Trooper who handles the police canine. Trooper Tracey, the Officer, indicates she has been working with "Deputy Shirley," the canine, for three years and she went through an intense training to locate explosives and ammunition.

Anni says to Little Miss, "I can't believe how talented some animals are to be able to be more productive than many people are." Little Miss chuckles.

They settle into their respective rooms after the check-in process, which was set-up as an alias, so no one would stake out the hotel unexpectedly. Anni realizes they put Little Miss' reservation under the alias to provide her some anonymity and relaxation during her stay. Anni meets-up with Little Miss in her room, which is the most luxurious suite in the building. It takes up an entire corner of the property and has three rooms within it. The luggage arrives and Anni goes on to collect her own bags in her room down the hall.

Anni thinks things could not get any better until she opens the door to her room and notices directly across the hall was the hotel exercise facility. Someone must have put the buzz in the Manager's ear that Anni is a fitness fan. I'm glad to be a part of this team.

* * * * * * *

A few hours later they congregate in the lobby to head out for the hospitality dinner with all the out-of-town visiting titleholders. Little Miss tells Anni, "You'll like the restaurant; it's Italian-like a homegrown Olive Garden." Anni knew she'd find it enjoyable, since she likes a variety of different foods.

As they are heading through town, Little Miss could not contain how happy she is to see familiar sites. She points out the window, "This is where the preliminaries for the state pageant were held and they will be holding this year's event there too with a new bunch of women. I'll have to check with May and see what kind of applicants she has received so far. Our executive committee is keeping their fingers crossed that they can find the next Miss Patriotic from our state and make it a three-peat!"

The limousine pulls into a shopping plaza and they arrive to the restaurant called Curcio's. The manager of the place opens a backdoor, so Little Miss could arrive without having to work her way through the regular dining room where the general public are eating. She enters into what looks like a Tuscan faux painted room with glowing orange-washed walls.

A few of the titleholders were assembled in the private dining area. Little Miss gives her pageant comrades big, warm hugs. They had just flown in and were telling Little Miss how tired they are from the travel delays and the flight in. They catch-up with her and find out how intense her schedule has been. "I travel roughly 20,000 miles a month," Little Miss told her pageant friends. "I can't believe time has passed so quickly, since you all swarmed around me when I was crowned Miss Patriotic at the pageant. That is a moment I'll never forget."

Minutes later other pageant women arrive after dropping their effects at their designated hotel. These wearied travelers put their game face on when they approach Little Miss.

Even her nemesis, the runner-up from Texas, acts cordially. Little Miss had told Anni previously, she did not think Miss Texas had competed for the right reasons and that there is something insincere about her. When the girls were bonding in California a few months before the January pageant Miss Texas was aloof and did not want to hang with the girls. She tended to be a loner and seemed to have a different agenda.

Anni wants to make all the girls feel welcomed at the hospitality dinner, so she makes a point of introducing herself to them and has intermittent conversations to explore what their lives are about currently.

Anni finds Miss Texas to be conversational. She purposefully looks straight into her eyes; Anni wants her to connect in the same way. Her eye contact is not returned, but she did open up, telling Anni she had just finished doing appearances in Texas for two Women's Correctional Centers and she found those women to be interesting because they have gone through a lot. Also, she mentions to Anni, "These women truly enjoyed my singing performance. They gave me an ovation. I didn't know what to expect."

At the hospitality dinner, Little Miss sits at the large table surrounded by her court and a few past titleholders that came to town to wish her well.

Anni claims a seat at another table where most of the Executive Directors and State Chaperones are seated. They turn out to be a very fun bunch. There is a guy who has judged a number of pageants and is also an Episcopalian Minister. It is wild to see how multi-faceted his personality is. He chatted on about being asked to officiate in some of his former pageant girls' nuptials and how angelic that was and then he transitioned into how kooky some of the girls are. He highlighted how some of the women who tried out really had no talent. There was an applicant who played the spoons and he found it puzzling to determine how they could possibly judge such a "non-talent."

Seated across from him is another state level judge, who is a professional hip-hop dancer by trade. This young, dark skinned, African-American-guy with jeri-curled hair, named Rodney, and is clearly in touch with his feminine side. He is all bedazzled at the dinner with a glittery scarf, rings on many fingers and multiple necklaces and a few dangling earring in his right ear. Anni overheard the others at the table refer to him as "Cheetah." Someone suggested she ask how he got his nickname.

Rodney was reluctant at first, but liked the attention it began to yield him at this dinner event. He relayed he was at a pageant fundraiser event at a prestigious golf course and country club, which predominately had a white, male membership base. Rodney was trailing along one of the holes behind some of the other attendees at the fundraiser and a club member assumed he was the green's keeper.

Rodney replied to the member, "I'm Cheetah Woods, Tiger's cousin." The country club member was speechless…

His punch line causes the table to roar with belly laughter as Rodney laughed along at himself.

Meanwhile the pageant table clucks with assorted girl talk. A few of the ladies turn towards Anni's table to see what is so hysterical. After the dinner, the ladies line-up for photo opportunities and Little Miss suddenly has to dash with her police entourage to run an errand—she needs to sit for her passport photo, then later hook back-up with her pageant sisters at their hotel to hang out with them while they are in town.

Little Miss is slated to get her passport photo, since many Miss Patriotic's do some overseas appearances as part of the USO Tour. Little Miss and her parents have some major concerns about going abroad, especially to the Middle East during wartime. Serberus had proposed to Little Miss to appear at a base in Kuwait to visit with troops stationed in the vicinity. Serberus indicated her experiences in Kuwait, "were some of the best" in her travels, because the Kuwaitis treated Miss Patriotic and her associates like royalty. Yet, Little Miss feels overwhelmed by security issues.

* * * * * * *

Little Miss is thrilled her parents come by to help her settle into her hotel room for the evening and her Mom brought a carload of clothes and gowns. Little Miss' Mom, Shannon, reflects to Anni, "I can't believe how much stuff she has acquired from winning the crown. We transformed her old bedroom into a big closet. There are racks and racks of clothes and boxes of items she was given so far. We had to remove her bed and furniture to make room for all this stuff. Basically, she has no bedroom at home anymore. She'll have to sleep on the couch when she comes to see us…"

Shannon reaches into a plastic shopping bag and pulls out a variety of hot pink and black beverage cozies that have faux fur around the edges and are embroidered with "Miss Patriotic 2007." Shannon couldn't give them away fast enough, as a family friend went overboard and made a bag full. Shannon thought they are cute, but a bit over-the-top. She couldn't picture herself in public with this "blaring advertisement" wrapped around her soda can. So, she insists Anni have one and also pawns one for Sonny to commemorate the crazy days of Homecoming.

The following day, as Little Miss was getting dressed, Sonny suggests that she make sure her clothes are appropriately pressed, so Little Miss takes out the iron and board to press out the creases in her St. John knit suit.

Anni asks, "Do you need any assistance?"

Little Miss has it under control, as Sonny showed her how to do it. Anni was relieved, since she is not a whiz with the iron.

Momentarily, they leave the hotel, once again, with the trooper escort, to arrive at the Methodist Church for an official press conference and a series of radio and television interviews for the state media. Little Miss was able to handle the menagerie of interview questions in an unfettered way. Mostly they ask about her pageant and current experiences, her travels and what she represents. She already realizes any of them can throw her a few curves by tossing in her stance on the controversies of Harold Frump's pageant mired by underage drinking, drugs and things of the like. Little Miss responds by diverting the accountability toward the owner of that organization, "to do what's right for his people."

After the interviews, Little Miss is guided to the ground floor of the Grace Presbyterian Church, where the local Kiwanis Club honors Little Miss with a luncheon. This Club was instrumental in her rise to the national level, since they did a considerable amount of hometown fundraising. Also, more than 300 supporters came to Las Vegas to rally for the big pageant event. So, this luncheon is her chance to render face-to-face appreciation.

Even May Zander is in attendance with her legendary parents. She is a legacy to the Executive Directorship for the state pageant system. Her Father was well-known the Ohio State Executive Director for twenty years. Now he and his wife slowly approach the stage with a walker to assist them. As the reach the podium, a photographer snaps a photo of the pair with Little Miss. May Zander is in her glory that all her efforts paid off, as far as the prestige from her pageant girl who she mentored, winning the title, and her parents there to share in the glorious moment.

That evening one of the delegates from the state pageant board hosts a themed, welcome barbeque. The theme that evening, "Denim and Diamonds," and Little Miss was aware of it having received the invitation for this barbeque back in February. So when Little Miss had some down time months ago, she had shopped with Anni and Cheryl at the Jersey shore for a diamond-studded tank top. It was really decorated with large rhinestones, but it suited the theme just fine. However, upon dressing for the welcome bash, Little Miss bagged the diamond studded tank, and opted for an old pair of bedazzled jeans and cropped jean jacket that her Mom brought over from home.

The outfit looked a bit dated. I wore a similar a bolero, cropped jean jacket back in the 80's.

Besides the barbeque, the excitement of the homecoming events keeps mounting. The following day is a big one for Little Miss and the titleholder contingency. The vehicles pull up in front of the legendary crown jewel of Ohio, the Lakewood Civic Auditorium. Fifty years of proud performances have taken place here. Now, they are putting on a lavish revue with performances from the competition talent they performed in Vegas. Yet, this venue and stage was a relaxed, fun setting, because the ladies were not competing with each other, just reminiscing and highlighting the talents of their national pageant experience.

Anni sits in the front row during the afternoon rehearsals. She's thrilled to see the little flirty, friendly signs of affection the pageant women show each other from center stage, while the other ladies sit in the audience to cheer their fellow titleholders on during rehearsal. Winks, air kisses and hand gestures are the rage among them. This is the first time they could spectate each others' talents, as they were all prepping and rehearsing anxiously back stage during competition.

One of Little Miss' good friends from the pageant is Miss N.J. This gal, Georgie made a nice name for herself while meeting people in her home state and during Homecoming. She is so down-to-earth, and has no issues walking around after an event with no make-up and mismatching sweatpants. At the state level, she could get away with it, but she's mixing with national. Georgie comes across as your sister or a friendly girl who lives on your street - rather whimsical.

When Anni asks about her life's ambition, Georgie has visions of grandeur heading to law school, but you'd never pick-up on that merely having a conversation with her. She seems so simple, even though there's a lot going on. She's an accomplished violinist and does not believe she is a talented vocalist, but Anni finds out otherwise.

During rehearsal, Georgie was unable to procure her violin that she shares with her sister back in N.J. Her sister needed it for another performance, and there was no time to rent or borrow another one, so Georgie opted to sing "a little ditty" instead.

When the rehearsal is complete, the ladies shuttle to the lavish, private country club at Muirfield Village. This luncheon is arranged at this upscale locale, because Little Miss' boyfriend's parents, the Woodmans, are members at this prestigious, private club. Muirfield Village is well-known among the pro golf community - Jack Nicklaus designed the course.

The honorary luncheon is held in a room decorated distinctly for a women's group. Anni walks in and sees magenta colored Gerber daisies clustered in the center of the three banquet tables. Everyone comments how beautifully the floral arrangements complement the tablecloths with same Gerber daisy, graphic designs on them. This illusion looked like the heads of the flowers were strewn on the cloth and softly, blanketed with a tule overlay placed on top. The accompanying pea green linen napkins are folded in a pouch formation which blankets the silverware and a matching flower peeking out of it.

It is real girlie venue with all the pink Gerber-daisy décor.

While hour'dourves are passed by the wait staff, Mr. Woodman, chats with Anni and asks how the tour is coming along. Anni responds Little Miss' connection to his son has been important in keeping her upbeat and secure. Anni indicates how Little Miss is all aglow after she visits with him.

Mr. Woodman replies Anni, "Call me Darnell," as he hands her his business card. "I'd like you to keep me posted on things from your perspective, especially as it relates to the two of them. They're both great kids. All my contact information is jotted on it" and reiterates with a serious look, "Please keep me posted about them."

Anni agrees. She thinks it's admirable how involved he wants to be in the life of his children and the people they associate with. Mrs. Woodman tells Anni how they enjoy family trips to South of the Border with all three of their kids and spending time at their lake house. "I heard Little Miss say how much she enjoyed times she spent their too."

In addition to the hosts, Mr. & Mrs. Woodman, the parents of Little Miss' boyfriend, also seated at their banquet table during the lunch are: her own parents, Anni, Sonny and Donna, the former traveling companion with her husband David. This was the first opportunity for Anni to get to have a conversation with Donna and her husband David who are intrical in their state system as volunteers.

I want to understand what the mystique is about, after all I uncovered dealing with Serberus and their interaction with the former Miss Patriotic...

Anni notices Donna's outfit. It looks as if she was wearing the infamous St. John's knit, but it does not look contemporary, like it is from an older collection with sparkles on the lapel and the knit is a bit pilled. Also, instead of carrying a nice handbag, rather Donna holds a cheap plastic beach tote bag that she displays wrinkled pictures of her grandkids through the clear vinyl inserts across the front of the tote. Anni could not appreciate how Serberus had previously attempted to defend Donna's sense of style. Perhaps, her tastes were no longer keeping up with the times...

Both Donna and David pull their weight during this Homecoming, chauffeuring the young ladies around town, to and from events and the airport.

During Friday evening of the big Homecoming Revue and Gala, Anni is very attentive to Little Miss by carrying her gowns and accessories and helping her with her wardrobe changes. They arrive at the auditorium and Anni takes the assorted gowns out of the garment bags and arranges them for Little Miss' easy access costume changes. Even though Anni notices there's no garment rack to hang the items, so innovatively, perches each hanger from the gowns on the door frame of a locked electrical closet.

Little Miss mentioned to Anni prior to arriving in Ohio, that her runner-up, Lindsey, was always so jealous. This most recent competition was Lindsey's final chance to stake her claim to fame in the state pageant, because she just reached the maximum age to participate. Little Miss feels Lindsey carries herself with an air of importance and comes across arrogantly. Through the rumor mill that reverts back to Anni and Little Miss, Lindsey has been telling people that she knew she is more talented than Little Miss. They both are vocalists, even though their sounds are very different.

Minutes later, the assistant to the current Miss Ohio, observes Anni's handiwork and proceeds to take Lindsey's gowns out and hangs them on the same closet doorframe as Anni did, so now the area is crammed with lavish fabric hanging on the narrow precipice. The overcrowding causes a few of Little Miss' gowns to teeter off.

This simple act solidifies the constant rivalry between the two women. The runner-up, Lindsey, who resumes the state title, when Little Miss won the national title acts like she and "her people" are entitled to everything Little Miss has. There's certainly an awkwardness sharing the same dressing room.

The assistant to Miss Ohio has good intentions for her titleholder, but it came across like she's encroaching on Little Miss' space and her garments. In the dressing room they share this evening, it seems like Lindsey is attempting to upstage Little Miss by spreading her stuff all around and placing big bouquets of flowers on the table that Little Miss thought were delivered to her, but are really Lindsey's.

Perhaps Lindsey was trying to make the most of this event, since this would be the biggest venue for her to perform among her pageant peers during her reign that she obtained by Little Miss moving up to the national level. In the meantime, Lindsey has been introducing herself to the community as "the current Miss Ohio." Lindsey's assistant tells Anni, "I admire how confident Lindsey carries herself."

In actuality, it is here at Homecoming that protocol requires Little Miss to invite her runner-up to take over her former state title and associated duties. It is kind of like getting knighted or named a Lady by the Queen. Little Miss feels Lindsey has been claiming the title before she was formally asked to take over and Little Miss is certainly slighted about her presumption of duties.

With all the chaos this particular evening, Little Miss is overwhelmed with emotions. After being homesick for the past three months, now she's back in her home state among friends, family and the Chairman of the Miss Patriotic Organization Board. He flew in from Hollywood to introduce Little Miss prior to her performance and to attend the Gala banquet as an honored VIP.

Anni notices Little Miss shaking like a leaf in the dressing room. She asks, "Are you alright?"

Little Miss gets choked up, she is having difficulty finding Lenny to get her hair styled for the show and is worried her dress is not fitting snugly. Anni tells Little Miss, "No need to worry, I'll get people to help find him and go to the wardrobe people to get some safety pins to fix the gown. Everything will be alright."

Now I've got to make it all work. It's a tall order, but that's my job.

Anni provides Little Miss some breathing room to collect herself, while she did the footwork looking for Lenny and some safety pins, so Little Miss' could relax and enjoy her Homecoming performance.

Anni runs down the hall to collect a few safety pins from another dressing room, but is having trouble getting any signs of Lenny. So she heads back to the dressing room and offers to pin Little Miss in her gown. As Anni is pinning up Little Miss' gown, Lenny storms in to the dressing room minutes later and doesn't bother to knock even though Little Miss was not fully clothed. Lenny doubles back then reenters when Little Miss gives him the "OK."

After Lenny cavorts with Little Miss during the hairstyling session, Anni peeks in and notices all seems right with the world again based on Little Miss' demeanor. Little Miss never did uncover where Lenny was when he was scheduled to start styling her hair at 7:30 pm, but she seems to accept him, as delinquent and abrasive as he is.

When she's stage ready, Anni offers to assist Little Miss by lifting the train of her gown, in order that she can glide down the steps leading to the stage. From there, Anni indicates to her there is a seat near-by, so she can be close to the stage door and assist her with her other costume changes.

Sonny had told Anni earlier that there was "no way" to reserve her seat, since the auditorium was sold out. Anni was not worried about it, as she knows how to be resourceful.

Anni enters the auditorium from the side door on stage right in the audience area and sits in a seat closest to the backstage door, so she can make a quick exit as Little Miss leaves the stage each time to change. Each of the titleholders were doing their individual performances and returning to the audience to sit in the

VIP area and watch their other peers perform, so Anni had to shift seats a few times to accommodate the ladies returning to the audience. She did not mind, since her priority was being available and making sure things went as smooth as possible for Little Miss.

Wouldn't you know, Georgie, Miss N.J. performs the little song that she did at rehearsal and it turned out to be the biggest HIT of the night! It was sultry, sarcastic, witty and fun and the audience felt she was making it up as she went along. She told a story of young girl living along in an apartment distracted by the other sounds emanating around her from the other apartments. Her body language mirrored the hysterical lyrics as if her movements represented various characters she sang about, complete with multiple voices and vocal stylizations.

The emcee of the show, Mingon, is a close friend of Little Miss'. She was a part of the pageant world too, as she had won a state title back in the 80's, so she and Little Miss have that common thread. Also, it helps that she currently practices law, so Little Miss queries her by phone often to get sound advice regularly.

From the standpoint of hosting this revue, it all makes sense. Mingon and Little Miss have an existing bond, and she is extremely witty. This trait makes her transitions between performances humorous and sharp like a chef doing pristine knife work.

Following the big revue, (which is like living a dream to Little Miss) there is a hospitality suite waiting for her and all her fellow VIP's to cut loose and catch-up. The state chaperones and executives from the state pageant committee also stop in. Anni accompanies Little Miss and sits at one of the four tables in this VIP suite that is a couple of former hotel rooms transformed into a small meeting space.

The pageant companions were all starving from performing earlier and not indulging in the dinner at the gala, so they decide to get take-out from the nearby "In & Out." They are craving the greasy stuff: onion rings, mozzarella sticks, cheeseburgers, fries and milkshakes. The ladies are so glad not to have to be concerned with diets and competitive impressions. Little Miss also joins in on the food fest. She asks her friend, Macy, on the pageant committee if she can drive her car through the drive-through, since it's been so long since she has driven and off they went.

Here is another instance, Little Miss gets a ride in a vehicle not $1MM insured for liability.

In the hospitality suite Anni socializes with the other officials, as the group chats about the bloopers and outakes. The emcee, Mingon, was alive with anecdotes how she ad-libbed her transitions between acts here and there to buy some time for the ladies. There were a few technical difficulties. The most obvious was the lack of audio for Miss Utah's electronic violin. After some adieu, Miss Utah nearly played acoustically, but following a few dramatic moments the audio was restored.

For additional levity to the evening, Rodney, stops by the hospitality suite carrying a life-size poster of himself and his alleged cousin "Tiger Woods." The poster is homage to him crafted by the lead promotions guy from the Ohio state pageant committee. Anni rouses the group, by telling all the late arrivals to the hospitality suite to ask Rodney to meet his famous relative!

* * * * * * *

The week long Homecoming festivities are still unfolding. Saturday night is the big hometown banquet at the Commander's Club at the Wright-Patterson Airforce Base. There is a lot of nostalgia here. Little Miss' Mom is a teacher on base for elementary school kids and a lot of the town's population is driven by the influx of military. Little Miss rides in the limousine with her boyfriend Ron by her side.

Anni also rides with them and has a chance to speak with Ron. He tells Anni it is surreal taking a ride in a limousine with his girlfriend, since he looks at her as a normal girl. "She's not a celebrity or a rock-star to me, even though the life she currently leads is. It's hard to comprehend the whole thing," he softly comments.

Anni exits the limousine first, so the media has a chance to get in position to take Little Miss entrance photos. She and Ron walk in together, as she is greeted by 600 community leaders, friends, family and supporters that paid a hefty admission to be a part of this lifetime town event. A few minutes after she arrives, she is told that Brady Quinn, the football player of the Cleveland Browns stopped-by to wish her well. They are both alumnus from the same school system. She makes her way over towards the throngs of sports zealots to say hello to him. Brady does not stay for the dinner and performance, but wants to make a stop to support her accomplishment. A few years ago, he was drafted to the Browns after a successful career at University of Notre Dame where he attended on an athletic scholarship.

Anni overhears their exchange. Briefly they reminisce about the old high school. Quinn mentions he had heard of a young man from their school, whose mother had died and caused him to have a turbulent life until he was mentored by one of the guidance counselors. Based on the mentoring he received, this kid, Jamal opened a fortune 500 auto parts enterprise. Little Miss was glad to hear the positive outcome for Jamal.

The performance at this banquet begins when Little Miss sings a few songs dedicated to her supporters. One of the tunes she performers is a duet with Robert, one of the state pageant officials, who had helped coach Little Miss during her state competitions. He gets sentimental and teary when they perform together. Robert appears to be very dramatic and actually takes a turn for the worse as he nearly passes out during the vocals. While performing their song, he takes a seat on stage, because his legs got weak and nearly collapse from under him. Later, he chauks it up to a combination of the humid climate and his overwhelming emotions. He considers Little Miss his protégé' and is filled with raw sentiments seeing her in her prime.

In addition to their duet, Little Miss' childhood friend, Coley, delivers a purposeful soliloquy titled, "Journey to the Crown." He mentions how they found inspiration in each others' friendship. During the speech Anni can see, Ron, Little Miss' boyfriend is not completely comfortable with the nature of their friendship, especially now that she continues to cry on Coley's shoulder over the phone and tell him what's happening in her life. Ron wants to be the exclusive"shoulder" for her.

The next morning, after all the hoopla, Little Miss intends to go to Sunday church services with her parents and family. This is the same church she has been attending since she was born. The church community is a major support system for her and had raised a lot of funds for her to go to the national system. They had rallied for her to win the state and national level titles and are overwhelmingly proud of her. To give back to the congregation, the Pastor asks her to sing a hymnal with the Children's Choir at the service. She accepts the honor and this becomes a very emotional moment, leaving an indelible mark on her psyche.

After church, Little Miss' Mother, Shannon calls Anni, who stays behind at the hotel for Little Miss to have personal family time. Shannon cordially invites Anni, upon Little Miss' request, to join them for lunch. It is their family tradition to get Mexican food for lunch after church each and every Sunday at their favorite place: Celia's. Anni is delighted the family invite her to attend!

It was a blazing, hot sunny day and they say their hellos in the desolate restaurant parking lot. The asphalt is pot-holed and mud caked. There was an arid breeze blowing through and Little Miss had to hold her BCBG mini skirt down as she approached the doors to her all-time favorite Mexican haunt. At the restaurant, Anni greets all of Little Miss' grandparents, siblings, and her parents. Shannon makes a gesture to Anni to sit next to her, so she can get some scoop about their travels. Anni offers Shannon her personal contact numbers, so she may have direct access to her, if she is ever unable to reach her daughter or just wants to see how things are going. Shannon gives Anni a big hug in appreciation.

Shannon tells Anni she has a headache from all the excitement of her daughter being in town and their home phone ringing off the hook with media, neighbors and friends all wanting to share in the excitement. Anni immediately pulls out her stash of migraine pain reliever and tells Shannon, "Please take it. I have to be prepared for headaches on the road, so I know how you feel."

It is ironic to step in to care for Little Miss' Mom, not just Little Miss, but the family is so welcoming, so it's appropriate to return the gesture.

While Anni tends to Shannon, Little Miss is in her own element squabbling with her younger brother about which queso tastes best: the white or green. They also mention Morgan's upcoming surgery. Shannon did not want there to be much talk about it, but Little Miss tells her family she arranged to stay in town to be with her sister, "especially when she is wheeled out of surgery." Little Miss proclaims, "I want to be the first person you see when you open your eyes, Morgan."

Shannon abruptly changes the subject. Little Miss' Grandmother hugs Anni at the end of the lunch and says, "Thank you for looking after our Granddaughter during her travels." Shannon reaffirms their appreciation.

— 25 —

Following a day of sentimentality for Little Miss and her family, it is back to business. She and Anni are dressed in business suits and get transported by the Captain of the State Police to their Trooper headquarters. Little Miss' Dad shows up at the police barracks also to have some face time with his daughter while she is working nearby.

First, the police administration offers her a brief tour of the building, and then they settle into a conference room and have a working lunch over the packages dropped off from Panera Bread. Little Miss enjoys their selection, in addition to the fruit tray, sweets platter and beverages they generously assembled for her visit.

The tides of the meeting change when Little Miss gets introduced to a few special agents who focus on the Immigrations and Customs Enforcement (ICE) Task Force, they also were trained as part of Internet Crimes Against Children (ICAC). Recently, they have been tapped to probe child predator cases. The special agents feel the only way to give Little Miss a sense of the intensity, is by sharing with the group some of the busts they have been working on.

Unmindful of the graphic nature of their discussion, Little Miss' Father sat in the corner clearly shaken by their gripping tales of torture with young, abducted children forced to submit to misogynistic acts of terror. He wipes away tears that well-up in his eyes. Anni notices Little Miss as she is nearly gagging on the bread she eats and is beginning to get signs of the red hives on her neck and chest.

Special agent Jeff, mentions Innocent Images an FBI predator search group, whose mission is to identify and capture internet pedophiles. Jeff provides the majority of this graphic narrative inclusive of a file with statistics and facts. He offers to share it with the group. Anni, who is seated next to him, takes a look at the documentation and notices one report was prepared by an analyst at the National Center of Missing and Exploited Children, who has the same surname as she does: Seller. It gives her a reason to remember the name, because she finds the connection so ironic and she may run into that individual at an upcoming meeting there when they are in D.C.

No one else wants to read the stats as they had enough of the disturbing realities they all just heard. At the conclusion of the meeting, Anni asks Little Miss' Dad if he's OK.

He replies, "I did not expect the meeting to be so horrific."

Anni comments, "The truth of Little Miss' platform to protect kids from the danger associated with the internet is harsh…It's more than what happens from one keyboard to another, sometimes it crosses the line as we see from the evidence the agents provided."

Anni finds it interesting how Little Miss' Dad periodically shows-up when she is working within a driving radius of where he may be. He has the freedom to come and go as he pleases, since he is an independent insurance representative, where he racks up lots of miles to visit accounts in a few states.

Following the meeting, Captain Teckton of the State Troopers chauffeurs Little Miss to the State Capital for presentations to the House and later to the Senate. Some of her local state politicians were formulating legislation to tighten the penalties for internet crimes, especially those involving children.

In the corridor of the Capital building, Anni observes a young girl who wants to meet Little Miss. The unique quality about this particular girl that Anni sees is that she has no hair. Her mother whispers to Anni, "She has been fighting an unusual strain of cancer for four of her seven years, but will be considered cancer-free if her next screenings come out negative for the next nine more months."

Anni responds, "What a relief that will be for her and your family. I will ask Little Miss to arrange to meet your daughter and say hello."

Anni whispered to Little Miss the heroism of this young girl. Little Miss briskly walks toward her and kneels down to eye level and says, "Hello there. What is your name? Would you like to try on my crown?"

The little girl, named April, gives Little Miss a big hug around her knees, as Little Miss was standing soon after asking her those simple questions. April nods excitedly with the thought of trying on her crown. Little Miss has her sit on her lap, so a photo of the two of them can be taken. Anni snaps the picture with the bald little girl wearing the Miss Patriotic crown. April tells Little Miss, "I want to be you when I grow up!"

Little Miss tells April, she wants to have the spirit and love the little girl has.

There are a handful of other kids who also want to meet her, since school is out and some of the state employees decide to declare a "Bring your Child to Work Day."

Afterwards, Captain Tekton drives Little Miss back to her hotel three hours away and tells Anni some of his men will be by in the morning to escort Little Miss to the city hospital where her sister is scheduled for surgery. Captain Teckton mentions they will be onsite to avoid any unwanted publicity, as Little Miss intends to be there for her family in a private matter.

Anni mentions to him, they will have checked out of the hotel that morning too, being that they are headed back to the capital the day after her sister's surgery. "I suppose I will stay in the lobby here at the hotel, since our rooms will be checked-out to give Little Miss privacy with her family," Anni says to the Captain Teckton.

He responds, "You can probably come to the hospital." Anni does not want to overstep her bounds. She would occupy her time someplace else, but in this prairie town they are staying there is nothing around for miles.

This town is no metropolis and there is no public transportation for me to occupy myself.

Little Miss tells Anni, "My Mom wants you to stay at our family home, while we are at the hospital or you can come directly to the hospital."

Anni asks Captain Teckton, "Will it be any difference in terms of the transport, whether I stay here in town or at the other locations, since your department is driving us both across the state back to the Capital?" She asks. The Captain said his men will do whatever is needed to complete the job.

Little Miss' Mom decides it may be nicer to have her come along than be completely alone for hours and hours. So the conclusion is made, Anni will accompany them to the hospital and she assures Little Miss' Mother she will not be in their hair. Anni is used to keeping herself occupied, while Little Miss is involved with her events and appearances.

Fortunately, Anni likes to read and enjoys being a computer user, from updating her reports to headquarters at record speed, uploading photos she takes to keep the travel log current of the national website and corresponding with her family and friends. They're all glad to hear about the exciting things she witnesses along her journey!

As Anni checks them out of the hotel that Tuesday morning and, she sees the hometown newspaper in the box by the front door, the photo caption is the one from yesterday: "Little Miss and April, (the young girl who has fought back cancer) got a chance to wear the Miss Patriotic crown!"

At the hospital, Anni settles in an alcove that is across from the pre-surgical area that Little Miss' family is converged. Not only her parents and brother, but their Grandparents, many neighbors and friends from church come in support of Morgan's imminent surgery.

Anni is delighted to see the solidarity of the family and the extended community. She has not experienced this phenomenon, since in her hometown neighborhood; people isolate themselves and live independent of everyone else around the block.

Little Miss' Father sees Anni feverishly clicking on her laptop and walks over to say, "Good morning." He sits beside her and she shows him photos that were posted on the photographer's website; images from the banquet held at the base. She briefly scrolls through some shots that have some of their close family in the pictures with her. He looks really proud when he sees these shots. He thanks Anni and indicates "I'm going back across the way to wait for more of our relatives coming by to pray for Morgan."

No sooner does he depart from the vestibule that Anni is stationed when Little Miss' Grandmother Tess comes by and asks Anni, "Do you want to look at this newspaper?" Anni thanks her for the offer and says, "She has a copy of it."

Tess is the Grandmother who befriended Anni at the family luncheon after the Church service. She just wants to say hello and mentions to Anni, "You don't have to sit all the way over here by yourself; you're like family to us, so feel free to sit in the other section with us."

Anni responds she wants to provide them time to deal with this family matter privately, even though she notices a steady stream of community people, neighbors, congregants carrying gift bags and baskets. She is amazed by the amount of floral deliveries that have arrived. So far, she has counted eight of them and the surgery has not been performed yet.

Little Miss' Mom also waves to Anni and motions for her to come over to the waiting area the family is camping out. She says some friends brought bags of snacks and hands them to Anni and tells her to help herself. Anni notices a plastic shopping bag of that has a pile of newspapers strewn in and around it. Anni asks if she may look at them. Grandmother Tess interjects, "Help yourself."

Anni sifts through the various papers to do a quick search for any photos and articles that mention Little Miss. She carefully sets aside the mementos, so her family can assemble them in a scrapbook or file for posterity. Little Miss' Mother, Shannon tells Anni she has been so busy with all the excitement and work, she has not been up-to-date collecting every article, so they appreciated Anni doing that.

Shannon said she relies on her friends to monitor the headlines for her and just assumes she'll eventually get a copy of all the media containing her daughter. Shannon comments, "The Miss Patriotic Office can send me copies of everything I don't already have."

Anni wonders if that is a service the headquarters will provide?

Little Miss and Shannon, pull the lead nurse aside to request that Little Miss get special dispensation to stay with her sister Morgan in her hospital room, prior to wheeling her in for surgery. They plead, since Little Miss is in town for a few hours to be here to support her sister who is like her "little shadow."

Their request does not follow hospital rules, but they made a special exception for her. So, Little Miss is whisked back to the pre-operative room, where Morgan is lying with IV's and various monitors attached. Little Miss climbs in her bed and snuggles beside her sister.

Anni asks Justin, their younger brother if he is interested in seeing his sister too. He replies, "Dad forced me to be here. I'd be out hitting golf balls, until they tell me she came out of surgery, if I had my choice!"

Anni comments, "It's nice your whole family is together to support your sister." The surgery was scheduled for early morning, but got postponed a few times, as other emergency cases preempted her non-urgent procedure allegedly.

Meanwhile, Morgan's paternal Grandmother, Florence, was markedly sullen. Anni asks her, "Are you alright?"

She comments, I drove three hours to be here for my Granddaughter and I asked to go back to her hospital room, and they let her sister in, but not me. I don't understand why they bent the rule for her…I am her Grandmother!"

Anni commiserates and mentions, "These are some unique circumstances."

Hours go by and the family gets word that Morgan's surgery time is rescheduled for around 1pm. By that time, Little Miss had to say her good-byes to her sister, as no one was able to go into surgery beside hospital staff.

Little Miss gets very anxious and hungry, so she takes a ride with her Dad, brother and church friends to get some fast food for lunch at "Jake's." She asks Anni if she'd like anything. Anni declines the friendly offer. Little Miss insists you have to try one of "Jake's" famous cherry lemonades or root beer floats.

Anni smiles and responds, "Since you insist, I will try the souped-up lemonade." She tries to hand her some money, but Little Miss' parents say, "Let us get it, you are like a family member." Anni feels honored.

They come back with bags of food and drink and have an impromptu picnic in the waiting area of the hospital. Two of Morgan's surgeons appear and ask her parents to come into a nearby conference area to review the surgical findings. After the talk with the surgeon, Shannon approaches the cluster of friends and family waving surgical photographs of Morgan's newly removed cysts. Anni can not believe how candid Shannon is with her daughter's excised growths.

Shannon tells everyone, with the images in hand, "They removed a grapefruit sized cyst that has hair and teeth," as Shannon then passes the pictures around.

Little Miss is obviously disgusted. "Was there a small person growing inside her?" she asked. Shannon indicates, cysts have the make-up of human organs and material. Little Miss feels nauseous after eating fries and pizza with her best friend Coley, then seeing the explicit pictures of her sister's cyst!

After a few hours in recovery, Little Miss is the first one to get the OK to visit with Morgan. Again she jumps in her bed and lies beside her. Anni remained in a waiting room separate from her family to give them space.

Yet, she could hear them asking, "Where is Anni?"

She walks around the corner to let them know she was in another section of the waiting area, which provides better internet connection. Shannon indicates she is interested in knowing about Little Miss' upcoming travels. Anni confirms she will pull-up the information, to provide her an update.

Anni walks outside to get cell phone service and then dials-up Serberus. She asks her that Shannon wants to know the phone number of a hotel on the West coast that Little Miss will be traveling to, so she can arrange to ship a bulky gown there for her daughter in advance. Serberus was not eager to look-up a phone number when Anni asks.

Anni mentions, "You can get back to me when you have some time. You don't have to drop everything and find it this second." As she has this exchange, Anni's the cell phone beeped, signaling a voicemail was left on another line. After finishing-up with Serberus, Anni attempts to retrieve the message and the voicemail system keep telling, "Please enter your login." Anni had never had to login on this phone before. Apparently, Sonny had programmed a voicemail passcode when she upgraded the phone and neglected to share it with Anni.

Why was there a code now?

Anni calls Sonny at her home number, which is the only contact phone number she has for her. Sonny's answering machine is on, so Anni leaves a concise message requesting the code and to call her on the work cell phone as soon as she receives the call. About six hours later Sonny responds. She was away visiting her Grandkids and thought she told Anni how to access the voicemail using, "M-I-S-S." Anni said, "No big deal, it must have been an oversight."

* * * * * * *

Anni writes down the next few weeks' worth of travel plans for Shannon's reference. She is excited to hear about it all. The family then gets word they can visit Morgan in her room. Anni stays behind, but tells Shannon to wish her a speedy recovery.

In the meantime, Anni takes a walk to the hospital cafeteria and picks-up a tossed salad. She wants to keep her energy up, as they have a three hour drive back to the state capital that evening with Captain Teckton.

Shannon peeks into the waiting area that Anni is working and motions to her. She mentions she wants to speak with her. Shannon leads her down the corridor in the direction of Morgan's recovery room. She tells Anni that Little Miss is overwhelmed by leaving her sister behind and having to go back on the road. Shannon indicates when her daughter gets hysterical like this, which is not often, it is best to let her cry and give her space.

As Shannon is providing Anni those guidelines, there is Little Miss sobbing profusely in her Father's arms in a small medical office near Morgan's room. Little Miss is wiping her eyes and nose on her own sleeve, so Anni pulls out of her expansive work bag, a Kleenex with a cute, smiling Snowman design on it and hands it to Shannon. Anni tells her, "I hope it will cheer her up." Anni considers how Little Miss and her Mom initially told her how they are a "huggy family."

Now she prefers to have her space. I'll be very sensitive to this situation.

Anni remains in the hallway where the state troopers are positioned. These are the same troopers who have provided transportation and security while she's been in her home state for the Homecoming events. Captain Teckton asks Anni how things are going and what time they should depart. Anni lets him know, Little Miss needs some time with her sister to regroup and get in gear, before he drives them back to the state Capital.

Anni chats with the Troopers and Little Miss' Dad about watching some college football and they indicate how they love to chill out eating things like spicy sausage or knockwurst and cold imported beer. She kids the, "Too bad you are on duty now."

Within a half an hour, Little Miss appears from her sister's room. Her eyes are red and swollen. Anni asks if it is OK that she says "Goodbye" to Morgan.

The family says, "Sure!" Morgan was groggy but awake and Little Miss tells Anni, how Morgan had recently given the nurses a hard time by demanding a juice box and talking with a Southern drawl, "You get it, Girrll!" Morgan normally does not have that kind of accent. Little Miss recounts, "It must have been the anesthesia."

Little Miss slowly saunters down the hall with both parents at her sides and Anni following behind with the State Troopers. Her luggage has to be swapped out from her parent's vehicle, because her Mom is instrumental in taking care of her laundry, while in town and packing new outfits and more gowns. Little Miss gets in the back seat of the Captain's unmarked car beside one of the suitcases that did not fit in the packed trunk. She wants to just settle in by herself and sleep with her ipod on. After a half dozen hugs and kisses with her parents, the car was off.

Ten miles away, Little Miss pops-up, "I forgot to take the hanging garments from my Dad's truck!" The Captain pulls over waits for her to feverishly text message her Mom, and they confirm they can double back for the items. The two vehicles converge in a gas station parking lot and the exchange is made. Anni jokes, "This is a covert operation, to handoff some garments. Really Little Miss strategized with her Dad to get a few extra hugs." They all laugh.

— 26 —

On the three hour drive back to the capital, Little Miss sleeps most of the way. Anni and Captain Teckton talk-up a storm to pass the time. The Captain tells Anni how the state is in the midst of upgrading communication systems and technology and he is doing extensive research on wireless internet service. He asks Anni what service she uses with her laptop. Anni indicates her new laptop has had better connectivity with the internet, which is her major means to keep in touch with data, reports, images, etc. She mentions him in certain places there has been intermittent outages, but overall the service is sufficient.

Captain Teckton wondered if her laptop would receive a signal in the midlands. Anni is glad to give it a test, so at the next rest stop, she pulls her laptop out of the carry-on case and boots it up. The connection instantly linked in. The Captain was impressed and plans to consider that type of service for his Troopers if the economics fall in line.

Anni notices Captain Teckton is driving about 90 miles an hour on the highway, but she does not question him, as he is a professional. She makes sure her seatbelt is fastened. Even as they approached the toll plaza, where drivers normally yield, the Captain whizzes through. Anni tries to focus on the conversation to avoid the realization how crazy-fast they are traveling.

To pass the time and avoid the worry, Anni asks Captain Teckton about some of his life changing experiences in law enforcement. He recounts how he worked with children who faced some extreme situations when violence abruptly took family members from them. He said one particular girl wrote an essay after hearing a presentation he made about law enforcement and emergency personal responding to the 9/11emergency. He wrote protocol for some emergency response systems and was honored for his efforts. The Captain was shaken by the magnitude of the fallen law enforcement and civilians.

In the report the mysterious girl had written, she thanked him for his hard-work, because her uncle was seriously injured as result of the terror attacks. She reminded the Captain through her written words that each day will shine new light on the world. Recalling, the words of this young student has the middle-aged police Captain in tears. He was stirred while recounting the story for Anni. He removes his glasses and wiped his eyes. He said that was five years ago and he wanted to respond to the little girl for being so positive, but the essay had been forwarded among piles of letters and assignments from various elementary students assignments on life, coping and hope.

A couple of years later the Captain was attending at a law enforcement convention and among thousands of men, he runs into an officer who last name on his badge was the surname of the little girl. But, he and the other cop were heading in different directions. Later on in the week of the convention, he crossed paths with the officer in a training session and mentions the story of the little girl who affected his life positively by giving him the right to grieve for the victims including her uncle who was hurt. The man confirmed, "I am the Uncle of that girl who wrote that essay."

The Captain could not believe he coincidentally met him in another state. Captain Teckton tells Anni, "It really was not a coincidence, but a meeting that was supposed to happen; intended by a higher power."

Three hours later they arrive in Cleveland back at the Regency Hotel, where they had stayed at the beginning of Homecoming. Since it is after ten at night, there is less pomp and circumstance. The Troopers do not take the bomb sniffing Deputy dog Shirley through the hotel as they did the last time. Instead, Anni quietly registers them back into their respective rooms and they settle in for one night.

Anni calls Serberus to connect with her about the tour status. Serberus tells her there are some itinerary updates being faxed to the hotel. She stipulates to Anni, "Be advised our long-standing relationship with Premier Travel is now over. I have to find a new source to handle the Miss Patriotic business."

Anni asks, "What caused the change in travel agents?"

Serberus answered, "Judy at Premier Travel said they need to work with accounts that give them larger amounts of travel arrangements. We have been working with them for years! Apparently, they don't they realize how much business we gave them over time, and I have noticed and the service has been slipping. She doesn't call back as quickly as she used to."

Anni comments, "Travel agent business is shrinking as many professionals opt to book their own travel on the internet through many different websites."

Maybe Premier Travel realizes Miss Patriotic's travel heyday was slipping away and they can use their services more effectively with more gracious accounts who pay promptly.

Anni walks down to the front desk to the retrieve the revised travel itinerary from the other travel agency.

The following morning Little Miss has her gear selected for a photo shoot with her favorite state photographer, Ken Lowes. All their other stuff needs to be packed-up too, as they are leaving the photo shoot at day-end for the airport, back out to their next destination. During the photo shoot, Little Miss is in her element, she is surrounded by May Zander, the executive director, who mentored her through state and national pageantry; Ann, a close friend and matronly volunteer from the state pageant system; Lenny, her home state hairstylist and Anni is among them too. Within an hour of Lenny primping Little Miss' hair and make-up, she gets a text from her Dad who drove across the state, to visit her on location. Conveniently, he appears around lunch time and has a surprise visit with his precious girl. He admits how much he misses her since they just parted ways at the hospital the day before.

Little Miss has fun at this photo shoot, wearing fashions by the gown designer who outfitted the pageant. She looks darling in an ethereal-looking silk wrap blouse, matching camisole and satin-black tuxedo pants. Lenny sets her hair in big, soft curls.

She has an updated Farrah Fawcett look about her.

As the shoot winds down, her Father said his good-byes and leaves to attend to some business in town. Little Miss is in better spirits seeing her Father and ready to be back in work mode.

She declares that she will use some of the photos from the shoot as content for the upcoming pageant program book. Ken puts the images up on his large computer monitor, so the group can admire his work and select which photos, she should use. After the informal vote and review, Ken does some quick airbrushing and editing of fly-away hairs, quirky shadows, and crops the shots, so her unsightly fingernails are not visible.

Following the magic of technology her selections are perfected and it was time to dash to the airport, enroute to their next stop.

— 27 —

As the finality of Homecoming comes to pass, Little Miss and Anni, fly that evening to Bedford County, Virginia. There Little Miss is slated to work with law enforcement supporting her internet safety mission. The Sheriff's Department introduces her to the State Attorney General John Brownlee and a retired FBI official who now heads the Corruption and Crime Commission, an organization that seeks out white-collar crime and holds executives accountable. They are pleased to meet Little Miss. She is not very upbeat that morning and tells Anni her throat was achy.

So Anni tries to run the proverbial ball for Little Miss by carrying on most of the conversations in the meet-and–greet breakfast. Anni also suggests Little Miss drink a little orange juice to help ward off her ill feeling. Little Miss objects to the juice idea, since she does not like juice. Anni persuades her just to take a few sips to help boost her immunity level.

Upon conversing with VA Attorney General John Brownlee, Anni learns how he holds his boss, U.S. Attorney General Alberto Gonzales in high regard. Anni comments to him that Little Miss is scheduled to meet with his boss during the upcoming week, so she can send his regards. State A.G. Brownlee's young daughter came to the meet-and-greet at the Sheriff's Department to meet Little Miss and she was delighted to have her picture taken with her. Anni suggests Little Miss have the little girl try her crown on and that certainly made for a great photo opportunity, one the little girl and her parents will not soon forget.

Following the morning conference, Little Miss attends an intensive ICAC (Internet Crime Against Children) training, where the Sheriff and special agents logged into live chat rooms posing as 14-year old girls to see what conversations would develop. This is a real-life lesson for Little Miss to witness how prevalent internet trolling is by predators. Within seconds of logging in, the imaginary teenage girl is contacted by a handful of "wannabe friends." Without any encouragement, the screen names morph into a series of conversations and many are older men, looking for a vulnerable and curious, young girl.

It's unfathomable how exorbitant the response rate is and the chat logs get weird and suspicious.

Little Miss could not have imagined how prevalent the pool of online predators is. Through this experience, she witnesses it firsthand. During the training session the agents and Sheriff barrage Little Miss with statistics and data. Anni notices Little Miss is losing engagement and her attention, possibly because her energy begins waning. Anni steps-in and asks questions, to make the session more interactive and to show that Little Miss is involved for a reason.

Eventually, Little Miss gets reengaged in the discussion when she meets a 23-year old woman, who attends the session; a former victim who had fallen prey to a pedophile. The woman arrives with her Mother to the session and shares her story with Little Miss. The young woman, Vanessa, tells how she went off from a friend's house to meet this boy, who she thought seemed interested in her. It turns out the alleged boy was a 37-year old man, who sexually attacked her, drove her to an unknown area, violently beat her and tossed her out of his moving vehicle and left her to die on the side of a darkened roadway. She is a survivor and came out to champion the mission of internet safety her surviving living through such a devastating experience. Little Miss is moved.

After Vanessa's shocking testimonial, Anni requests the Sheriff's Department break for lunch. Little Miss was starving and needed to recharge her batteries after this intense presentation.

When the Sheriff's Department concludes the training, they deputize Little Miss as an honorary Deputy Sheriff, along with legendary Basketball Player Shaquille O'Neil. Now Little Miss is off to Lynchburg, Virginia. There she films public service announcements regarding internet safety and also invites Vanessa to participate. A handful of deputized celebrities are the spokespeople for this campaign. Little Miss is slated to make a statement also.

The PSA's are filmed on the campus of Liberty University, founded by the legendary Dr. Jerry Falwell.

Anni asks Little Miss, "Are you familiar with Jerry Falwell?" Little Miss is too young to know who he is or his influence over Christian fundamentalism coinciding with televangelism. Dr. Falwell, along with other leaders of the University hosted a private reception for her. From the reception, Little Miss is being transported by Dr. Falwell's private jet to Washington Dulles for more work in the D.C. area.

Anni looks over at her and she appears to be a bit tired and congested. Little

Miss asks, "Is it OK, I sit down as the guests filter out of the reception?" She whispers to Anni, "I feel like I am getting sick." Anni offers her some water to keep hydrated and a plate of crackers and cheese to snack on.

Anni thanks Dr. Falwell for permitting Little Miss to travel in his plane. He said it was no problem and some of his personnel accompany them on the short flight from Virginia to Washington, DC. This is the first time Little Miss was aboard a private aircraft.

Flying by a private jet certainly has its privileges, because, they are driven through a secured gate immediately onto the tarmac. There are no X-ray machines or security lines; rather they step out of the van and directly onto Dr. Falwell's jet.

As the forty-five minute flight nearly ends, Little Miss stretches from the brief nap she was taking and gets a few more minutes of downtime in her reclined seat in the far back of the jet. Her trusty ipod with pink cover is positioned in her lap, as it usually is when they flew place to place. As they prepare for the landing, Dr. Falwell's assistant collects the empty water bottles and the tarmac was suddenly in view. Anni asks, "Do you feel any better?"

"Not really."

Steps of the jet extend to the ground as Little Miss is guided down where she sees police escorts on their motorcycles beside the aircraft. The police briefly want to say hello and get photos taken with her around their motorcycles. She obliges. Then the motorcycle brigade asks Anni if she'd like to sit on one of their bikes too. She demurely refuses, but they insist. She complies with their friendly urging to try it. Anni climbs on a bike and they take her picture too.

Also, standing-by is the ever-loyal Dick Zweber. He appears on the tarmac driving an immaculate black Escalade waiting for Little Miss. Dick helps load the bags into the Escalade and they are off! The police lead the escort during rush hour, so they ride with their strobing lights flashing through the traffic. As the result, the lanes of cars part like the Red Sea. Little Miss is amazed about the escort treatment she is receiving. Zweber adds, "The police do not usually provide this type of escort unless it is the President, obviously, or a high level diplomat, and certain celebrities like Steven Spielberg."

Anni said, "It's moments like these that would be great to capture in a journal about your experiences on the road and how you felt at the time."

Little Miss nods, but decides to take less effort by calling her Dad. She tells him about the traffic pattern, to share the excitement and hope one of them will remember this for posterity.

— 28 —

As they arrive downtown, all of the traffic along the highway continues to separate like their vehicle has the power of Moses. Little Miss was sitting on the edge of her seat. Dick told her this is really unusual. He had not seen this take place in a long time. The entourage pulled up to the Ritz Carlton. Little Miss and Anni approach the entrance as the doormen offer them, "Our warmest greetings."

Little Miss' health has steadily declined. Her eyes are watery and a bit puffy and her head feels like it is submerged in a fish bowl. Anni is quick to respond.

Before Dick departs from the driveway of their hotel, Anni asks if he knows where the nearest pharmacy is. He is unsure, so she asks him to wait with the vehicle, while she queries the Concierge. While she is waiting for the answer, Anni rapidly contacts Little Miss' Mother to get their family doctor to write a script, and then to fax it the local pharmacy she was trying to identify for Little Miss.

Anni calls Shannon back with the particulars: the pharmacy fax number and the address for their Doctor to respond.

At the Ritz Carlton, the ladies approach the reception area and Anni quickly navigates through the check-in process, as part of the itinerary was being billed to the government via the USO, and the other portion is on the Miss Patriotic Organization's tab. Anni speaks with the Eastern European representative at the desk to inform her of the split billing, but tries to do this in a demure way, so as not to concern Little Miss. More importantly, she requests their rooms be adjoining and to provide the larger one to Little Miss. The associate indicates both rooms are the same as she provides Anni the coded keys. Up they went to their assigned private floor, accessible only by this coded hotel key, otherwise the elevator sits motionless without it.

Anni attempts to get Little Miss to her room, so she can take a nap.

They arrive at their rooms, Anni expresses, "Call me if you need anything. I'm going to the pharmacy to pick-up some medicine for you, and then get a quick workout in on my way back. I can help you with anything you need to get ready for 4pm. Try to get as much rest as you can."

"Thanks, Anni, I'm taking a nap as soon as I shut the door," Little Miss responded.

A few minutes after entering her own room, Anni hears a knock at her door. She wonders if it's Little Miss. "Who is it?" she asks. There was no reply. Cautiously, she opens the door and sees a Ritz Carlton Hotel associate with a room service cart. "I did not order anything."

In broken English, the worker indicates, "From hotel, for Miss Patriotic." Instead of having him intrude on her brief, quiet time, Anni accepts the cart in her room. Minutes later she calls Little Miss and tells her the Hotel must have mixed-up the room numbers as they sent a complementary fruit presentation with bottled iced teas and waters, along with a fresh floral arrangement of exotic tiger striped orchids.

"Enjoy it. I don't like fresh fruit much and I'm sure you'd eat that healthy stuff," Little Miss responds. Her observation is right. Anni is overjoyed Little Miss offers the fruit basket to her. Now she did not have to run out to grab breakfast, as she could pare the variety into a nice fruit salad.

Anni especially enjoys the fresh floral design, because it reminds her of the time she spent last Summer in Hawaii, where she got married.

This unexpected delivery certainly put me in a great mood!

Anni gets back on track and zips back to the lobby and in the waiting SUV with Dick to find the pharmacy. When they locate it, she tells Dick to wait curbside, to avoid the hassle of finding a parking spot downtown. Anni figures she just has to pick-up and pay for the meds. Yet, the pharmacist inside, had not received the fax from the Ohio doctor. Anni calls Little Miss' Mom to inform her that the script has not transmitted here yet, so she "lights a fire" under the doctor and Anni hears the fax machine beep as the transmission is received in minutes.

"This is a rush!" Anni informs the Pharmacy Tech, as he asks her questions regarding the insurance processing. Again, Anni calls Shannon to confirm the insurance ID numbers and the script is now filled. As the tech is ringing it up, Anni grabs a few bags of Halls Vitamin C drops for Little Miss too. She also knew she would not eat at the gala, so she asked Dick if she can grab her some food next door at Subway. He nods and Anni asks if she can get him something too. He gave Anni his order and they rounded back to the hotel. Little Miss is relieved how well Anni expedited the response to her not feeling well. Her Mother was even more at peace with Anni's ability to "save the day." There certainly is no time to be sick when you have a tight schedule and you're living on the road.

* * * * * *

Some executives from the USO offer to arrange a hair styling and make-up session for Little Miss to primp for the gala.

Apparently, as they both find out, Little Miss did not have a say in the matter, when Anni gets back from the fitness center and starts to undress then to jump in the shower, her phone rings. "Miss Patriotic, I am here in the lobby for your hair and make-up," the caller mentions.

Once again the front desk must have confused in their registration log that Anni's room is Miss Patriotic's, so Anni advises, "I am her assistant and will be down momentarily to let you up to her suite."

"Are you ready for hair and make-up? The stylists are in the lobby and called to get started." Anni calls Little Miss to give her a head's up.

"I thought they were coming for 2:45pm, they're early..." she trails off.

"Since this appointment was arranged by our hosts, I don't think there is room to negotiate, if you know what I mean?" Anni wanted to level the playing field. "I'll be back-up with the stylist in just a few minutes."

First, Anni had to throw some clothes on and try to look presentable to go down to the lobby. Their timing was awkward in a few ways, but as Anni tells Little Miss, she can't pass up the opportunity as the hair and make-up were pre-arranged by a Board Member of the USO.

The stylist arrives with two assistants: his sister and cousin. They must be related, they have similar features and look very edgy with drastic hairstyles. Alejandro, the hair stylist has jet-black spiky hair with sculptured side burns and a rock-and-roll uniform of black, fitted jeans and a distressed leather jacket. His sister, Sylvinia, sports sleek black hair and lots of make-up. It was not evening yet, but all of their looks are nightclub worthy. Their cousin, Gina, also looks similar, but a few years younger.

Their appearance reminds me of high school in the 80's: Big, big hair, also jet black, with thick, black eyeliner and at least five coats of mascara.

Little Miss' eyes open wide, as she answers her door in the heavy, cotton robe provided by the Ritz Carlton. She was wiping the sleepiness away, when she sees the "rockstars" enter. They ask to see her gown and shoes for inspiration of the cosmetic color palette for the evening. Alejandro inquires whether she has a vision in mind for her hair. "I have not given it any thought, you can have creative control."

"I see your long blond hair in tons of spiral curls cascading all over," as he professes his idea. Little Miss is not excited about it, but lets him give it a try.

In the meantime, Anni offers to get the steam iron ready, since Little Miss' gown needs pressing before wearing. "I can manage it," Little Miss responds.

"OK, I'll finish up getting ready myself and come back over to see how you're doing in just a bit," as she dashes to take her 10 minute shower and prepare.

I assumed that for black tie, we'd have ample time to get ready, but it's really a 50-yard dash to get her all situated, before getting myself together.

After taking the briefest of showers and dressing rapidly, Anni bolts back to Little Miss' room. Hopefully she was left in good hands. Little Miss looks frazzled as Anni sees her sitting at the desk where Alejandro has crafted a ton of curls bouncing around her head. He is using a tool Anni never saw before; it is a ceramic curling iron with no clip to hold the hair around it. Rather, Alejandro holds the twirled hair in place around the intensely heated barrel of this iron using a bright yellow heat- resistant glove.

It is Michael Jackson Thriller-esque.

Sylvinia and her cousin, want to put some intense eye color on Little Miss. Anni could see she is a bit uncomfortable with their selections. "I bought some Bare Minerals products just the other day here at the Mall. I'd like to give these colors a try," Little Miss peeps.

"We can make this work," the pair of cosmetologists corroborates.

The hairstyle was coming to completion and Alejandro proclaims, "This hairstyle is perfection!" When Little Miss slid into her turquoise, silken gown with brown appliqué' on the straps and plunging bodice, he adds, "You look like a goddess!"

Anni notices Little Miss' facial expression, she is clearly not in agreement. The look is way too dramatic for her. She whispers to Anni, "I really don't like having curly hair." Time had elapsed and there's no slack to redo the style, so this corkscrewed concoction is now her glamorized look for the next few hours.

Anni tells her how amazing she looks. "It's a different look, but it fits the bill for this formal event, I am partial to curly hair," being that her own hair consists of thick looping locks.

As the stylists pack-up their gear, they complement Anni for her sophisticated black, fitting gown. Sylvinia offers to line Anni's lips with a complementing color to accentuate her green eyes. Anni accepts the offer for the "ten second pampering." She looks in the mirror to witness the touch-up. The liner makes Anni appear as if she had collagen injections in her lips making them look fuller and enhanced by the shiny mauve lip gloss they apply.

As hair and make-up is now complete, Anni gives Little Miss some of her 8.5"x11" promo shots to autograph for each of them, and then Little Miss and Anni go on their way to the sound check for the gala at which she was performing later with other celebrities. When they arrive at the auditorium level of their hotel, the search is on to locate a Manager in charge of Production or someone who has a clue about the sound check. They enter a banquet room, with a flurry of activity, as workers weave in and out placing hundreds of tables and accompanying chairs around for the 600 person gala.

Anni identifies an event assistant who pages another official to assist with Little Miss' music and sound level adjustments. The assistant indicates, "The contact you need is not around until 4pm, the designated rehearsal time. I know your time is precious, so I'm trying to get them to start your sound check sooner, then you can finish rehearsal as soon as possible."

"It's a shame you had to be in full hair and make-up and no one else is on time for you," Anni comments to Little Miss. Little Miss frustratingly nods in agreement.

As usual for Little Miss, the rehearsal takes just a matter of a few minutes.

Anni attempts to be proactive by locating their seats for dinner. Anni realizes there is a chance Little Miss will be sitting with the other "esteemed celebrities." Laura Bush is slated to attend and will be receiving an honor, so Little Miss may be dining with her after the receiving line with the other celebrities.

The event assistant, who Anni checked-in with earlier, verifies Little Miss and Anni will be situated at table six, not at the First Lady's table. Their particular table is sponsored by AOL, the internet provider. She also mentions, "Due to time limitations; the First Lady will not be in a pre-Gala photo shoot with the other celebrities." Little Miss was looking forward to meeting her, but was confused about the entrance they had planned for her and the other dignitaries. Anni tries clarifying the details if this is now in lieu of the receiving line, but it seems as if these plans are changing on a dime, minute to minute. "You'll just play it by ear," she tells Little Miss.

The start of the gala is getting closer as the hotel is infused with hundreds of Secret Service personnel.

First, is a cocktail reception to kick-off the Gala. Various guests and dignitaries schmooze with Little Miss and a few offer her cocktails. She politely refuses. Anni makes sure Little Miss has a glass of water, in a regular looking glass, to keep her hydrated, so it does not look like she's imbibing a cocktail, to avoid rumors.

Many higher-ranking military officials and political figures chat with Little Miss. She leans toward Anni and whispers, "Boy, do I hate cocktail parties, I don't like trying to make small talk with all these people who I don't know and the fact that they're bombarding me."

Anni responds, "Most people find it awkward entering a room full of strangers, but in retrospect, there may be some conversation you have today that you think is inconsequential now, that eventually turns into some future opportunity. Bear with this, it can reap rewards later."

I recall being at functions, networking with professionals as a Consultant with Dale Carnegie and subsequently became a keynote speaker for a prestigious group months later from a contact I had made.

An announcement reverberates through the corridor for everyone to make their way into the banquet hall and find their seat, so the honors may begin. Little Miss dashes to a separate area to make her grand entrance with the other performers, Daniel Rodriguez, an operatic Tenor who was a former emergency responder in NYC on September 11, 2001, and Trace Adkins, a country music lyricist who wrote a song transformed into a video promoting the hard work of the soldiers fighting the war and the support of USO's services, also involved is a comedic impersonator, who specializes in Presidential impressions.

A color guard, with bagpipers wave on their brigade from the hall toward the stage then in the procession Little Miss follows suit and sings the National Anthem.

The AOL executive, of Korean heritage, sitting next to Anni at the table, was not familiar with Miss Patriotic. He did not know about her title or that she is a powerful vocalist. He mentions to Anni, "I am so impressed with her singing."

When Little Miss arrives back at the table, Anni gets up and gives her a hug for the job well done. The AOL executive proclaims he is delighted to introduce her to his wife, when she finishes her performance. Seated next to them is an Army General, who had been stationed near Little Miss hometown while on base there for eight years. "What a coincidence!" Anni exclaims. "This is like one of those seven degrees of separation from Little Miss. She always runs into people who are from various places or times of her life."

The General and his wife, Betty, are enamored by Little Miss and their common connection. Betty pulls out her drugstore disposable camera, snaps handful of pictures of her husband with Little Miss and switches so she can pose with Little Miss in some pictures too. "My neighbors will fall over when they see us having dinner with Little Miss!" Betty squeals.

Diagonally to the right of their table, the guest of honor is announced and arrives flanked with a swirl of Secret Service. First Lady Laura Bush, waves as she arrives. Anni has goose bumps on her arms as notices she has a perfect view to Mrs. Bush's seat. Anni catches eyes with Mrs. Bush and lip synchs "Hello" to her. Mrs. Bush acknowledges and gives Anni an obvious one-eyed wink to respond back.

The Army General's wife chimes-up to anyone who would listen, "Do you think I can go get my picture with her?" Anni responds, "Her security detail is rather intense, it's probably better to admire her from afar instead of breaching the suroundings."

No sooner did Anni complete her statement, Betty steps away from the table to test just how close she could get to Mrs. Bush. Two security guards posted immediately behind Mrs. Bush deter Betty from her mission and recommend she go back to her own table and let the First Lady enjoy the dinner program in peace.

Surprisingly, Mrs. Bush remains for the entire dinner and then accepts her honor following it.

I'm surprised the First Lady participated in the meal, I figured she'd arrive for the presentation of honors among wounded U.S. soldiers.

Yet, her instincts on this one were wrong.

— 29 —

While they were still in Washington, D.C., Anni is advised the CEO from the Miss Patriotic Organization will be connecting with them to accompany Miss Patriotic to a meeting with the National Center for Missing and Exploited Children and there is also a tentatively scheduled meeting with the U.S. Attorney General.

Well, the meeting to see the U.S. A.G. is put on indefinite hold, as his office is under scrutiny by Congress determining whether Alberto Gonzales' office is leading a cover-up of alleged eavesdropping and intelligence recording related to the terrorism our county is concerned with.

Anni finds out the Miss Patriotic Organization CEO drives to D.C. for the meeting. He drives frantically through the beltway traffic to make the meeting. Pearson in her smiley-centric way takes the train and arrives in a more leisurely manner for the meeting. He meets Pearson at the train station and they both arrive over to the Ritz where Miss Patriotic and Anni are staying, so he can carpool the group for the meeting.

Anni observes the CEO is clearly anxiety-ridden by driving down to the DC-area. He is all-flushed and clearly not comfortable with the driving directions. Pearson is sitting in the front passenger seat, but is not helping reduce his anxiety, as she is not paying attention to relevant highway markers, signs or landmarks to arrive at their destination.

Anni offers to help navigate, when she sees Pearson get noticeably stressed, perhaps a reaction to the anxiousness of their driver, the CEO, so she agrees to switch seats with Anni. Yet, Anni senses Pearson is sort-of reluctant to switch places.

I do not want this to be construed as overstepping my bounds.

Anni hopes Pearson does not read into Anni's action, which is purely helpful. She hopes Pearson does not think she is implying she is incompetent to navigate the group to the meeting location.

In the meantime, Little Miss text-messages feverishly on her Blackberry and does not get involved in the dynamic during the drive. With Anni's guidance, the CEO finds the address. He parks the car and they all stop for a bite to eat for lunch. At the cafeteria-style lunch stop, they make their food selections and reassemble at a table nestled in a corner. Ravenously, they take their first few bites.

Suddenly, the CEO puts his sandwich down and says, "I want to make an announcement." His tone of voice was stern and wavered slightly. Little Miss and Anni notice his expression and manner and determine this must be very serious. He makes the disclaimer, "You both should keep this news to yourselves for now." He goes on to mention he nearly canceled today's meeting, because "I just got word last night the country television-station which the organization was in contract with until 2011, just decided to pull-out of the partnership."

Now Anni realizes why the CEO looked so flushed and anxiety-riddled, in addition to fighting the traffic. He is preoccupied by the loss of the TV partner. This has huge implications for the future of the organization.

Anni concludes the TV alliance is the source of funding for the non-profit.

Suddenly Little Miss looks worried. Quickly she asks, "When will the next pageant be held?"

"I do not know right now," the CEO did not have the answer at that moment, since the pageant schedule is dictated by the TV partner producing and sponsoring the event and show. She gets instantly concerned, "That means there is a chance I will have to remain Miss Patriotic and be on tour beyond my normal year?"

Anni says quietly to her, "You have a contract, so regardless of how this plays out with a new TV partner, you can have your representation abide by those terms."

That comment does not resound well with Little Miss; still she is nervous.

Quietly Anni wonders how this will play out and if this will have an impact on the budget or more importantly employment with the Miss Patriotic Organization.

The CEO mentions, "We are already looking at a handful of options. It's been a rough series of years with the pageant and its TV partners, but we'll work through this."

After lunch, they vow to change their solemn tone back to their energized selves to see about doing some cross-publicity for kid safety. Miss Patriotic is overwhelmingly quiet all during the meeting, other than shaking hands to say hello. The National Center for Missing and Exploited Children make detailed presentations for Little Miss and the group. She is overwhelmed by the dramatic content they share regarding exploited children. The executives speak about current cases they are investigating and show graphic images of some clues found on the internet. Much of the facts, visibly shake Little Miss to the core. Anni notices Little Miss' torso cave in with disgust.

She regains her composure when the presentation ends and they tour the internet safety division. Little Miss is overjoyed to meet people there, who she communicated with, years ago when she first was researching her internet-safety platform five years ago, as she begun to get into the pageant circuit. She says to one contact in particular, "It feels like we're old friends, because we've e-mailed and talked for a few years now and you supplied me with a ton of great educational material to address the kids in the school assemblies I conducted."

After the tour of the internet safety division, they depart the facility and Anni asks Cheryl, "Are you staying in town?" Cheryl abruptly retorts, "NO, I am heading back as soon as my car arrives."

Anni is unsure why Pearson replied in such an abrasive tone, she was wondering if she planned to accompany them to dinner and any other activities. She figures, Pearson is stressed about the news that the CEO disclosed earlier.

— 30 —

The CEO gives Little Miss and Anni a ride back to their hotel. He mentions he has arranged a dinner with Miss Washington DC, her state director and his daughter that lives and works in the region. So he will confirm the reservation and call back to advise what time to be ready. Little Miss did not want to eagerly go, but she was not going to turn down the CEO's arrangements. He mentions he'll be calling in about two hours, as he needs to take his suit off and take a nap from all the overwhelming events of the day.

It is surprising how candid he is being an executive of a high-profile organization and not having any endurance. He needs to run to his young daughter's apartment to carve out some time to nap before dinner... so much for being an energetic leader.

As he indicated, the phone rings two hours later to confirm their 7:30pm dinner. He swings by the hotel and drives Little Miss and Anni a few blocks from their hotel to a newer restaurant in the Reston, Virginia area.

Little Miss sees Vicky, Miss Washington D.C. and her State Pageant Executive, Terri pulling up in her silver Mercedes convertible. They both step out of the vehicle once the valet opens each of their doors.

As opposed to the CEO, who finds a curbside parking spot a within a block of the restaurant. Little Miss, Anni and the CEO walk- up from his vehicle.

The CEO's twenty-something-year old was waiting in front of the establishment. Stephanie, the CEO's daughter is a pudgy, unmemorable-looking girl. Her clothes are unsophisticated and lacking in detail.

Anni asks the CEO if her feels refreshed from his nap and he indicates, "It did a world of good."

They say their hellos and enter the restaurant. It is crowded inside and their table is identified in the center of the tall-ceiling dining area.

At their table, Terri hordes the conversation immediately. She talks about how influential she and her investment lawyer husband are in this city and beyond.

She is dripping in couture fashion and accessories. Her make-up is perfect and hair-salon fresh. Terri sits next to Anni and the CEO.

She may as well have been at her own table seated on a golden throne, because her mannerisms reflect that she believes she is better than everyone else.

Even Little Miss, who is the most well-known of the group, is not able to interject much to the discussion, until Terri asks her questions directly.

There is such a dichotomy between the simple, plain, everyday person the CEO and his daughter are to the high-profile Terri exudes. In the middle of the spectrum is Anni, who is polished and professional in a modest way. Then there's Vicki-Miss Washington, D.C. who Terri is trying to mold into her assertive muse. Little Miss is somewhere in between. She holds the title, has the beauty and is accomplished, yet she carries herself in a more down-to-earth way. Finally, Terri, who believes her larger-then-life, cheeky, persona, owns the place and is a model of perfection. What a unique assemblage of dinner guests at the table!

Terri uses this dinner as a forum to highlight her accomplishments in her state pageant system and has the arrogance to say she is adept at finding the next perfect contestants.

She spots a table across from theirs consisting of three women. Terri sashays to that table and asks one of the women, who appears to be the youngest among the diners, "Have you ever modeled before and do you have any talent?"

The young lady is obviously speechless and bit embarrassed why this dolled-up and coiffed woman is interrogating her, while she is having an intimate, birthday dinner with her friends. She feels singled-out and is uncomfortable at this moment. Terri turns and points, "…well this beautiful lady seated here is Miss Patriotic and the lady next to her is Miss Washington, D.C. You could be next, and she hands her a business card."

Next, Teri summons the Executive Chef to greet Little Miss table side and rallies some other Washington, D.C. characters that she deals with to also say hello. After they finished eating a lavish dinner including dessert, Terri insists a group photo be taken with the proprietor. Anni offers to take the photo. A gentleman passes by and whispers to her, "You're too pretty to be the photographer; you need to be in the picture." Anni stood by on the sideline, to let Terri have her moment wrapping around the pageant queens and the restaurateur. The CEO awkwardly stands in one of the shots.

It's ironic how the CEO gets his daughter in on a business-related dinner and pays for her on the business tab. For a non-profit, he makes some special rules from time to time. Come to think of it, many of the Miss Patriotic executives seem star struck in a way. Between the MPO staff, they take their turns to bring Miss Patriotic to their homes or to eat with their families as the CEO does in Washington, D.C., so his daughter can boast having dinner with Little Miss, Cheryl did by bringing her to her home for dinner. Anni assumes Sonny eventually will take a turn too, bringing Little Miss to her neighborhood…And who knows what Serberus will do?

— 31 —

While in the D.C. area, Little Miss gets invited to place a wreath at Arlington National Cemetery. This opportunity is a high honor not offered to just anyone. Typically, dignitaries, celebrities and people of influence are part of this elite ceremony. The most formal of this wreath laying procession, happens in August when the President or other high ranking designee is selected for this honor to mark Veterans' Day or Memorial Day. Yet, the public can try to make a formal request to attain this approbation, yet, official events take precedence.

Earlier in March, Serberus had told Anni, there was a possibility the wreath-laying would take place, but she would verify the likelihood. When she did, Serberus was sure to indicate to Anni, "I had had this privilege witnessing a handful of Miss Patriotic's performing this honor." Also, Serberus stipulates, "You will have to stay behind and stand on the steps where the public gathers. You won't be able to be as near to the Memorial as she will be."

Anni heeds her message and thinks; she'll assess her precise position when she gets there.

Little Miss is informed through headquarters that she would have this distinction. Anni describes to her how many heads of state, dignitaries and Presidents have performed this tradition. Little Miss then begins to realize the magnitude of her task at hand.

As Little Miss and Anni are once again in this DC region, Dick Zweber, is their driver, a loyal patriot of the USO and a close acquaintance of the Arlington Cemetery Superintendent. Because of his connection to the austere Superintendent Jack Metzer, Zweber is able to provide Little Miss an insider's view to this historic ground. Zweber keeps his fingers crossed as they approach the base to have a non-invasive security check.

He clamors to be on time. The opportunity to perform the wreath-laying is part of the meticulously synchronized changing of the Guard at The Tomb of the Unknown Soldiers. This event happens 365 days a year; essentially every hour on the hour.

It is 1:45pm, Zweber begins to sweat. His balding head reflects the beads of perspiration, enough so that Anni notices him dabbing his white handkerchief all over his face and scalp. He tells them there is no leeway to be late for the wreath-laying. Little Miss is scheduled for the 2pm time slot.

Upon their drive to the Fort and adjoining cemetery, Zweber had told them how the most recent soldier's crypt added after Vietnam, from the Tomb of Unknown is currently empty. There were three soldiers buried here. The tombs had held the remains of unidentified fallen heroes, but the remains were exhumed from the Vietnam burial chamber and matched through mitochondrial DNA testing with its rightful family. The kin of US Airforce First Lieutenant Michael Blassi challenged the government and military to preserve their family's honor by reburying their son in their home state of Missouri.

At the checkpoint, there is one vehicle ahead of them, and the soldiers have the driver step-out as they check the contents, scrutinize his identification, as well as, swipe the underside of the car he is driving with mirrors mounted on long poles. He gets the "all clear" and proceeds. Zweber anxiously hopes they do not have to disembark, but his hope fades, as the soldiers want everyone out to inspect the vehicle and they use the mirrors a bit more swiftly than the previous entrant's car.

The soldiers notice Little Miss who cautiously steps down from the shuttle steps in her three inch silver grey heels wearing a fitted, powder blue St. John's knit suit with three kick-pleats in the bottom of her hem line.

The guards are somewhat distracted from the formality of the security check...

They make it on base! Zweber breathes a sigh of relief. He drives cautiously through the grounds telling them about the Generals and Colonels who reside here and pointed out the posthumous citizenry. Within just a few minutes they approach the Memorial Amphitheater, where Little Miss is greeted by Superintendent Metzer, Elaine Rodgers, the President of the Washington, D.C. Metro USO, as well as a staff photographer. Metzer proudly offers Little Miss a brief tour of the amphitheater, where he helps them imagine how different the setting is when it is full with politicians, diplomats and soldiers when a few Presidents had made statements here. Metzer allows them to stand in the box where the President presides.

Then he points out the bronze memorials for the fallen NASA astronauts from the Columbia, Challenger and Discovery. Anni asks Little Miss if she recalls any of the space mission incidents when astronauts died during their mission. She responds, "No I have no memory of that." Anni puts things in perspective as Little Miss was born in 1986.

Anni has an awe-inspiring moment looking at the American flag at half-mast near this memorial and seeing the multitude of funerals happening right at that moment.

Metzer indicates, "There are about 25 funerals occurring each day, while we are in wartime." The mood is extremely somber as Anni hears the horses pulling the caisson of another fallen soldier.

Steadily, the Superintendent unlocks the door to the Memorial Museum that is closed to the public for upkeep, but provides Little Miss the opportunity to see the archives of memorabilia including gifts from foreign heads of state: unique weaponry, coins, and commemorative flags. A quick photo is snapped, as the Superintendent unlocks the back door overlooking the Tomb of the Unknown.

Little Miss looks into Anni's eyes glaringly, wondering how the procession is handled. A National Park Service officer, promptly briefs Little Miss, how she is to walk down the steps one foot at a time in a slow, but steady pace. This takes place after the three guards complete their ceremonial duties.

Anni immediately asks Zweber, "Where is it appropriate for me to situate myself in order to take photos of her?"

Zweber confirms with the Superintendent and the Park Service official said, "You can stand right upfront where the other media and journalists are positioned." The staff photographer graciously leads her through the cordoned off areas for the public and allows her beyond, which makes her parallel with the Tomb of the Unknowns.

Chills run down my spine realizing the kind of unprecedented access I just attained.

The commander signals the start of the ritual, as a rifle is unlocked by the relieving commander. During the process, each of these men dons Ray-Ban, mirrored, aviator-styled sunglasses.

The inability to see their eyes makes this ritual seem very perfunctory.

There is a salute and a thorough inspection by a gloved, blue-uniformed soldier holding another rifle. The third is the sentinel. The three soldiers salute the three tombs, representing the Medal of Honor.

As Anni witnesses the ritual, she believes each step they take is astonishing. She wonders what Little Miss' perception of this is like.

With each of their steps, there is a tap sound on the hallowed grounds, as they give distinct orders and do a color-guard-style rifle exchange, touching and passing each instrument a multitude of times. They also emit a memorized passage of prestigious poetry. As the processional from the tomb site continues, the guards keep their rifles on the shoulder closest to the visitors to represent them standing between the tomb and any possible threat.

Little Miss is escorted by one of these impeccably uniformed soldiers to place the wreath on a standing wire frame. Anni captures Little Miss' part with some photos of the wreath placement. Following the brief, but powerful ritual, Little Miss departs prior to the crowd dissipating. As she does a Mother, asks if her handicapped son may have his photo taken with her. She agrees and Anni takes the picture for the child, who is elated to see Little Miss. He was here visiting the hallowed grounds to honor the memory of his Dad who was killed in the line of duty.

Following the photo, Little Miss is lead towards the sentinel's chambers, where the steadfast soldiers are in their quarters "hanging out." Little Miss is shocked to realize the two men approaching her to shake her hand were the two who she had just witnessed doing the intricate rifle exchanges. They were wearing t-shirts with their uniform pants, but they now look like real people. Anni enjoys their friendly, nonchalant demeanor, she thought they looked so rigid during their duty up outside. The soldiers open the locked gun cabinets and permit Little Miss to hold one of the real rifles they use in the procession. It is a lot heavier than she thought. She is amazed how they could maneuver these with such ease and have a reflecting saber at the end. It certainly is a treacherous task if they were not so well-trained.

Anni asks how they became a part of this elite brotherhood. They tell her, they are a volunteer force that has to meet and maintain a handful of requirements including: physical stature, weight, be part of the 3rd Infantry, possess a meticulous military record and go through an interview and trial process. Following that, they have to diligently study seven pages of poetry and history about Arlington Cemetery and be able to recite it verbatim. They are retested over a series of months before they are a full-fledged member of the Old Guard.

It is fascinating to get this perspective from the current guardsmen who are so passionate about their objective to honor the memory of fallen soldiers.

Following the visit to the sentinels' chambers, Superintendent Metzer guides Little Miss, Zweber and Anni around the grounds of this national landmark. As

Zweber shuttles them around, Anni asks Metzer, "Did you think you would be involved in this profession as a young boy?"

Metzer very humbly answers, "I had no intent to carry this on as my Father had. I saw myself growing-up to do other things, but I had the opportunity and later decided I should carry-on the legacy my Father was so proud of." Anni is so impressed from his candid response.

Anni notices as Little Miss struggles to walk around the sloping trails of the cemetery in her high heels. She offers Little Miss her arm, so she could support her on this monumental guided tour. Slowly, she walks at a comfortable pace for Little Miss to make it to the sites Metzer and Zweber were eager to identify for them.

He stops to show various sections of the hallowed grounds where some prestigious people are buried including: an actor who appeared in American western movies and a Hollywood Producer who his Father was good friends with. The names are unfamiliar to Little Miss and Anni. Zweber also remarks there are only two Presidents buried here. They look as the eternal flame burns in front of the Kennedy family plot. Distinctly, Robert Kennedy is buried by himself and has a white cross marking his grave.

There is such power in witnessing the abundance of headstones and they had a variety of symbolic designations.

Most identified the religion of the deceased, which were intuitive. There were a few icons Anni asks about that wre unusual. Metzer clarifies there are Wiccan, Jehova's Witness and other affiliations demarcated too.

She points out to Little Miss how extremely young many of these lifeless patriots are. They both feel a sense of grief and despair as Metzer leads them into the section dedicated to soldiers dying from the current war in Afghanistan and Iraq.

As they pass by the abundance of graves in view of the Pentagon, Anni questions Metzer, "What were your experiences like during September 11, 2001?"

She asks as Little Miss is in earshot, so she could get this firsthand testimony as well.

Metzer recalls being in his administrative office on a seemingly, industrious day, as most of his days are. He received a call from some facilities staff about a plane that just literally clipped the roof of the maintenance building. As he recounts the situation, Metzer points to the building that was 800 yards from where they were standing at that moment.

The flight pattern was leading right up to the Pentagon. Metzer said the tone of his day entirely changed as they had to go into a crisis management role. "It is a day I'll never forget."

Anni feels her breath taken away with the thought of standing in the same direction that chaos took place. Little Miss yawns, but learns a great lesson that day putting perspective on human tragedy.

— 32 —

Little Miss is still in the D.C. region for a few more days to continue the episodic journey, but now has to switch gears. Her events are now under the guise of her Goodwill Ambassadorship for the national children's charitable organization. The group has selected a child from each state to represent various parts of their demographic to assemble in Washington, D.C. with their parents to experience some greatness in the nation's capital en route to a bigger party at Walt Disney World in Orlando.

Anni makes sure she and Little Miss have all their effects as they went from one hotel they stayed the past few days to the designated hotel for these events. The children were arriving and Little Miss was in a different state of mind. She likes dealing with kids, yet she knows these children have a variety of physical challenges, so she has to be extra patient, kind and caring.

Anni escorts Little Miss to her room, where she was set-up in a large suite. Right away, Little Miss flicks her thumbs across her Blackberry to determine which one of her friends is in town for her to get a dose of normalcy when she could sneak in some downtime. As usual, she was successful.

Little Miss gently knocks on the door that separates her suite from Anni's adjoining room, to mention, that she has arranged to grab some food that evening with her friend who goes to college in town. "It is truly amazing how well-connected you are to so many people around the country and have the knack for visiting with them in most of the cities we've been," Anni commends Little Miss.

"We are a close knit community. Many of the people I know are from my town, school, and even more are people I met through the pageant process and they keep in touch. It doesn't hurt that I have this title, because they make themselves even more available when I am in their town nowadays," Little Miss replies.

"I can see how that makes a great story for them to tell their friends and coworkers how they just had lunch or dinner with Miss Patriotic," Anni responded smiling wide.

Anni reminds Little Miss that she needs to tell her where they are heading and what time, for her safety. (Serberus went so far as instructing Anni to walk Little Miss out of any hotel after meeting her guests in the lobby). Anni said, "You know the drill. We're just trying to do the right thing."

Reluctantly, Little Miss nodded. In meantime, they had a couple hours to relax until Little Miss had to greet the kids to kickoff the welcome event at ESPN Zone a few blocks away.

Anni went back to her work on her laptop. She is diligent about writing-up event and appearance reports and submitting them to Serberus following each segment of the tour. She has to summarize the client and sponsors role in the events, the venue, the results and the impact for the groups involved. Anni incorporates the timeliness of the program, the attentiveness and responsiveness to Little Miss, how she conducts herself and her overall presence: look, manner and professionalism for each event. Also, Anni makes recommendations if the organization should continue to work with each client, in what manner and identify other opportunities.

As Anni is completing her most recent reports pertaining to the long-standing USO relationship, she considers, does Serberus have Little Miss complete a similar report on her role in the process? It seems I may be on to something, because some of the points that Serberus mentions to me are things that she must have questioned Little Miss about.

There is a double-edged sword, as Anni was hired to manage Little Miss on tour, yet Anni believes she is being managed, not by Cheryl Pearson, her boss, but by Serberus pulling Little Miss' strings to get dirt through Little Miss. This circumstance is compounded by the influence Little Miss' Mother has on her too. The discussion she had with Anni back in the hospital about giving Little Miss some space when she was homesick, was reported back to Serberus and became another ding on Anni's proverbial record.

She finishes uploading photos for the Miss Patriotic Organization website and formatting her reports. Then she moves on to selecting an appropriate outfit to wear, which she had to press, in order to get that traveled, wrinkled look to disappear. As she was going through her errands, she hears a knock at her door. It's one of the coordinators from the event; dropping off their badges and materials for Little Miss. Anni asks her if she could obtain biographical information about all the children; including their names and where they are from. This will enable Little Miss to be even more personable when she meets them. Bridget, the coordinator thought Little Miss would have received their summaries from the Director, but in his frantic pace to get all the kids safely to the destination from their various home states, he hadn't gotten to providing it to Little Miss.

Anni hopes to get Little Miss that information when Bridget has a chance to access it. Five minutes later, Bridget is back at Anni's door with a few copies of the spiral-bound program highlighting each child's background. Anni complements Bridget on her expeditiousness.

She continues to get ready and freshens-up her hair and make-up. She knocks on the adjoining door to Little Miss' room to see if she was just about ready to depart and she is all set too. Little Miss was wearing a black form-fitting wrap dress and they were sure to take along her "hat box" since the kids would be thrilled to see her crown up close. In the hallway outside of their rooms, Anni notices a man, who is dressed rather stylishly with a nicely fitted button-down shirt, expensive looking dark indigo jeans and pointy cowboy boots. He is in the midst of wrangling up three young kids with his wife to head to the elevators too. His kids were playing tag with each other and trying to bet which one of the six elevators would arrive first.

Little Miss smiles as she sees the kids horsing around. She asked the man's wife, who also looked stylish herself, "How old are your kids?"

Suddenly her question opens a little bit of dialog regarding how the kids are a bit rambunctious just getting off the plane for this event they are town to support their Dad, Ritchie MacDonald, who is part of a program this evening. Anni and Little Miss, put two and two together to realize, Ritchie is another Goodwill Ambassador and is performing at the same series of events with Little Miss! It is a nice coincidence to meet him and his family prior to being at the first venue in formal business mode. Rather, they were able to chat and exchange pleasantries as his three kids swirled around like cats and dogs having a good 'ole time.

They all proceed to catch the van to whisk them to the ESPN Zone to rehearse for the welcome program for the special children. Prior to Little Miss' performance, Anni suggests she dash into a soundproof control room to get psyched for her performance. The kids and their families were still filing in. The Director of the organization stops in the booth, away from the growing crowds to take a reprieve and have a soda. When all of the sudden, he realizes they were behind schedule. His watch is set in a different time zone, so he pipes-up, "I thought we still had time to spare, but we are running a few minutes late." Then he accepts his own tardiness by indicating, "A few of the kids' flights were delayed, so twenty minutes isn't a deficit, maybe more of them will be able to see the show now."

As most of the children and their families arrive and settle in, Little Miss walks around to say hello. Many of the kids are too young to recognize who she is, or what her title represents, but when the show begins and she was formally introduced... the magic began...The girls especially gravitate to her crown, which Anni suggested they display on stage, as Little Miss generally doesn't wear it when she performs.

Afterwards, the kids were invited to meet Ritchie and Little Miss, get pictures taken and let the kids try on her crown. Some were reluctant to approach her, but she has such a child-like spirit that they ultimately are drawn towards her. She kneels to be eye to eye with them, whether they are small or in a wheelchair to make them feel special.

First, some little girls were "all about" trying the crown on and getting a "fairy-princess" photo taken, but then a handful of boys did too. One older boy, around fourteen, looked like Sanjaya from the show "American Idol." Anni asks if anyone every mentioned that to him and he shook his head no. Probably to divert attention away, but when Anni tells the emcee about the amazing likeness, he makes an announcement on the microphone that Sanjaya is also a special guest and the kids got even more excited!

Little Miss is escorted around to play video and arcade games with the kids for an hour or so, before calling it an evening. The kids really enjoy themselves, as this is a unique experience for them to frolic in an arcade like "normal" kids since this group all have physical obstacles they contend with. They embrace being among their peers, those who encounter similar impairments in each of their young lives. Little Miss is proud to be a part of the program and Anni finds reward merely observing all the interactions.

Finally, they arrive back at the hotel and Little Miss could let her hair down to spend time with her friend for a quiet dinner. She introduces Katie to Anni and she walks them out. Anni asks where they are going to eat, per Serberus' mandate. They were not sure where they were headed for dinner, so Anni compromises, "Please call me on cell when you settle on a place."

Qucikly, they went off and Anni decides that she wants to grab a bite to eat. She looks at the choices listed in the hotel and most did not appeal to her current appetite. So with her work cell phone in hand, she takes a quick stroll to see if there was something quick and easy nearby. A few of the places are fast food, which is not the fare Anni enjoys. Another place Anni steps into, is filled with cigar smoke, Anni being a non-smoker realizes that is not an option either.

Finally, she sets her sight on a café version of a steakhouse that she had eaten at before in other destinations. Anni enters and the hostess said there is a wait for a table, so she opts for some food in the bar area. This section is busy too and the bartender acts as if he couldn't be bothered. While waiting for some service, the man seated next to Anni starts to chat with her about her line of work.

"Funny you should ask, because it is something kind of unique," she responds. Anni tells him she currently is on tour managing Miss Patriotic.

He agrees that is unusual. He informs Anni he just transferred to the area, working for a major luxury hotel chain. He said he is always eating out at restaurants and doesn't remember the last time he made himself a meal. As he makes that comment his food was served, which he had ordered after Anni placed her order.

She is a bit annoyed and famished at this point. She flags the bartender over, who forgot about Anni's order and then scrambles to get it placed. When it ultimately arrives, Anni is disappointed. She had asked for a Portobello mushroom sandwich without the bread. Instead, she receives mounds of crusty bread: three layers, held together by toothpicks, but it looks like they neglected to place any mushrooms on the sandwich. Essentially, it is bread and pesto sauce sandwhich and a ton of fries. Anni is trying to reduce her carb intake, so to her this platter is a waste. She tells the bartender how dismayed she is, so he chirps back, "What do you want me to do about it?"

She responds, "The right thing!" He made things better by taking the uneaten platter off her bill and she heads back to the hotel. About forty minutes later, Little Miss knocks on their adjoining door to let Anni know she was back. Anni had not received "the call" regarding their dinner location, so she asked, "Where did you two end up?"

It turns out they were in the same steak restaurant café Anni had her poor dining experience! Fortunately, Little Miss enjoyed her steak and potato meal. They mutually comment, "What a coincidence, out of all the places around, we all ended up at the same one."

Of course that information later wound up in Serberus' arena. Little Miss must have conferred with her.

Serberus comments to Anni, "You did not handle the situation correctly, because Little Miss feels like you were checking-up on her!" In actuality, she asked her to call, based on Serberus' instruction, to know where she was in the event of an emergency, since they are in a different city and Anni is there to ensure her well-being.

The following day, Little Miss gets ready for the day's events, again wearing her powder blue, St. John's knit knee length skirt suit. They were headed on a city tour with the kids, then on to the White House to meet with President George W. Bush. The kids and their parents were herded onto color-coded buses to take the city tour of downtown D.C. The children, some with their leg braces, wheelchairs and special accessories were all in tow and ready for the ride to see the Washington Monument and the Mall, the Smithsonian, the U.S. Capitol Building, and many other relevant landmarks.

Little Miss sat amongst the kids on the Green Bus. One of the kids started a trend by asking not only Little Miss for her autograph, but also signatures and notes from the other kids aboard their bus.

How profound that a young child instinctively wants to make everyone feel special by remembering each and everyone getting an autograph in their own program book.

The other kids on the Green Bus, found that "neat" and a great way to interact with the others on their bus, so there was a sudden flurry of program books with assorted doodles and notes in addition to Little Miss'. Anni comments to Little Miss, "We can learn a lot from children; sometimes they have a great idea without having any life experience behind them. It's so pristine." Little Miss was reveling in her interactions with the kids on the bus, with the exception of the screaming toddler up front, who could not be consoled by his parents.

Keep in mind it was a major achievement to have flown lots of these kids out of their normal, safe environments, complicated by their physical and emotional limitations.

Midway through the tour, the rainbow cavalcade of buses converge and let all their passengers off near the beautiful display of Cherry Blossom trees blooming beyond the Capitol building. Their objective here is to gather all the kids on this tour to get a commemorative photo taken. It took fifteen minutes or so to get the mass of kids, parents, handlers and special guests to come together at the same statue by the Capitol Reflecting Pool.

I am concerned they chose this spot to take the group photo, as is so close to a body of water. Of course there are a few rambunctious boys rallying to get as near to the water's edge as possible.

The photographer and assistants had no method to getting everyone's attention when they were all en masse. So, through a series of "pass the message along," they attempt to alert the adults to get all the kids on the steps beside the statue to gather as a close knit, homogenous cluster for the picture.

Well, it was like herding feral cats, the kids were moving in so many directions.

Anni motions to Little Miss, "Try to get in the center of the action and let the photographer work his magic." In her powder blue suit and severely, high-heeled pumps, Little Miss, cautiously walks in towards the center of the cluster of 50+ kids. She was at the lowest part of the stone stair case, and takes it upon herself to sit down on the ground with the children beside her. Anni is shocked, because she is wearing a light-colored knit suit, with a very short hemline on the skirt. She thought it probably would have been more manageable to sit or stand on a higher step, so as not to run the chance of ruining her skirt and exposing herself at such a dramatic angle.

The kids didn't seem to notice Little Miss amongst them. They are preoccupied by their parents' whereabouts; a small child upfront is busy flinging a yo-yo all around narrowly missing some of the other kids surrounding him. The photographer snaps a few shots, while the kids were in a variety of precarious poses and expressions.

Now this event is captured through the indelible photographic imprint.

Anni walks towards Little Miss, she tried to make eye contact with her during the photo session, but Little Miss was distracted, so Anni could not dissuade her from the position she struck at the bottom of the stairs. Anni extends her arms to Little Miss to help her up and tells her to adjust her skirt. When she does, Anni sees there is some dirt on the light knit skirt from sitting on the stone step. Anni walks behind her, so the others would not see the dark smudge, while she insists Little Miss try to brush it off. After a bit of maneuvering the soiled spot was less obvious. That is critical, since the next stop on the itinerary was a private meeting with President Bush and a photo op with the kids in the White House. There was no time allotted to go back to the hotel and change outfit her outfit.

Back on the Green Bus, the remainder of kids finished their autograph session. This diversion comes in handy, as the secret service stops all the buses and were doing security checks of each.

They held long, wanded mirrors below the undercarriage of each bus; they examine exhaust pipes, board each bus and do a scan. This process happens while the kids were unaware of what was happening. Anni is glad the intensive security checks did not rattle any of the children. They were all here to have a week's worth of fun!

Finally, the bus driver was radioed the "All clear," and is able to advance closer to the White House. The buses let all the passengers off outside of the wrought iron fence at 1600 Pennsylvania Avenue. Once again, there was a procession of kids, strollers, wheelchairs, parents, escorts and others to security at the Northeast Gate. At first security did not have Little Miss and Ritchie MacDonald on the list, as having approval to enter for a meeting with the President.

After a few calls, the clearance is verified. Serberus had been sure to have Little Miss' particulars on file with security and even checked them with Anni the proceeding week to get her easy access into the White House for this high-profile meeting. Anni wonders how she will be able to gain access. Serberus did not provide dispensation for Anni to be involved in the meeting room. She figures she would go along with the protocol and find out what kind of accessibility she would get.

At the guard's tower, Anni also gains entry to the private entrance! She proceeds with Little Miss through the screening and loads her large work bag onto the x-ray machine. The group walks on a winding walkway offset by lovely, blooming Southern Magnolias along the perimeter of the East Garden. They walk past the administrative offices of Mrs. Bush which do not have public access.

Anni strolls along the corridors and looks at the photos on display of various receptions and entertaining that took place within the White House compound. Across the walkway is an immediate view of the First Ladies Garden.

What a magical charm the view provides.

One of the security personnel asks Little Miss, "Have you ever been here before?" She tells him this is her first visit. "Well, in that case you may want to peer into a few of the rooms." They make their way through the winding corridor. There is a large vestibule that once had a gift shop stationed here, but after 9/11, changes were made, security was tightened, and they disbanded the shop to minimize people lingering on the premises.

I am squelching the thought of the demise of society when the White House gift shop is considered a potential terrorist threat.

The subsequent path leads them to the rooms often seen by people who tour the White House. Anni peers into the China Room and is in awe of its majesty. There is an air of decadence with the various pieces of dishware on display. Across the hall is the Library, which was formerly used as the Laundry during the 19th century. Anni takes a quick peek inside, but scrambles to ask the security escort where she and Little Miss may find the nearest Ladies' Room. They dash through the Vermeil Room and make their way to an impeccably decorated restroom. Anni checks out the details: Brass fixtures and wallpaper with an oriental willow tree design.

It is so ethereal and unusual. The fixtures and counters inside are granite-like and framed by gilded edges. Even the hinges and toilet paper holders have this motif. As a keepsake from this visit, Anni saves the durable towel from the Ladies Room emblazoned with the Presidential Seal.

Before she departs, Anni asks her, "Do you have some ideas about what you'll discuss with George W.?"

Little Miss shakes her head that she is not prepared, rather, "I was going to let the executives lead the conversation and respond."

"I'm sure you'll do fine," Anni highlighted encouragingly, while trying not to come across overbearing. "I'll be waiting for you in the East Room. If you want, you can give me your things, so you have your hands free in the meeting to shake hands. Good luck!"

Little Miss hands Anni her purse and camera, as she makes her way back to the tour, Little Miss admires the grand floral arrangements in the rooms. Then she was off in the other direction she heading upstairs where she and some executives, on behalf of the children's organization, privately meet with President Bush. Anni strolls through the crossway, while Little Miss is maneuvered towards the State Dining Room.

Anni is unsure the best spot for her to wait, while Little Miss is attending the meeting. She sees a wave of children amass in the East Room. One of the security guards tells Anni there typically is not much furniture in this room as they hold many gatherings and press conferences here. She notices a series of bleachers situated in front of the mantle. Perhaps this is to assemble the children in an orderly fashion when President Bush enters the room to greet them. It turns into pandemonium, as the kids and parents wait for the President to complete his discussion with Board Members of the charity and its' Goodwill Ambassadors: Ritchie and Little Miss. Meanwhile, kids are blitzing in every direction

Anni wonders how the Secret Service will handle the roaming children with special needs, as the President approaches. In this room, Anni sees there are a couple of settees in the window boxes of the corners of this massive space. Anni saunters with the purses and cameras to the corner window overlooking the Garden and a clear view of the Washington Monument.

It's like I can reach out and touch the monument from this spectacular vantage point. What other historic figures glared out of this same window over centuries past?

There are velvet ropes on both sides of the East Room to delineate where the group should be to provide the President ample space to make his entrance, but since this crowd consists mainly of children, it is as if the golden ropes are imaginary as they blend in to the décor of the room and are not meant to set physical boundaries. The guards adjust the ropes to signal the group should get set and in position.

It seemed like an eternity waiting for this brief meeting to end.

Then the security detail removes the bleachers and places just a few golden-lattice backed chairs in a row. A handful of kids ran towards them, like an unannounced game of "Musical Chairs." Some of them were running in circles, others were trying to claim their territory, because there were about eight chairs and more than fifty kids. The commotion was in a roar and Anni considers, will the security and secret service hush the kids as best as possible when the President makes his entrance?

Meanwhile the parents, siblings and attendees, who try to stake their claim up close to the golden rope, started shifting around when the guards realigned the ropes. This caused Anni's clear view from the corner settee to become obstructed. She wants to identify another place to get a close view of the President as Little Miss welcomes the kids with him, to get a great picture of them on her camera. As the seemingly endless shuffling continues, all the sudden, President George W. Bush appears in the East Room, smiling and waving at the crowd.

I can't believe some Executive Staffer doesn't approve the President's entrance—he just walked right in. He went along the golden rope on the opposite side of the room and started a receiving line of handshakes, pats on the kids' heads and various welcomes. Many of the little ones did not know what was happening, so they still were playing musical chairs and running in and out of the Golden ropes to find their families.

One small 3-year-old, Black child named Brandon, with severe vision and hearing loss (as evident by the large hearing aid banded across his head), who was being held by his Father, jumped into the strolling President's arms. He may not have been able to distinctly hear the President's "hello," but he held on so tightly, he could feel the warmth of the President's body and feel his breath upon his face. President Bush is surprised how the child leapt from his Father's arms towards him, but he smiles and goes along with it by giving Brandon a friendly hug. The pose created is subject to a nice picture taken by the White House photographer and a series of clicks went around the room by parents and members of the children's charity.

Anni hopes President Bush would make his way to the opposite side where she and now the majority of the group were anxiously waiting, excluding the rembunctious children in the center of the room. President Bush walks slowly across the room and stops in front of the mantel where the kids are assembled.

A young blond spiky-haired boy, with wire-rimmed glasses and sparkly blue eyes sitting on a chair named Brady, dashes towards the President. George W. was in the midst of chatting with a cluster of kids when Brady, latches onto the President's left pant leg and begins tugging…lighly, then more aggressively to get the President's attention.

This is like witnessing a scene from "Little Rascals," as this scenario plays out.

Little Miss had not entered the room yet, she probably is finishing a photo opportunity in the State Dining Room with the executives. Anni looks toward the central doors and sees Little Miss and the men arrive, so now they could also witness the excitement of the children meeting the President.

Meanwhile Brady, got George W.'s attention and says, "Mr. President, I have a joke for you," very assumptively, as he stumbles on his words; still learning to pronunciate.

President Bush replies, "You said you have a joke for me? OK, let's hear it."

Suddenly, Brady is in performance mode. He scans the audience and folds his arms. "Why…" he began, and then starts over. "Why," he repeated with some hesitation. Brady runs diagonally across the expanse to find his parents. When he encounters his Mother, she appears in front of the Golden rope and cuffs her hand over her son's ear to assist with the big riddle. Brady gave her the "thumbs up" and runs back over to the center of the room, where he left his new buddy the Commander-in-Chief waiting anxiously for the riddle. On cue, he was hoping to execute the joke just right.

Take three, Brady says, "Why was the broom late for work?" The President repeated loudly so everyone could he what young Brady was attempting to say in a marbled tone, "Son, you asked, why was the——what?"

Mom exclaimed from the anterior of the great hall, "He said BROOM."

The President repeated, "Why was the broom late for work?" he said with outstretched arms in each direction.

"Yes," Mom agreed.

"Because he overswept!" Brady smiled with his toothy grin and extended his hands in the air. The President was completely entertained and shuffled into the center of the large room, like a vaudillian comedian and performed the joke himself.

He assumed a character, so unexpectedly. How unique seeing the President so laid back.

With arms opened wide to each side and pumping in and out, the President said in an overjoyed, animated way, "Why was the broom late for work?" President Bush's tone of voice was cartoonish as he repeated the performance on behalf of his new little comedic buddy, Brady.

President Bush gave a rallying motion with both arms and took a leap from the floor, as he exclaimed, "He overswept!"

It was an astounding moment to see the President so animated and full of life based on the energy the kids brought in the White House. Following his hugs and hellos with the children and Brady remaining at his side, President Bush continues to the front half of the East Room, where the other satin golden rope is delineated. Anni feels the hair stand up on her arm, as the crowd squirms to make their way towards the President.

Anni's mind is racing. She wants to have the opportunity, not just to shake hands if she had her druthers, but she hopes to make an impression on the President that is non-partisan, yet meaningful. Ten seconds later an idea flashes into her head, ask the President about his twin daughters.

Anni recalls reading how the twins, Barbara and Jenna, took a trip to Argentina where one got her pocketbook taken at a Buenos Aires café. This image stood out to Anni, since she had taken a trip to the same city in November, a month before starting her journey on behalf of Miss Patriotic. Also, Anni realizes that Jenna Bush had been doing work helping children in other continents through her affiliation with UNICEF.

So, along comes President Bush following the path of the golden rope, shaking hands and greeting the guests, when Anni, who is three people deep in the crowd, exclaims, "President Bush, how are your daughters doing these days with all their travels?"

At first, there is no reaction. Perhaps, the President did not hear Anni. He continued past her by two feet, then he looks up, with a delayed reaction, turns around and makes eye contact with Anni, then he doubles-back to respond to her meaningful inquiry.

George W. responds, "Thank you so much for asking about my girls! I am so proud of them and can't believe they have grown into such accomplished young women who continue to make me so proud. Can you tell that I am such a proud Father?" His eyes sparkled and there is a glow in his expression. The President converses one-on-one with Anni as if there was no one else in the East Room that day.

Anni continues, "I understand they have done some traveling to South America. I was interested to hear about it, because I was in Buenos Aires and made sure to be aware of my surroundings after learning about your daughter's purse snatching."

The President was glad that their experiences have made impacts on others and enabled her to avoid being in a similar predicament. As Anni speaks with the President, she can not believe, she is seeing his five o'clock shadow. His stubbly grey whiskers make him seem like a real person, not merely the iconic Commander-in-Chief seen on C-SPAN or the Nightly News.

A firm handshake signifies the conclusion of their banter as Anni closes the conversation with, "I hope you continue to find joy and inspiration from your twin daughters. It was nice to have met you."

"Thanks again for asking about them, it means more than you know!"

Anni looks deeply at the President who looked preoccupied by current concerns. Perhaps, over the perception of the war in the Middle East, the impetus to investigate the tactics of his fellow Texan and friend, Attorney General Alberto Gonzales and all the other facets of his administration.

Anni is thrilled to have seen things from this vantage point, both in looking at the view from the East Room and observing the President's interaction here as well.

Following the casual exchange with the President, Anni scans the center of the room for Little Miss. She is finished with the group photos and looks towards Anni, as if she was more than ready to wind down for the day.

She hands her her purse and digital camera and tells her, "I took a few photos for your memory of today!" As they make their way from the East Room to leave the White House premises, Anni asks Little Miss, "How was your meeting with the executives and the President?"

"OK."

"Well, what was the topic of discussion?" Anni curiously asked.

"The President asked about my year as Miss Patriotic, where I've been and the events. I told him about my hometown and that working with the kids has been the highlight of my year so far," she responded.

From there, they both go back to their respective hotel rooms and retire for the evening—Anni to update and submit her reports and photos, including an incredible group shot with the kids and another with Little Miss surrounding the

President and a severe close-up of George W. Bush as a precursor to their conversation.

Little Miss plans to see what movies she has access to and catches-up by phone and text of her daily dish with friends and family.

— 33 —

Early April, Anni goes to headquarters to follow-up with her boss and Serberus. The currents continue to change, now Serberus becomes less prone to sending Anni information in terms of how to plan for her month on the road. Also, the rules of engagement flip. Anni gets reprimanded for the speed in which expense reports are submitted and notices a slew of contradictions as expenses that were reimbursed a suddenly not being covered, as they were initially. Anni spent many long hours into the early morning to reconcile and transmit her follow-up reports for Serberus.

Anni's dry cleaning bills become a bone of contention with Serberus— even though Anni tries to be extremely contientious how much and how often she got her clothes laundered. She also takes her clothes in for dry cleaning when she noticed certain promotional specials to save the company some bucks.

Also, when Sonny hands off the cellphone and phone jack to Anni between months, she notices Sonny receives a cash advance envelope with much more funding than she does. Anni notes that Sonny is given double the cash advances for her months of the tour. So, I am under the parameter of doing more with fewer resources.

In addition, Serberus comments, "The organization had not determined whether Miss Patriotic needs to pay for all the movies she orders from Pay-per-view." This was unprecented that any Miss Patriotic sat in their hotel room and ordered nearly as many movies as she did. Serberus never provides Anni any definite answer, whether she needs to guide Little Miss with paying for those charges directly or submitting them through an expense report, so Anni was not itemizing them on her own expenses.

* * * * * * *

In addition, to Anni's great surprise, she finds out during the month of April, the Miss Patriotic Organization had opted to move forward with the televised sting operation! This was the outcome of the meeting Anni attended back in March, with the Producers of "The Nation's Most Wanted" along with her CEO, the Communication Director and Little Miss. She had since been reprimanded by Serberus about her "unnecessary input" at that meeting.

Anni was off- tour while the multi-day sting mission took place, but had been instrumental in making a sound presentation to the producers when they were conceiving the strategy a month ago and helped to enhance the sense of urgency to get the project underway.

Anni recalls there had been awkward ten minute silence among the CEO and Communication Director, who came across tongue-tied and ill prepared, when the Senior Producer had sternly asked the team, "So what is your purpose for being here??"

Nevertheless, the project manifested after some serious persuasion to convince Little Miss and her parents to feel comfortable with her safety on this mission. They needed to believe that her safety would not be jeopardized. During that stint in April, Sonny was on tour duty and took Little Miss to Long Island.

The tactical operation was carried out by the Suffolk County Police. Little Miss' role was to pose as a 14-year-old teenager who chats online and then by phone with some zealous respondents. During her efforts she was backed by the Long Island Police Department to catch internet predators in their lawless acts.

Since she did not see the episode as it aired, Anni checks out the video on the internet. On it, she views Little Miss posing as a 14-year-old in chat rooms, naively talking with the participants; men of varying demographics. Some of them didn't believe she is a real girl, so they requested to talk with her on the phone. She does, but the calls are wired by the police. The last and most risky step is getting the men to visit her at a police monitored house, where eleven men are arrested.

In the sting house, during the meetings, Anni notices, Little Miss is wearing a cotton-jersey, v-necked "PINK" brand shirt by Victoria's Secret, with a white cami underneath, jeans, tennis shoes and a matching pink baseball hat, with very minimal make-up and her hair in a loose ponytail. Little Miss does have a youthful quality about her, not necessarily enough to be 14, but kids do mature faster these days.

Little Miss sounded and looked weary, tired and a bit spooked in her video diary of the sting operation. Her voice was reluctant as if she is unsure she was out of harm's way. Yet, she tries to convince the viewers that this is part of her work as advocate for internet safety and if she can protect at least one young kid, it's all worthwhile.

Anni did not watch the original television episode of the sting to catch these criminals, but notices a lot of flap in the media. No sooner does the show air, there is commentary: "A beauty queen with no right to do police work." The Suffolk County Attorney General Tom Spota reports that Little Miss acted as "bait" in the sting operation but that she does not intend to complete the process by testifying against those arrested. The media brouhaha broiled to an intense level. As the story hit the Associated Press newswire, it reverberated through the internet, TV, newspaper and the gossip trails.

As things proceed from bad to worse, the Miss Patriotic Organization had "no comment" regarding the allegation of Little Miss' intent not to testify.

Anni is shocked to hear the reports. Little Miss has gotten in over her head and the organization is not backing her up! She needs a professional to provide damage control and crisis management.

Anni e-mails Little Miss to see how she is making out with the media frenzy. It is starting to wear on her, because she feels isolated, since the organization did not step in and take control. For days, they did not release or post a statement. "I never told anyone I would not testify. The DA's office made that up to get some publicity, since they were not a part of the sting directly, but they would be involved when the pedophile cases are heard in court."

Sonny affirms in a phone call, "Little Miss is not herself. This has put a strain on her. She's doing her best." Sonny neglects to say anything about the organization not responding. She's a veteran with the company, so she'd never question their actions or in this case inaction...

* * * * * * *

Also during April, while Anni was off the road, other contradictions come to light. Little Miss mentions to Anni that she and Sonny had stopped by Sonny's house. She mentions, "Sonny's development is nice where she lives and the extension she had built in her home is gorgeous. You should see the wall of fame of all the Miss Patriotics she traveled with over the past 18 years!"

Little Miss got her laundry done by Sonny, while she also took care of other personal errands.

Funny how I was commanded by Serberus, that I could not stop home while on tour, even if we were stationed locally. During our local downtime I could have arranged not to drive to avoid liability by getting some public transportation or getting someone to pick-me up for a few hours. I was refused, but Sonny was chauffer-driven to her house with Little Miss!

Also, why was my clothing selections second-guessed, when Sonny regularly traveled and went around in jeans and Keds sneakers?

Being the newest certainly puts me under a higher level of scrutiny…

— 34 —

May begins and the next leg of Anni's tour with Little Miss is set to kick-off. Anni starts the day drinking a cup of coffee and languishing over the newspaper as she patiently waits at her home for the limo driver to arrive for the 11:30am scheduled pick-up. Suddenly at 10:45am, there is a knock on the door. She opens the door to an overcast morning and sees the driver standing there. He is forty-five minutes early!

She knows her flight is not scheduled to depart until a few minutes before 2pm, so she makes a decision not to rush, to take her time getting all settled with her paperwork and finish her coffee. Anni tells the driver, "I will need a few more minutes and will be out and ready to go then."

He replies, "That's no problem, I'll just wait in your driveway." It appears to Anni that the driver really was unsure of the scheduled pick-up time and he clearly is not familiar with where he is in proximity to the airport.

Anni compromises and comes out with her luggage all prepared at 11am (so he is not waiting for a full forty-five minutes.) As she makes her way outside, she feels drizzle lightly fall on her face. She notices the driver has the hood of his sedan up and the engine is no longer running. He appears to be chatting with one of her neighbors about something. Anni questions, "Is everything OK?"

The driver responds, "For the some reason the engine will not turn over now." He continues to crank the starter and no ignition was evident. Anni asks, "Did you notify your Dispatcher or your office?"

"No, I did not get a chance, but I will," he indicates. He was wearing a suit and looked like a retired white-collar professional, who probably never changed a tire before not a mechanic. Quizzically, he looks at the engine of the sedan and did not know where the problem was stemming from.

Anni said, "Perhaps it's the alternator. What did it sound like when you tried to turn the engine over?" He said he heard only a clicking noise. She went on to say, "You really need to notify your company, because we are on a schedule and

I have to be at the airport for a flight." She asks, "Have you been in this situation before?"

He unaudibly responds. Anni already knew the car service company he is from is situated at the Jersey shore. Her home is nearly an hour away. She suggests, "Why not call in for your company to send another car that they can dispatch which is already inland or have them get a subcontractor take me to the airport."

The driver said they don't operate like that.

Anni indicates, "Some solution has to be found quickly. Time is of the essence now."

He responds, "This looks like a nice neighborhood, why don't you knock on your neighbors' doors and get assistance..."

Anni is shocked that is his recommendation. She is his client. His service was retained to pick her up on time and deliver her safely to her destination. Why now is he expecting me to get my neighbors to intervene?

Anni said first, she will look in her garage to see if there are some jumper cables handy. She figures the hired car would not be able to get a jump from her personal vehicle, as it is further up near her house facing the opposite direction.

In her nice business clothes, she trudges through her dusty garage and locates the jumper cables. She then tries to ascertain who she might find straight away to provide the connection to get the sedan started.

Anni takes a moment to dial-up Serberus to apprise her of the debacle. Serberus barks back, "It is the limo company's problem, let them figure it out...All I know is you better not miss that flight!"

This is not the response Anni was expecting or hoping for. Serberus did not offer to make some calls and determine how the limo company was prepared to overcome the challenge. She told Serberus that the driver had the bright idea she get her neighbors to help or give her a lift. Serberus wrapped-up the call by stating, "Call me when you're on the road."

Anni attempts to finish the conversation on a positive note. She says to Serberus, "Things have got to get better. We'll get through this."

Serberus shot back, "No, they don't," and she abruptly hangs up the phone! The phone went dead.

Anni's heart was pounding harder as she knows she has to solve the dilemma herself. I am relieved that I have proven myself as a problem solver, but now feel stifled by the lack of support from my company in this scenario. I am on my own to make this situation work.

Many of Anni's neighbors are at work; her immediate next door neighbors are physically impaired so they are not an option to provide help. One had a stroke, the other a heart condition. Her other possibility is Susan, the woman diagonally across the street.

She doesn't know her extremely well, but figures, she is running out of choices. Anni scrambles across the street and Susan pops out of her house in her sweat pants and disheveled hair. Susan is in the middle of scrubbing her floors as a diversion from all her professional work waiting for attention in her home office.

Anni apologizes for disturbing her, especially as the rain begins to fall harder, but appreciates her willingness to jump in, provide a helping hand and help jump the car.

Susan backs her champagne-colored Honda out from her driveway and does a K-turn lining her battery, as close as possible, with the hired sedan. She cannot align her vehicle in a straight line, but has to angle it in, since other neighbors' cars are parked behind the dead sedan.

With one brief flick of the ignition, the sedan's engine turns over and sounds effective. Anni thinks they should let the cars keep running for two minutes, so the sedan can garner more charge from the Honda's battery. The driver quips, "No, I think it's good enough."

All the sudden, he's a car expert?

Anni offers Susan a sincere "Thank you," and says I will have to speak to my company and limousine service about this to recognize your efforts. She says, "I don't need anything, your thanks is enough." Susan smiles and tells Anni to have a good trip.

Susan does not even know where Anni is headed or what she does professionally. She said, "We'll have to catch-up one of these days." Anni agrees.

The driver closes the hood to the sedan. Anni gets in the backseat of the vehicle, while Susan gets in her Honda to back away from the nose-end of the Sedan and head back to her driveway. As she puts her car in reverse, suddenly she bumps the neighbor's blue car parked behind hers and creates a basketball-sized dent in the driver's side door! She immediately puts her car in park, as does Anni's driver. Anni exclaims, "Wait here, I need to help her now, as she was our Good Samaritan!"

Susan is in tears. She can't believe this just happened. She thinks it was destined to happen, since fluky things happen in clusters.

The driver yells and points across, "Why don't you knock on their door."

"Him and his comments," Anni mutters. They both knew that neighbor was at work. The same neighbor who was dealing with a recent cancer diagnosis. Anni takes photos of the damage and the license plate with her camera phone. Susan said she'd leave a note on the door of their house. Anni gets Susan's phone number and tells her to try not to worry; she should not be held liable, since it occurred as a result of her good deed.

Anni assures her she would put calls out to her company's headquarters to work out something with the limousine company. "Someone needs to take responsibility, as the sedan should have been in good working order, otherwise we would not have been in this situation!"

Anni and Susan, both now very wet from the rain, part ways and Anni tells the driver to get going. She felt awful about the series of events that just took place.

She hopes this grey cloud is not indicative of the month ahead.

The driver approaches an intersection and was reluctant to put his signal on. Anni asks, "Do you know how to get to the airport from here?"

He is not sure. Anni has to navigate from the back seat of the hired car. As they were progressing on a straight run, Anni dials Serberus to update her on the additional mishap. She relays how her neighbor helped out as a Good Samaritan and then backed-up into the other neighbor's parked car.

Serberus immediately jumped down Anni's throat. "You better not have promised her anything! We are not paying her a dime and the limousine company does not have to either."

Anni responds to Serberus that she did not make any promises or guarantees with her neighbor, but she indicated, there needs to be accountability on behalf of this car service. "We are their client and they did not handle this pick-up appropriately. This is now compounded by the driver instigating that I should involve neighbors to assist. When one did, a ripple effect happened when she backed into the other car."

Serberus reiterates, "That car accident is not the organization's problem and the car service does not have to do anything about it." Anni retorted, "I will call the limousine-service owner there and review the details, because some action needs to be taken to right this."

Serberus' voice rises even louder, "You will not call the limousine company! I am the contact person. You will get me your neighbor's name, address, phone number and the details of the accident and I will put it in a memo to them. We have a relationship riding on this that I am not prepared to have ruined!"

Anni replies, "At this point they should offer a credit to our company account for the poor service in addition to making things right with my neighbor."

Anni can not believe Serberus was ultimately focused on her business relationship with this limousine service that has consistently proven to be lacksidasical: late for pick-ups, unsure of directions, multiple cars that were not in good working order.

In any case, she is now at the Philadelphia International Airport on her way to meet-up with Little Miss in Baton Rouge, LA.

— 35 —

Anni arrives in Baton Rouge on time and connects with Little Miss who just flew in from Las Vegas. Little Miss arrives wearing her pink and white striped Victoria Secret sweater and jeans, the identical outfit she wore on the TV sting episode! Wouldn't she try to put that event behind her, by not wearing the clothes that could bring unwelcome attention to her?

Little Miss is talking non-stop about the lack of support from the organization on her cell and doesn't stop to take a breath, while catching-up with her legal liaison, Mignon. A few minutes later she and Anni hug once again and head to their respective hotel, this one: a Holiday Inn.

"How are you holding up? Anni asks Little Miss.

"It's been difficult, not what I expected from the office."

While in town, Little Miss' schedule is intense. She needs to be dressed and ready for the Governor's Prayer Breakfast which begins at 7am. There, Little Miss is part of the esteemed guests sitting at the dais with Governor Kathleen Blanco and Mayor Kip Holden with other dignitaries. Following the ceremony, Little Miss gets interviewed with the Governor for various local news outlets.

Anni hustles across the immense banquet room to capture photos of Little Miss' participation in this 800-person event. She also has to keep Little Miss in tune with the itinerary, by transitioning her out of that venue discreetly to do a live radio show from the limo, en route to the Louisiana Capitol building.

By 10am, they are at the Capitol Building in Baton Rouge. This legendary façade was built in 1932, during the Depression era under the Governance of the often showy Governor Huey Long. The Art Deco building claims to be the tallest Capitol building in the U.S. and constructed with a 5 million dollar tab.

Little Miss is greeted by numerous Senators, their assistants, spouses and children prior to her being presented in the Senate Chamber. Here Little Miss makes a statement regarding her Internet safety platform. Coincidentally, the Senators are elated her message is concurrent with legislation they are in the midst of formulating about tracking predators.

It also happens to be "Bring Your Children to Work" day, so among the Senators, there are clusters of kids both on the Senate floor and high in the balconies, seemingly on assorted field trips to see how government works. They all got the unexpected treat of seeing Miss Patriotic during their visit.

While still at the Capitol, Little Miss is whisked to the House of Representatives for a Presentation among the Congressmen. It is a similar drill, with a different batch of politicians. Little Miss receives Proclamations for her efforts to condemn predators preying on children through the internet.

Upon reviewing the schedule, Anni notes there is a lunch and then a teen summit in between the two Capitol building presentations. In confirming the locations with the host, she confirms it is more convenient the two events are merged, so they did not have to go back and forth to the same location in a single day. Sometimes an effective business decision helps to expedite Little Miss' hectic day.

After the Capitol, hundreds of student teen leaders are assembled for a forum, where Little Miss addresses them on how to be safer when surfing the internet. The students admire her ability to share her own experiences when she was thirteen and was approached by a stranger online. Her and her girlfriends told their parents, so the trouble did not escalate beyond a grown man socializing with young girls in a chat room. It certainly could have gotten scarier if they made other decisions.

Anni finds a seat in the back of this banquet facility with a table of corporate sponsors from a signifigant cable company. The executives are very hospitable. They offer Anni a boxed lunch. She also puts one aside for Little Miss after she completes her presentation.

Anni responds, "Thank you so much for your generosity. It really is not necessary to wait on us. We'll grab some food, when she's all finished. You've really gone out of your way already with the lovely flowers in our rooms and the gourmet snack basket for Little Miss."

"It's our pleasure! She is really quite engaging for this audience. The kids can relate to her."

"You're absolutely right, she has a way with kids and has a whimsical quality about her," Anni adds.

After Little Miss is finished, Anni takes a few pictures of her interacting with the kids who wanted to meet her and thank her for her talk.

Anni whispers, "Are you hungry or thirsty, because I have a boxed lunch for you?"

"I'm mostly thirsty, right now. Also, do you have a Sharpie, so I can sign autographs?" Little Miss comments.

"Yes, here you go It is a commemorative Miss Patriotic pen. You did a nice job today. The cable company sponsor likes how you interacted with the students."

They exchange smiles.

Following the lunch and summit, Little Miss is slated for a few more interviews. These are more in-depth with correspondents who write features on her work as it relates to current Louisiana legislation.

An Assistant District Attorney and an Internet Crimes Task Force Agent arrive to hear Little Miss maneuver through the press junket. This Task Force Agent feels obliged to tell Anni, "I do not agree with her prior participation in the Long Island sting, where she went undercover as a young teen girl in a chat room as bait for potential predators soliciting kids after inappropriate chatting." He went on to explain, since she is not law enforcement, she is not appropriately trained to handle the delicate nature of those cyber communications.

Anni mentioned, she did have some training by various ICAC (Internet Crimes Against Children) Sheriff Departments from a few states.

He still held firm to his opinion, that she should not have been involved in that environment. "Not everyone considers her work heroic!"

This was something Little Miss and her parents struggled with prior to her participation—the safety of being in an environment crossing paths with criminals. As it turns out she did not just text in chat rooms, which she originally thought would be her "part," but she spoke on the phone to set-up phony "dates" with two dozen men of many ages and demographics. Then she tried to dress in a more juvenile way to answer the door of the designated address to have the invited guests drop-by into the police infested house and meet their demise.

Anni had interesting banter with this agent and considered it's best to keep his opinion between them. She did not want Little Miss to get barraged by this alternative viewpoint. Little Miss was already struggling to deflect the bad press she received as a result of taking part in the Long Island sting in April.

Anni has the complicated job of keeping Little Miss upbeat and stress-free from the post sting commotion.

Following these interviews, Little Miss has to regroup for her appearance at the Governor's Mansion. This event is by invitation only. The Publisher of The

Picayune Times newspaper is there and other important guests, some of which brought their daughters to meet Little Miss. She enjoys talking with the young ladies and Anni is sure to bring in the crown box, so the curious could inspect it and try it on! What a delight, even the Publisher got in a photo with Little Miss and the crown.

How captivating to be walking into the foyer of the Governor's Mansion! Anni notices a mural that wraps around the entire area. It is a landscape with Louisiana Bayou, beaches, farmland and varieties of state vegetation and wildlife. Anni inquires to Karmen Blanco, the Governor's eldest daughter, "What is the significance of this mural?"

She advises her it is representative of six gubernatorial administrations. There are symbols in each section that are meaningful to that particular Governor.

Anni find this art very thought provoking, as she was told about some of the symbolism including personal pets, their musical instruments, silhouettes of Governor's spouses and even an infamous mistress! As the Governor's reception wraps-up and Little Miss was already in overdrive working twelve hours, Anni notices she gives her "the look."

Anni comments to Karmen, "Excuse me, I think Miss Patriotic is ready to go. We had a wonderful time. The reception was lovely!"

Anni makes her way to the State Drawing Room where Little Miss is still conversing with the dwindling crowd. She said her goodbyes and left for the limo back to the hotel.

Anni figures by now Little Miss must be famished. This was a 12-hour workday and when Little Miss is working at events, she rarely eats. She does not like to eat in front of the public, because it will smudge her impeccable make-up or she may get food caught in her teeth, as well as feeling rushed, so back at the hotel Anni hands her various Room Service menus.

— 36 —

The following day, they were departing Baton Rouge around 10am for the airport on their way to Dallas where Little Miss is slated to do a fashion shoot for an upcoming alliance with a dairy cooperative.

That morning, Anni receives an abrupt call from Serberus indicating the organization is sending a bouquet of flowers to Miss Patriotic to be delivered to her during their next stop on the tour in Dallas. Anni asks, "What is the occasion?"

Serberus snaps, "Just because we decided to send her something."

Without further explanation, this must be a gesture on behalf of the organization in regret of not being more supportive during the media stir; when they neglected to place statements to deflect the rumor that she never intended to testify as the situation may dictate.

Anni changes the subject and tells her that Little Miss has been incurring overweight luggage charges for the past two flights. Serberus affirms, "Those are her responsibility. She has to follow airline regulations."

They were still in Baton Rouge and leaving in a few hours. Anni wants to be sure Little Miss is up and ready to depart, as she had informed her the night before, "I will have the bellman up to pick-up the luggage at 7:45am for an 8 am departure to the airport."

Promptly at 8am, the bellman knocks on her door. Little Miss answers in her PJ's and towel wrapped on her hair and responds she needs five more minutes.

So, Anni releases the bellman from waiting, so he may answer other calls and make tips in the meantime. Ten minutes turn into fifteen and the women have to shuffle their own luggage down to the lobby. It would have taken too long to wait for the bellman to return back up to their rooms.

As they were getting all their gear from the rooms, Little Miss' room phone rang but she did not stop to answer it, then Anni's suddenly rang. She was wondering who was trying to reach them. Anni dashes in to answer the phone, and it is the front desk indicating, "There is a delivery here for Miss Patriotic."

Anni acknowledges, "We are in the midst of checking-out and will receive it when we pass through the lobby," which they were in the process of, on their way to the airport.

This delivery is at a nonopportune time. How are we going to consolidate this new package with our luggage and transport it along? We are already scrambling to meet the driver.

As they approach the front desk, Anni is shocked to see a cardboard box for Little Miss the size of a medium-sized appliance like a microwave!

Suzanne, their limousine driver, was pacing in the lobby, because they are cutting it close to the departure time. When she sees them come off the elevator she assists in getting the bags loaded in the vehicle.

Suzanne looks very anxious, Anni thinks. It should not be the timing, because they still had ample time to be checked-in at the airport.

Suzanne asks Anni if in the process of transporting them the past few days, "Have either of you seen a red, beaded charm bracelet?"

"No, I have not," Anni replies, but asked why she inquired.

She believes it broke off and fell upon dropping them off at this hotel in the first place a few days ago.

After the exchange, Anni notices a pair of dark sunglasses in pieces on the asphalt. Suzanne looks down, releases a subtle sigh and said, "There is something else I broke."

Anni kids, "These are occupational hazards in this line of business." Suzanne nods in admission.

The process of loading and unloading the vehicles always took some doing, since each limousine is individually customized. The layout of trunk space and in the cabin differs, the seats and consoles always makes it a unique puzzle how to fit all their gear appropriately.

Today happened to be a humid Louisiana day and Suzanne, their driver, is wearing her knee-length black waistcoats. Anni asks her if she is alright, as she noticed her struggling to configure the bags in each part of the car. She says, "I am doing OK. I've been doing this for awhile," yet Anni could see the beads of perspiration welling on the sides of her face.

In the meantime, Anni mentions to Little Miss, "Let's open this package out here on the Doorman's stand to see what you received, determine who it is from and how we can get it transported."

Anni thinks this spot is good because there is room to maneuver. Little Miss doesn't want to open the box outside. Anni figures she does not want bystanders looking over her shoulder to inspect her delivery, so they squeeze the cumbersome box in the limo to get on their way.

In a tight compartment, Little Miss attempts to open the box. Anni gets on her work phone with the organization to see if they had an idea where the package was from. Maybe Ann Jo's delivery to Dallas has shown up at the wrong destination?

Anni asks Little Miss, "Were you expecting any deliveries?" She could not think of any. Immediately, she text-messaged her boyfriend at college to see if he sent her a "just because" gift.

Anni quickly calls Serberus for clarification. The tides immediately get very rough. Serberus goes ballistic over the phone call, when Anni attempts to determine if this package received from a national floral company was sent on behalf of the organization or not.

While on the phone Serberus reiterates, "The delivery is a surprise for Little Miss," so Anni is careful to respond in a way they would not ruin the surprise for Little Miss.

When Anni asks Serberus if the package from the company could have arrived early, she didn't want to confirm. Anni was trying to determine this, since there are no markings on the package.

Little Miss concludes, no card is attached, nor a packing slip.

As it turns out, the package is not flowers, even though the box is imprinted with 1800-BOUQUET on the outside. Upon unwrapping all the packing material inside, Little Miss finds the package is not an arrangement, rather it's a bath spa set.

Anni inquires, "Is there anyone you can think of who might have sent you a present?"

She asks Anni if she had an idea who it may be from.

Little Miss thought it could have been from her boyfriend and was waiting for the text reply. Her Blackberry buzzed, the verdict was in. The delivery was not from her boyfriend. He was now also curious...does she have an admirer?

Little Miss mentions to Anni, "I'll dial up headquarters to see if they had any idea." Anni was trying to be coy, in case this was indeed the floral delivery Serberus alluded to her earlier that may have been delivered too prematurely and mispacked with a spa set instead.

The Suzanne, their driver, lets them off upon arrival at the airport.

Curbside, at the Baton Rogue Airport, Little Miss and Anni attempt to repackage the basket and were trying to assemble it in order to get it shipped to the next destination: Dallas.

Little Miss cheerfully talks with Serberus. "Hello, Sweetie!" Serberus greets Little Miss (the volume on her cell is loud enough for Anni to hear.) "No, I have no idea who sent the delivery to you, Sweetie."

Anni makes a gesture, she'd like to follow-up with Serberus. Little Miss hands her the phone.

On the phone, Serberus gives Anni the third degree. "First, why was Miss Patriotic opening the package herself? You should have screened it for possible explosives or hazards! I told you flowers are being sent to Dallas. No need to question what I tell you! Where is that packing slip? I've received a ton of flowers and I know they always arrive with notes and packing slips. Look on the underside of the cardboard box, by the flaps and take out all the packing materials and search underneath!"

Anni responds, that both she and Little Miss searched, no card is attached, nor a packing slip, which the unpacking posed a challenge being in a tight, confined space of the moving vehicle.

There was no sense in responding to her claims, since Little Miss has had tons of items and baskets in her many hotel rooms and suites at the majority of destinations and Sonny had never opened the packages to "quality control" them before giving Little Miss the "thumbs-up" to enter her room with: "All clear." Nor did Anni want to second guess Little Miss, who told her there was no card or slip at all.

Next, Anni realizes in this scenario, their main priority is for them to catch the flight, as this package arrives inconveniently as they are heading out from Baton Rouge to Dallas. They are in overdrive: multi-tasking to determine was it is, where and whom it came from and the next issue what to do with it.

At the end of the call, Serberus took a severe, nasty tone with Anni and growls, "You think I'm a moron!!"

Anni tries to recover by responding, "Where did you come up with that statement, I have not called you any names?"

Serberus slams the phone receiver down on her end and disconnects the conversation. Anni pulls the phone away from her ear to see what the status of the cell phone was. She sees the: Call ended message and icon.

Little Miss looks over at Anni quizzically. Little Miss heard Serberus' voice rose and noticed that the conversation abruptly ended.

"We had ascertained, no packing slip was attached to the cardboard box,"
Anni mentions to her as if her tail hung between her legs. She feels verbally beaten up and it was obvious to Little Miss that Serberus inflicted proverbial punches on Anni.

Anni knows she has to instantly collect herself and appear unshaken to Little Miss. Anni wants to make a point of being poised and in-control of the tour as much as she can. So, she reaches the check-in counter with Little Miss to ship the box and the luggage.

At the airport, the skycap assembles their 5 pieces of luggage. Anni asks, "Do you have some sturdy tape we could close the box tighter for shipping." The skycap obliges by brings a roll of tape, but first, Anni looks at Little Miss in a final act of compliancy to disassemble the package again in its entirety, to see if Serberus had some merit that ALL floral deliveries include a card or packing slip. Once again they find no note. Nothing is inside; again the basket saw the light of day in Baton Rouge before heading back into the cardboard darkness for a trip to Dallas.

As Anni straps the packaging tape across the box, she tries to remove the prior bar code labels from the last shipping route and there she notices a plastic, peel away decal. Behind it is a tiny slip of folded paper smaller than 1"x2" saying, "Thanks, from the Communications Group." The mystery is solved! This is the corporate sponsor Little Miss just completed the Teen Summit appearances on behalf of.

What a fiasco this unnecessarily to out to be!

Little Miss has to ante up her credit card to ship this package and all her overweight luggage to Dallas. This is the third time the airlines have charged her for overweight baggage, beside the extra piece. She intends to meet-up with her Mother to help diminish some of her anxiety, homesickness and take the damn gift box back home in her car.... She also hopes the Miss Patriotic office will reimburse her for the heavy luggage charges...

At the kiosk for check-in, Little Miss rang-up Serberus. They exchange cutesy greetings, "I miss you too, Little Miss replies to Serberus' comment. She cheerfully tells Serberus SHE solved the mystery of the unknown delivery. Anni does not hedge, because she knows it is a leadership quality to let others take the credit and feel important.

"Yes, you give all your luggage receipts to Anni to submit for reimbursement for you," Serberus iterates.

I can't believe she heard Serberus go back on her word accepting the additional charges for her, when I was told that is her responsibility just this morning!

After Little Miss briefed Serberus on the sender of the package and they again exchange pleasantries, Anni asks Little Miss if she may speak with Serberus on her phone.

Immediately, Serberus' tone flipped completely. She roars at Anni in disgust, "I have no time to speak to you!"

Anni responds, "The package turned out to be a nice token of appreciation for Little Miss and the conversation between us did not need to be sour."

Serberus scowls, "I have too much work on my desk to talk AT you."

Anni indicates, "You cannot avoid me, as you are my point of contact and we need to work together!"

Finally, Serberus ensues, "The only time I will talk is with witnesses present."

I didn't realize I was being tried for a crime and that the case needed to be heard…What was she so overwhelmed and afraid of???

There was a dead calm, when the phone call ended. Little Miss and Anni looked at one another. Anni said, "Can you believe that reaction?"

Little Miss cautiously shook her head in confusion.

— 37 —

They settle in aboard their flight to Texas. Little Miss is seated one seat in front of Anni and pops in her ipod and covers-up with her Miss Patriotic black fleece blanket and drifts to semiconsciousness.

Meanwhile, Anni observes the people around her. Out of the corner of her eye, she sees a woman, who appears to be in her late 20's or early 30's seated with a child. He must be around three-years old and carries on a Winnie-the Poo backpack that he snuggles with at his seat. Anni overhears the exchange. "Just a little longer and we'll soon be home."

A man across the aisle reaches across and tells the woman, "We can switch seats, if you want to rest and I'll watch him." The man is the child's father.

A woman sitting on the other side of him asks, "How old is your son? Is this his first time on an airplane?"

His response intrigues Anni.

"Well, actually today has been his first experience flying, but this is his forth flight during our twenty-six hour journey bringing him home form Russia. We just adopted him today!"

Anni peeks through the space between the seats, since the little boy shifted over to sit on his Father's lap, so Mom could get a little bit of shut eye.

"What is his name?" Anni inquires.

"Alexander," the man replies.

"Congratulations to you both! That's so wonderful." Anni felt an immediate sense of harmony in the fact that these folks traveled around the globe to make a home for this little boy, who is leaving behind an entirely different world. "Do you understand each other?"

"Well, we learned a few phrases: love, hugs and family in Russian, but mostly we have an unspoken language mostly through gestures and eye contact."

Anni is comforted that there are still people who rise up to do good in the world.

* * * * * * *

When Little Miss and Anni arrive in Fort Worth, TX, Anni notices her coordinating via text a meeting with her Mom. Little Miss chirps, "My Mom wants to know the address we're staying, because she is driving there to meet us and will stay in my room."

Anni is surprised that she sprung this on her, but she complies as she pulls out the itinerary and points out the address of their hotel in Fort Worth.

As she finishes her call, Little Miss comments, "My Mom is coming to Dallas to visit me, plus she loves the shopping here."

"Isn't that far for her?" Anni asks in a puzzled manner.

"She enjoys taking road trips to the Dallas-area. She does it a few times a year, usually a "girl's weekend" with her friends to do power shopping. This time she's coming to spend time with me, since we are in town and she has some things for me."

"Maybe you can hand her off some of the clothes you picked-up on the road and the package you got in Baton Rouge, so you won't continue to get assessed overweight luggage charges," Anni indicates.

"That's what I was thinking too. I told my Mom to be prepared to take stuff off my hands and drive it back home with her, so she knows."

Forty-five minutes later, the vehicle pulls up and Anni sees Shannon's white SUV circle by in the parking lot. "Your Mom is here…right on time too!"

She approaches the car where Anni was getting out and gives her a big hug. "Nice to see you again! Your daughter is sitting on the other side."

Shannon anxiously approaches Little Miss as her daughter exclaims, "It's so good to see you in person!"

"You too honey."

In the meantime, Anni gets a couple of luggage carts, since no bellman were at the facility working at the door. She hoists various bags and Shannon tries to help. She takes one of the carts to her SUV to hang a bunch of garments and gets a series of luggage pieces on too.

Anni checks in for both rooms and feels heated as she is trying to maneuver the luggage carts. She pushes from the wrong side of the cart, since the set of wheels that roll in a single direction should be in the back, as the ones that pivot should guide the cart left and right. She struggles a bit, then builds momentum. By the time she reaches the third floor, she has worked up a light sweat. Anni opens the door to the first room and sees and hospitality basket with pink tiger lilies. She assumes this is Little Miss' room.

Upon opening the door to the second room, the same arrangement is there too, so happily she realizes the host presented each of them this gift, so it did not matter which room was which. She offloads the luggage—the pieces belted with the pink straps are Little Miss'.

When she went back into her own room, she notices a narrow, yet tall plain vase with yellow daisies in it. The infamous flowers from Headquarters Anni suspects. The card attached is for Little Miss, so she takes them next door and knocks gently, while she heard Little Miss and her Mom talking a "mile a minute."

"I believe these are for you."

"I'll take the luggage cart downstairs out of your way, while the two of you catch up." Anni comments.

Shannon, "You know what, I'll take a walk with you and help."

"Sure." So the two women push the empty carts down the hall and Little Miss' Mother indicates, "I wanted to have a word with you. My daughter was upset about some things."

"So that must be why you're in town to cheer her up. It's been stressful for her with the media backlash from the internet sting in April." Anni observes.

"In addition to all that, she's been working very hard and she is a great kid. Even when she was young we never had to worry about her as much as our other two. She never got in trouble with cigarettes, smoking, or other things. Everyone generally has a vice, but her only outlet to relieve her stress has been by biting her nails."

"Look, if I hurt her feelings by commenting on our flight she should not bight her nails, I was not saying that out of malicious intent. I was thinking of her image." Anni interjects.

"Well she said you hit her hand when you said, "Don't bite your nails!""

"I believe this is being taken out of context. I mentioned how her hands could look better, as was evident when the photographer in Arkansas said to keep her "man hands" out of the shot. I didn't want her to receive that kind of criticism, if she can avoid it. As I was talking about that I made a swatting motion towards her hand. I did not slap her! It was a gesture to accentuate my point."

Anni fells herself choking-up, as tears begin to well-up in her eyes. "I am so sorry, she felt I hurt or disrespected her. That was truly not my intention," Anni pours out.

"I believe you. There is no need to apologize. I wanted to let you know you there is never a need to touch her, just let her bite her nails, we tried to talk her out of it years ago, but we'd rather her bite them then be stressed out in other ways."

"I understand and once again apologize if you think a line was crossed." Anni mentions this as they are stepping back off the elevator. At the landing on the third floor, Anni feels compelled to mention, "I'm glad you mentioned this situation with me directly, but Little Miss must have already reviewed it with Serberus, as I have been handed an ultimatum as a result of this and my job is hanging in the balance." Anni said this in nearly a whisper, because she was getting choked-up.

"I wouldn't worry about it; it's over. You won't lose you job over it. Mark and I are so proud overall of the care you take of our daughter on the road."

Anni perks up a bit and makes that comment more tangible. "I'm glad we were able to get a hold of your family doctor to fax the prescription to the pharmacy I located when she and I were in Washington, D.C. She was rather flu-like."

"You handled that like a pro!" Shannon affirmed.

By now Anni had a major knot in her stomach. From the time she noticed the daisies in her room, (that she speculates were from Serberus) that she get railed into about when she thought the package in Baton Rouge was the arrangement they sent, and now this encounter with Shannon.

In front of Little Miss' everyone was friendly and acting normal. Separately, there was another layer of half-truths, misconception and altered expectations. Anni feels dismayed that Little Miss contacted Serberus before approaching Anni about feeling uncomfortable about Anni talking with her about her nails.

Instead, this situation was elevated through the chain of command and Anni now is operating on eggshells, because Serberus had her written-up with a 90-day warning. Little Miss' Mother excused the legitimacy of Anni's job being in jeopardy.

* * * * * *

That evening Little Miss and Anni join the executives from the Dairy Farm Cooperative to a steak dinner to discuss their objective and use Little Miss as a pitch woman for their campaign. Anni asks some targeted questions about their area of influence and it turns out their educational endeavors cover five states in their co-op in which they educate children using a roving "Moomobile."

Anni recommends they synergize their programs with Little Miss, as she has plenty of experience presenting to school children and connects with them very well. Their reaction is pure excitement. Anni tells them how to review the schedule and develop the necessary contract with headquarters of the Miss Patriotic group. The exectutives are delighted Anni identified such a phenomenal pairing to enhance they traveling educational initiatives.

The true purpose of Little Miss being in Fort Worth is to shoot a photo spread for the Dairy Farmer Cooperative campaign the following day. Shannon asks Anni if she can tag along to the studio. Anni stops-by Little Miss' room to indicate she got the OK, for Shannon to visit at the photo shoot after she checked with their executives.

While Little Miss and Anni were attending the dinner the night before, Shannon went on her Dallas-shopping spree. Shannon intends to take her own vehicle to the studio, since she plans to leave few hours later, now that she switched out her daughter's clothing providing her some fresh garments and gowns.

Little Miss' Mom has a set of new luggage strewn right beside the doorway and had a pile of brand new clothes too.

"Someone must have been shopping?" Anni says jokingly.

"Now you know where I get it from," Little Miss adds.

"I couldn't resist. I heard she was having trouble fitting all her gear in her luggage and she's been using it for months now, so I found some larger cases and the set was only $79.99.

Anni, look at these cute little numbers I picked-up for her today! The weather is warming-up, so I know she'll need some cute things for the warmer weather. Take a look at this dress. I got it at Tar-she' on sale."

"It will look lovely on her," Anni commented of the knee length, chocolate brown, eyeletted, starched, cotton frock.

Little Miss interjects, "I don't like it. The fabric is scratchy."

Shannon had insisted she try it on and it looked fabulous. Anni agrees.

Little Miss tells Shannon, "I feel uncomfortable, because the dress is really stiff and itchy."

Anni responds, "The things we have to do for beauty." Her Mother laughs and agrees, "You'll get used to it and it travels well. It's wash and wear."

"OK, I'll try it," Little Miss reluctantly says.

In addition, Shannon brought her a whole new set of rolling suitcases that are larger, since Little Miss grappled with the luggage requirements. Shannon's rationale is, "These new cases are easier to pull around." Little Miss had no problem wheeling the other cases, but Mother, like daughter they both have a knack for shopping and Shannon wants her to have the freedom to pack any extra things she bought along the way.

During her shopping excursion, Shannon got herself a new pocketbook. The day of the shoot Shannon wears a really large print black and white blouse that made a statement carrying the new black courier-style bag with zebra fur on the front flap in the shape of an eight inch crucifix bordered by rugged, turquoise stones. Some of the flamboyant consultants on the set commented how great her handbag is. She certainly could not lose it in a crowd easily how crazy the design is. It was really loud! Nearly shouting if zebras could.

In the studio, Little Miss is provided a fashion stylist and hair/make-up artist. She is in her glory, since she likes the attention and consequently loved the clothing choices the stylist had prepared. So much that she called Shannon into the dressing room to beg her to purchase some of the garments. Suddenly, they must have forgotten the point of Shannon's visit: to lighten her load.

Without much persuasion, Shannon grabs her checkbook to write a check for $600 for another cocktail dress, tee shirt, skinny jeans and the stylist "graciously" through in a couple of bangles. What a bargain!

At the shoot the photographer, takes creative liberty and poses Little Miss in different ways to capture a variety of moods. They attempt to incorporate drinking glasses of milk to promote the product. During a break Little Miss confides in Anni, "I hate milk. I never drink it, unless I'm handed a bowl of ice cream." Although, the campaign intends to have her as a milk advocate mentioning how she drinks glasses everyday!

Fortunately, they did not have her drink the product, just hold it in a variety of outfits. She is excited they intend to make billboards out of some of these photos. Little Miss was anxious to see her own image loom high above many interstates she is familiar with.

The sponsor had lunch catered in and to Little Miss' delight, they got Mexican. (Anni had told the assistant that is the kind of food she likes best.) Little Miss ate a few bites, but held back from her natural appetite, since the photoshoot was still in progress and she wants to look fantastic in the "skinny jeans." Shannon scooted out from the studio to head back home. They embrace as if they won't see each other again. In reality it was just a few more weeks until she had some time home again for Easter.

— 38 —

From the Ft. Worth location, they fly to Washington, DC to take part in a black tie dinner to support the National Center of Missing and Exploited Children initiatives. The Miss Patriotic CEO comes to town with his wife to attend the function. Little Miss is anxious to reunite with him, but he is delayed, so she gets involved in the VIP photos with Richard Belzer, Stephanie Match and others. After a few photos, she sees the confused CEO walk hesitantly into the reception area. Anni determines she is seated with Little Miss at a VIP table at the gala, but the CEO pulls Anni aside and says he revised the seating arrangement to sit with Little Miss among the Senior Production team of "The Nation's Most Wanted," Ernie Allen of the National Center, his wife, John and Reve' Walsh and U.S. Attorney General Alberto Gonzales and his wife Rebecca.

Anni escorts Little Miss to her table and then converses with the CEO's wife seated beside her. The CEO's wife is certainly star-struck, she asks Anni, "Should I approach the Attorney General to take his photo?"

"Maybe introduce yourself to him beside your husband, so you don't come across like some random groupie." She felt reluctant to interrupt her husband at his table, so Anni, as the liaison, walks over to A.G. Gonzales and mentions she has regards for him from one of his State A.G.'s John Brownlee. He was appreciative of the complement she relays. She then asks if the CEO's wife may take a picture and he accepts, so she flags her over to take it.

Anni enjoys her experience at this gala as she is seated next to the emcee, Brian Cranston, who was the Dentist on "Seinfield." He is a family man, dining with his wife and daughter. He makes some comical presentations, yet the tone of the gala is somber to raise more awareness of internet predators. A few surviving victims talked about their horrifying experiences and are presented honors by the Walshes.

After the event, Anni and Little Miss had to gather their gear from one Fairfax-county hotel to move to another for the next day's appearance for the Lupus

Foundation. Back in D.C. they are situating in yet another hotel. No sooner does Anni have them checked-in, Little Miss' Blackberry is buzzing a response that some friends want to stop-over to visit. Anni tells her to make it brief, since she has to be camera ready by 6:30pm.

As Anni gets into her own room, she notices the television is not working and calls the front desk to send an engineer for it. Her phone rings a minute later, so she suspects it is facilities trying to make arrangements with her about the broken set. Instead, it is the sponsor Kent, who wants to visit with her and Little Miss to introduce himself. Unfortunately, Anni had to inform Kent, Little Miss just jumped in the shower and does not have time. He still wanted to see Anni, since he has something for them both. She asked if she could meet in ten minutes. He agrees.

As soon as she hung up the phone, a very dark-skinned man approached the door. "I am the hotel engineer to look at the television."

Anni notices a heavy African accent and asks where he is from?

"Guyana. I came here to study and now work here."

She asked if she needs to be present while he trouble shoots, and he confirmed in his thick Guyanese accent, "It is not necessary if you have other things to take care of."

Suddenly, her cell phone rings and it's the PR coordinator from the office telling Anni, "We are updating passwords into the computer network, so when you log on, be sure to update yours. Do you know what you will change it to, so we have it on file to trouble shoot?"

Anni said, "I'll update my login to : CROWN06."

"That'll work," she acknowledges.

Anni dashes to the lobby to meet Kent, the sponsor and see what items he so urgently wanted her to have. She doesn't find any man, who appears to be waiting for someone. She walks back and forth through the large foyer until she sees some vases with flowers at the information booth set-back from the other areas. Anni approaches a man was on his cell. "Are you Kent?"

"Yes, I am. How are your accommodations?"

"Well, I just left an engineer in my room, since the TV is broken, but aside from that we're doing fine. Sorry we were not expecting your visit, or else I would have prepared Miss Patriotic to be available, but we did not know."

Kent mentions he is running around like a madman from various hotels and the venue where the gala is to get all the VIP's settled. "Oh, have you seen Shiloh? She's staying here too for our gala."

"No, I haven't seen her yet."

Anni had seen a change on their itinerary that they were slated to stay at the hotel where the gala is being held, but either it was overbooked or the expenses made it less feasible, so there appeared to be a last minute update.

Kent hands Anni two floral arrangements. There is one for each of you. The roses are for Miss Patriotic. Behind the desk, he had placed more novelties for them. I know you're hands are full, so I can carry the rest of the items that were to have been delivered to your rooms earlier today, but with the changes it just did not happen. Kent trails along Anni with exotic treasure boxes of teas and cookies for each of the woman too. "Thank you for your generosity," Anni mentions as she enters her room. "It appears they got the TV back in working order.

The Kenyan engineer poked his head around the corner and indicated, "No, we just replaced the whole thing, since we did not want to inconvenience you any further."

"See you in a few hours Kent!" He departed and Anni settled in to get ready for the formal that evening.

Little Miss knocks on Anni's door. "Does your iron work, because mine doesn't?"

"You know I have not had time to check it yet," Anni responds, yet she knows she would have to, since their luggage was crushed from Dallas to here. She looked in her closet and hands Little Miss the iron. "Here you go, let me know if you have any trouble. I'll need it back when you're finished to steam my garment. By the way, our sponsor for tonight's event called me and wanted to meet you, but you were in the shower, so I met with him after attempting to get my TV fixed and he sent along some gifts! These roses and this treasure box of teas are for you."

"OK, thanks." As Little Miss reenters her room across the hall, Anni sees two friends sitting inside on her bed watching TV.

After forty-five minutes there is no sign of the iron, which Anni desperately needs, since her dress has some deep creases in it. She knocks on Little Miss' door, who forgot all about bringing the iron back. Anni introduces herself to Little Miss' buddies who stopped-by with some fast food to eat with her. She was glad, since she never eats at work functions. She is all dolled-up in a short, power blue, babydoll cocktail dress. It looked awfully cutsy, but slightly glamorous with the slinky, metallic heels she paired with the dress. Her friends are thrilled to see how pretty she looks. Anni offers to take their picture together on Little Miss' new digital camera and one on their camera phone, then she excuses herself to get ready.

They reconvene and Little Miss' friends walk them to the elevator and to the lobby. There Little Miss is dumbstruck when she sees, her runner-up from the Miss Patriotic Pageant, Miss Texas.

Anni did not mention they are staying at the same hotel in attendance for the gala. She figures headquarters would have noted they are both making the appearance. Shiloh approaches them. Anni gives her a big hug, "Nice to see you again, since Homecoming."

Little Miss gets in the spirit and hugs her too. Shiloh reaches in her bag and responds, "I have something for you. I never had the opportunity to formally congratulate you for your winning the title, so here I want you to have this!"

Little Miss was speechless as her jaw dropped and no words came out. Shiloh hands her a card inscribed how happy she was for her earning the crown and the gift- wrapped box contained a necklace with an emerald on it.

Little Miss is in awe. She could not believe this exchange just happened, since all along she concluded Shiloh was jealous of her from the pageant, as she didn't get involved with the behind the scenes serenade, she didn't make eye contact during "the final two" or mix in socially with the others at the competition. This act of goodwill is overwhelming!

Shiloh grabs her camera and hands it to Anni who takes a photo of the two women. The two beauty queens along with their managers ride to the gala. At the event, Kent scurries by and says, "Oh, you all found each other. We are a bit behind, but make yourselves comfortable in the lounge and the VIP room will be situated for photos soon."

In the meanwhile, Anni asks Shiloh how things are progressing in her world. Shiloh makes eye contact as she indicates how blessed she's been seeing the great state of Texas, earning some scholarship money and getting a better sense of what she wants to do with her life. "I put my studies on hold to carry-on my duties as Miss Texas, but I am looking forward to pursuing my musical career. You know I tried out for "American Idol" twice and did not make it as far as I hoped, but now with my experience and maturity I am ready to pursue a recording contract."

"What about college?"

"I thought that was the route I needed to go, or maybe my Mom did, but I think my music is calling me to take advantage of some opportunities that I may not always have."

Little Miss has nothing to say. She is still surprised Shiloh is in town at the same appearance.

In the banquet, Little Miss is seated at a table by the stage. Anni is all the way towards the back, as is Shiloh and her escort seated at a different table.

The gala is highlighted by a presentation by Will and Jada Smith and a performance by Jennifer Hudson, a newly attained Grammy winner. She sang a few songs with a piano accompaniment and wanted the audience to participate in some lyrics. She decides to get even bolder by requesting a few people from the crowd join her to sing background on stage.

Immediately, Shiloh barrels across the banquet floor after she is handed a wireless microphone and belts out a line from the chorus. Others try to do the same, but Shiloh holds the mike hostage and continues to sing the rest of the song in nearly a duet with Jennifer. Little Miss is also on stage, but is lost in the crowd of others. Shiloh in her lime green, satin-sheath, floor-length gown glows and she stands front and center, now with her arm around Jennifer.

Anni makes her way to the Ladies' Room and calls headquarters to leave Serberus a voicemail about the combined appearance.

When the gala ends, Little Miss looks dejected as the crowd approaches her runner-up, Shiloh to discuss how powerful a voice she has and how tremendous a performer she when she stole she show!!

* * * * * * *

The next day at 7:30am, Anni follows-up with Serberus who obviously had not been apprised of Shiloh's involvement at the fundraising gala. It is disconcerting, national headquarters does not know others from the pageant system are involved in appearances along with Miss Patriotic and in this case she became invisible under the circumstances.

Anni also speaks with her to review an anomaly with their hotel bill. Serberus' tone is pretty ordinary, while Anni explained the glitch in the billing. Serberus did not have an answer how the billing is to be handled but feels this needs to be reviewed with the sponsor. Next, Serberus growls that Tony Bowls never did get final approval on the proofs for his campaign which is running in the current Crowning Moments magazine. Shouldn't Pearson have policed that material, before it was published? How is that my problem? The final point Serberus makes in their early morning conversation, is that the CEO would be contacting Anni when she arrives in NYC that afternoon to have a talk. Anni responds, "Sounds great."

— 39 —

They hit the road from Washington, DC heading to NYC. The driver is extremely late meeting them at the hotel, causing them to get backed-up in Beltway traffic and Holland Tunnel jams. The five hour ride turned into a good, solid six. Anni is anxious and struggles to read any of the newspaper while anticipating they arrive safely, so she can meet up with the CEO and later attend Tiki Barber's private birthday party with Little Miss, where he is raising money for a children's charity. Bon Jovi is slated to entertain at the event.

Little Miss wakes-up from her five hour nap stretched out in the back of the stretch limo with her ipod purring. Anni had watched her lying prone to the car seat covered with her fleece Miss Patriotic blanket. A bit disoriented, Little Miss yawns after Anni tells her, "We're pulling into the hotel driveway. You probably want to get ready." Little Miss grabs for her make-up case to touch-up. There is a lot of traffic around Times Square on this 10th day in May. The driver has to circle a few times to get access to the front entrance.

Anni collects their things, as the bellman advises, "Good day ladies, I will put your bags in storage until your rooms are ready." Anni kindly declines his offer, because she wants to get Little Miss checked-in right away. So, the bellman guides them to the eighth floor to the lobby area. Anni proceeds to the VIP check-in to find out they have arrived an hour and a half sooner than standard check-in time of 3pm.

Anni tells the clerk, "I am here with Miss Patriotic and she needs to get assembled in her room, since she is in town for an appearance later today." The clerk taps on her keyboard and said, "For the time being, I'll give you keys for her room, but I cannot get you into a room until 3pm."

She agrees and is handed Little Miss' room key and then dials Craig, the sponsor of the event to tell him that they arrived in town and the rooms are not yet available. He indicates he's in a meeting in a café on the other side of Times Square, but will meet them in the lobby shortly.

In the meantime, Anni explains the situation the hotel is asking her for her credit card for incidentals. Craig promptly calls the hotel to make sure the rooms are billed to the sponsor's account directly. He straightens things out with the Marquis staff.

Within minutes, Craig appears and verifies their two rooms are billed to his company when he checks with the clerk. Meanwhile, Little Miss is curled-up on a bench near the elevators, texting like madness to her friends about arriving in NYC to attend a celebrity party that Jon Bon Jovi will be performing live!

Anni waves to her and shows her she has a room key. After Little Miss finishes furiously messaging, Anni tells her, she will escort her to the room, get her settled and also mentions there is not another room for her until 3pm. She asks Little Miss if it is acceptable to have the bellman deliver all of their bags to her room, so it does not get confusing with separating them and putting half in storage for a few hours. It would make tipping the ballman simpler. Little Miss agrees. Little Miss hops on her bed with navy and brown comforter and tells Anni, "Feel free to hang out here. We can order room service and I'm going to watch a movie until I have to get ready for tonight's party."

Anni thanks her and replies, "If you don't mind, "I'll get out my laptop and my gym clothes and be out of your way, so you can relax in peace." Little Miss was on her phone already chatting with her Mom, so she nods in agreement.

Anni gathers her gear into her carry-on and waves to Little Miss and mentions, "Relax and enjoy yourself and I'll be back in around an hour. Call me on cell if you need anything."

Anni wants to give her some privacy and wants to be accessible to receive the CEO's call to confirm their meeting. In the meantime, Anni goes to the fitness center, where she changes into her gym gear and has a good thorough workout. She has the work cell phone right there, so she is reachable all along. Anni enjoys the time by doing a rigorous cardio workout on their high-tech machine and reading a magazine. It feels good to move around, after sitting in the limousine for nearly three hours in traffic.

The phone is still silent, so Anni moves to the weight area and does a lifting series for her arms and another for her leg workout. Then she makes her way to the exercise ball to work her core. These exercises are meant to build strength in her lower back and abdomen to provide good posture.

Just as she is settles on a ball in the center of the mat, the cell phone rings. The CEO comments, "I'm in town with my wife and we're having lunch, so I'll meet you at the lobby bar in forty-five minutes." Anni is upbeat and looking forward to it. She responded, "Enjoy yourselves, see you soon!" He immediately hangs up.

She was famished and thought he would have asked her to join them, but he did not. Anni is not sure what they were meeting about, but now that her workout was nearly done, she is energized and ready for it.

After she does some Yoga postures to stretch out and cool down, Anni grabs an apple to tide her appetite for the time being and gets assembled back to her work apparel. She still had time to spare, so she makes her way to the business center back on the eighth floor and organizes her expenses, receipts, and tour reports by copying and collating them. The clerk asks to see her room key and she verifies she is a hotel guest, but her room had not been assigned due to a backlog of check-outs. The business center representative accepts her explanation and offers to copy her materials at no charge. Anni thanks her graciously for the assistance, when the cell rings.

The CEO is on the line telling her he is now at the lobby bar. "OK", Anni answers, "I am across the aisle in the business center completing my reports. Be right over."

The clerk did not know she was on the phone as she affirms, "Enjoy your stay and let us know if we can help you further."

Anni places her folders in her case and zips it up, as she wheels it out of the business center toward the lobby bar. She walks briskly towards the café tables and does not see the CEO or his wife. She doubles back and sees him wearing all black at the very first table. He motions to Anni to come to that table with no emotion displayed on his face. Anni wonders why he wearing all black and she still is unsure what the agenda of their meeting is about. Anni approaches smiling and says, "Nice to see you. Did you enjoy your lunch?"

He could barely respond. Only abruptly mutters, "Yup, yup."

From around the back of where Anni is standing, Serberus appears wearing a black blazer and white blouse. The CEO looks toward her and says, "Would you like me to begin?" She clears her throat and says, "May as well."

They ask, "Where is Miss Patriotic?" Anni tells them, "I was able to get her immediately checked-in, but was unable to get the other room since their policy is a 3pm check-in time, so I am waiting for a room. I had them make an accommodation for her, since she has to relax for tonight's festivities."

Serberus jumped in, "What are you talking about?" Anni once again reviews how the hotel did not offer early check-in because they were overbooked.

Serberus looks at Anni glaringly and asked, "Then where are your bags?"

"I left them in her room, so we wouldn't have to play cat and mouse with the bellman in splitting the luggage up and tipping him twice. She was OK with that."

The CEO steps in and indicates, "The reason I called you for this meeting, is it's been decided your help on the tour is no longer needed." Anni looked up towards the beautiful glimmer of sunlight across the windows above. She was processing what he just said. Serberus sat there silently.

Anni inquires, "Is there an explanation for this?"

"No, it's just a decision that has been made. I don't like what I hear and I'm tired of it," the CEO indicates.

"Tired of what?" Anni questions.

No explanation is offered. "Out of professional courtesy, I am due some information."

The CEO's reply, "I'll take care of you next week."

The CEO had no other reasons to offer. He says, "There is a car waitng for you outside, so drop-off all the company items here, get your luggage, then you can be on your way. Let's schedule a meeting for Monday in the office and I will take care of you then."

Anni quips, "I don't know what you mean by "take care of me Monday," What does that mean?"

He repeated, just call to schedule for Monday and that's it. Apparently, there was no opportunity here for discussion.

Anni opens her carry-on pulls out the computer laptop, work cell phone, adaptor, the corporate credit card, remaining postage and a pile of Ann Jo Serberus business cards. She places everything in one big pile, and then dashes to the bank of elevators, trying not to trip on her carry-on and large satchel purse. There were a ton of people on the floor, since it was now just after 3pm. Anni jumps on an elevator which had just stopped. She hopes it was the correct one, as there are a series of elevators that stop at certain segments in the hotel. As the elevator doors were shutting, Serberus jumps on behind her. Anni did not say a word.

When she arrives on the fourteenth floor, Anni hustles back to Little Miss' room. She was pretty sure, Serberus had called ahead to prepare her what is taking place.

Little Miss answers her door and Anni says, "I'm here to say goodbye and introduce you to your new Tour Manager," as Serberus stood in the doorway with a snarled expression. Little Miss grabs Anni around the neck and gave her one firm and final hug and tells her, "Thanks for everything!"

Anni did not want to make a production; she darts in the foyer of her room to find her bags.

Serberus tries to appear she cares about Anni in front of Little Miss by asking, "Do you need help with your things?" Anni shot her an optical dagger and silently took a hold of her two cases and tried to configure them with her large purse and carry-on. She awkwardly maneuvers back to the bank of elevators to the ground floor.

Serberus trails behind and said, "The driver who brought me here and is waiting to take you home." She handed her the driver's card with his cell phone number and walks away.

Anni's heart is pounding through her chest, she can not believe the tour for her just came to a screeching halt. Her whirlwind job has crashed and there is no way for her to have avoided this bombastic demise.

The sound of the traffic from Times Square is so loud it creates white noise in the soundtrack of Anni's tragic job demise. She sits on a concrete bench outside the hotel exit and sits motionless around all the cars, taxis and limousines swirling around her. She abhors the cigarette smoke the fills the air, but she realizes the bench she found is the smoker's lounge.

Her stomach revolves in overtime. She is angered that the driver is not waiting at the door, as he is meant to be. As she crosses the driveway to access the convenience store to get some nourishment to stabilize her ill-feelings during the unexpected drive home, she sees the sedan with the familiar license plate of the limo service the company always uses.

She makes contact with him and confirms this is her driver. He comments he had to keep moving the car, being that this is the busy time in the city and the cops keep traffic flowing. Anni tells him, "Do what you have to, but I need to grab some water and food for the ride. I'll be right out." Anni notices how overpriced the items were at this spot here in Times Square, but her mouth felt like a desert and she still had some petty cash left on her final work day.

On the return ride to her home, Anni replays the conversation with the CEO that she just had, over in her head a few times to process what just took place. She can not understand why her boss, Cheryl Pearson, was not in on this meeting, either in person or on a conference call.

Well "next week" came and went and no explanation: electronic, by phone or by written correspondence ever manifested. There is not a voicemail, e-mail or memo from Pearson.

Anni sends a few e-mails to query the CEO and the Chairman of the Board, as to the status that she did not voluntarily come off her duties as Tour Manager and to determine "how she was to be taken care of."

After a few rounds of passing the buck, the CEO's assistant leaves a message for Anni to travel to see him at his convenience at headquarters. Anni uncovers he initiated some reorganization at the Miss Patriotic Organization… First, the Director of Scholarship, who was a 30 year veteran with the company was relieved of her responsibilities 45 days earlier. This came after phone lines were shut down, the square-footage of headquarters was minimized and he was ultimately negotiating a move out of Atlantic City after 85 years in town.

Anni believes the CEO needs to reach out and contact her directly with the update. She affirms it is unnecessary to exhaust three plus hours in commute time for a discussion that could have been held in N.Y. or as a follow-up conference call.

— 40 —

Summer 2007. 'Tis the season for state pageants to take place. These young women are vying to receive the title representing their state on the journey towards Miss Patriotic. Anni recalls, Serberus conversing with Little Miss that she could chose six states she is interested in attending state pageants. Little Miss and Anni were clamoring to include some exotic places like Hawaii, since she knows the current titleholder and they visited at Homecoming in Ohio. In addition, she definitely had on her short list South Carolina, the home state of her best pageant friend (who she confirmed she'll be in her bridal party when Miss S.C. ties the not).

Certainly, Serberus had to lay down the law and simply bust Little Miss' bubble. She responded that attending the pageants depends on time, cost and whether the former Miss Patriotic already attended pageants in those particular states. If so, Little Miss would not be heading to the same places this year. So, the list changes. Little Miss ends- up attending her home state's pageant, which was a memorable seeing the State Director and crew again. She went to Texas, where Shiloh, her runner-up is from, to uphold polical correctness. They still had a strange acquaintanceship, but Little Miss cannot shake the assorted comments and cold body language which deter her.

In addition, Little Miss went to Arkansas and Louisiana in support of those state pageants and a few others for good measure.

While they were in Ohio, back in March for Homecoming, they had interfaced with all the current state titleholders Chaperones and Executive Directors. Anni had befriended a few and chatted with the New Jersey contingency. The Chaperone for N.J. is Sally, a bubbly and witty character. She shared silly stories of life on the road, primarily in New Jersey, working with her exuberant state titleholder. Since Anni was also from that state, Sally extended an invitation to attend the upcoming state pageant in June. Anni wasn't sure if she would be able to attend, inititally it would have been her time off the road, as well as, time to celebrate her first wedding anniversary. As it turns out she was no longer affiliated with the organization by June.

So, the N.J. state pageant arrived. Anni's connection with national elapses, she now had a series of other commitments, so she passed on attending the N.J. pageant event.

Anni learns through the news Georgie handed her state legacy on. The winner of the current N.J. pageant was announced: Amy, a 22-year old from a Central N.J. county. Ironically, she also promoted a platform of protecting children from online predators (the same timely mission that Little Miss has been touting this year.) Amy, the newly crowned N.J. titleholder, has some physical characteristics similar to Little Miss: sandy blond hair, diamond-shaped face, brown-penciled in eyebrows, petite frame and features.

Within a month of her newly installed role, Amy receives odd packages of photos containing assorted pictures that SHE had posted on her social networking page: FACEBOOK. Many young adults use this tool and form of communication to keep in touch and make new friends around the globe. The downside is internet creeps also enjoy making friends and meeting new people too.

Little Miss had a biographical page similar to Amy when she was at the state level. National opposed her keeping the page or having her own personal site that they could not control or police. So, now Amy had her posting while working through the state system, which limited viewership to friends and family-so she thought.

Perhaps hackers know how to bypass those filters or some of those folks are not "true" friends and family she can trust. Others speculate this was manufactured by her "people," so she could fast-track on the publicity trail. Well, this photo collection of unladylike poses from her page was downloaded and sent in the mail with ransom notes calling for her resignation as Miss N.J.

A few more weeks into her reign and another package of similar content showed- up in her hometown. Her lawyer, Caruso, appears on the media press junket to dispel rumors her "people" are manufacturing publicity. He claims someone was attaching disturbing captions to her personal photos in an attempt to damage her credibility and career.

Amy and Caruso proclaim the photo spread is no racier than the images of her in the bathing suit portion of the pageant she just completed. There she represented herself in a red, sweetheart top bikini. They just feel the FACEBOOK photos should be withheld as they were directed to a limited audience and not meant for mass consumption and viewership. Amy stumbles on her words a bit, since she is not clearly a media hound yet. She is new at maneuvering through questioning which the media had in store. This experience has forced her to go from "ordinary life into an extraordinary situation."

There are similarities with Little Miss and the newly crowned and mud-smeared Miss N.J. Both had aspirations to be Broadway actresses, both came from very supportive families, both wanted to protect children using the Internet and both didn't realize if you post personal items even for private consumption, it could be used against you or for illicit purposes. Now The Committee to Save Miss Patriotic is pillaging and stampeding through Miss N.J.'s title to make a point how easy it is to manipulate images posted on the internet. Certainly a harsh, life lesson, giving these women firsthand experience regarding the underbelly of the platform they are attempt to uphold and warn others about.

Caruso indicates the state board needs to settle this matter along with the support and direction of the national Miss Patriotic Organization. On multiple inquiries, national has not made itself available for comment.

In the meantime, Cheryl, the smiling Cheshire cat-like Communications Director, is busy crafting news releases that the national headquarters moved. She backpedals, since a number of media connections she arranged fell flat. The red carpet segments that Little Miss was a part of with the country music cable station were edited out and never aired, similar to the Extreme Home Makeover episode, in which Little Miss was flown in to her home town (under the radar before her official homecoming) to be a part of the dedication. Unwittingly to Cheryl Pearson or the Miss Patriotic Organization, ABC executives cut-out her portion of the project. Perhaps, as a result of ABC choosing not to renew its contract with the organization two years ago, they opted not to include this content. Also, a PEOPLE magazine interview that Pearson had leveraged never went to print, but received a nominal mention online instead as a "controversial topic of the week."

When Anni had spoken with Little Miss she said softly, "I could not believe these things were cut or not included as they were intended." She was clearly upset and not prepared for these outcomes. Little Miss was under the guise that when she completed the interviews and television appearances that all was a go ahead. No one explained to her that there is no guarantee the material is used in every case.

Little Miss' depression deepened. Her need to be close to home and near her parents continued. She did not know how much her life would change as a result of the title and how many times things did not happen the way she assumed. She no longer wants to pursue a Broadway career, but is thinking going back to continue her college studies in state.

The Miss Patriotic Organization also took a hit in the entertainment columns, whereby reports highlighted, "Miss Patriotic is further abandoning her roots, by leaving the birthplace of the pageant." The residents already felt alienated over the past two years when the pageant transplanted to the West, moved to a cable station, (in which the specific channel is not available on their cable system) and now headquarters is gone too. The reporter said, "This contributes to the oblivion of this eighty-six year American tradition."

During this confusing publicity, Miss Patriotic HQ was fielding inquiries regarding its move out of its native home of the organization to a no-name town in a strip of office spaces. A sound bite was granted by the PR coordinator, who in the report was listed as, "Official spokeswoman."

"We wanted to stay in A.C., but it wasn't feasible."

Ironically she is scheduled to be unavailable on maternity leave, but they scramble to keep "All hands of deck," while maneuvering through these bumbling issues.

So, much for seizing an opportunity to place an upbeat message with the media.

* * * * * * *

The Summer's winding down, as vacations are in high gear and families are considering school-related preparations. In the news, The Miss Patriotic Organization announces a new "multi-million dollar" television contract with another cable station-TMC. The station will carry the pageant, a related-documentary surrounding Little Miss' yearlong endeavors and a hyped-up reality show. The next pageant will take place in Sin City to propagate the Hollywood-chic and style, but at a different resort and the date of the big show is still a moving target.

These announcements are a surge that the tides are changing; this being an American institution-which was the pride of Atlantic City, N.J. Its new persona is continuing to evolve into something else.

* * * * * * *

In the meanwhile, as the current crown is "getting tight," Little Miss has been under hairdresser, Lenny's spell. She appears on various media with his latest hairstyle—an exact replica of her predecessor: Miss Patriotic 2006.

Lenny is a one tune stylist, Little Miss had told Anni months ago. He intends for every pageant girl to have his signature color and "the flip" in front style and he accomplishes this with Little Miss. The style, way too mature for Little Miss, takes away her natural spunky, glowing youth and transforms her unnecessarily into a thirty-something mature woman with helmet hair.

Little Miss is booked to be a hostess on one of the televised-shopping clubs. How these appearances will springboard her career or even show her in a favorable light as a leader, only Serberus and Pearson can decipher.

Little Miss is on the first of a three hour program pitching Technobond. Actually, the fulltime hostess throws the pitch and rambles on about nothing. Little Miss just sits there as the hostess does ALL the talking. She has no opportunity to comment on any products or more importantly anything she represents.

When the hostess indicates, "She loves to wear gold jewelry any chance she can," Little Miss initially replies "Ah, ha."

Then rebuts her own knee-jerk reply with, "No actually I wear sterling silver mostly." Perhaps the cable network could have reviewed Little Miss' preferences and the hostess could have beefed-up on relevant points of interest with Little Miss. Fake gold is clearly not her thing.

The hostess does not have Little Miss say anything meaningful. You could tell she is not interested, as all her feedback includes small one syllabled answers: "OK", "Yeah," "Ah, ha," repeatedly.

Fortunately, Little Miss had the wherewithal to have her nails manicured before the show. There is a tight close-up of her hands holding some "liquid gold" earrings, nicely offset by her red polish. It wouldn't have helped sales if the tight shot revealed her drastically bitten fingernails. The whole hour episode evoked one single message: it perpetuated dumb blond beauty queen stereotype....

— Epilogue —

Currently, Anni is going through life with her shades on. "Yes, I am the first one to mention they are rose-colored, because life is good, each day is a gift," Anni states proudly. There seems to be such a dichotomy between high-profile lifestyle and the everyday. Yet, many people you come across may teach you life's lessons on either side of the spectrum. Life is filled with blessings. Keep focused on both big and small happenings, whether they are high-profile or not, just find the beauty in these presents.

It is evident among young Hollywood starlets; girls like Brittany Spears, Lindsey Lohan and Paris Hilton, who treat their assistants like scapegoats making all kinds of requests and at times placing them in precarious situations. These behind the scenes staffers work to try to keep their celebs on schedule, on point, image worthy and in the limelight. Sometimes fame causes life to become a bit distorted.

Anni realizes as the Tour Manager, she was essentially the personal assistant to a celebrity, which certainly has both perks and pitfalls. Anni learns it is a deficit to look good or better than any Miss Patriotic. "It's all about them, so if I inadvertently captured attention it was unacceptable." Being noticed is scorned by Little Miss and in turn, spurned Serberus, because she was not pleased how people on tour gravitated to Anni.

Anni's dynamic interpersonal skills and well-kept appearance were too overwhelming to Serberus. She ultimately wanted someone to speak on cue, when spoken to and to look clean, but ordinary and not to stand out of the crowd. Serberus preferred someone who would take a backseat, but chime-up only when problems need diverting. Although Anni held the distinctive Tour Manager title, the organization, with Serberus leading the charge, did not want to relinquish control and every decision Anni made became second-guessed.

Being Tour Manager provided an all-access pass to the behind the scenes of theatrical productions, meetings with dignitaries, politicians and an inside view interfacing with various communities across the country. Along the way, Anni got to see a few young women, begin the transition from an everyday girl to celebrity, and visited vast destinations. She saw firsthand, the Miss Patriotic women receive lots of attributes and trinkets, flowers and collectibles along the way. It is interesting for Anni to observe people who need things least, get the most for merely having the right title, because privileges come along with the territory. Whether it is selecting any item available at a Country Club gift shop to receiving CD, DVDs and items from Oscar winning actors, or piles of designer furs, coats, clothing and accessories, it all is offered along the way.

Serberus wanted Anni to be a "silent" figure head, to report back to her and Cheryl with limited authority. In no way was Anni to respond to the media and give them sound bites direcly. On the other hand, Anni confirmed Sonny was quoted in the media including the prestigious New York Times about giving the media access to Miss Patriotic and made off-the cuff remarks about the idiosyncrasies of the women she traveled with over her eighteen years.

Although Sonny appeared in a handful of photos taken by the press and others, she was well-received being extremely conversational and ended up making many connections over the years. She was not considered a threat because she is an aged woman. Her looks were faded, teeth yellowing and she was Grandmotherly in demeanor and in life. To Serberus, Sonny can do no wrong. There is certainly an incongruous nature between Sonny's role and Anni's.

Anni observed, over her brief stint with the Miss Patriotic Organization, that Sonny dressed outside the realm of business casual. This style went against the idealism of Serberus' guidelines for Anni, made obvious after she was ridiculed for her choice in outfits. Where as, Sonny frequently traveled in her Keds sneakers and jeans.

Another taboo Anni witnessed along the way, Sonny pulled the last-minute cancellation of her responsibilities as escort to Little Miss to the midnight interview on that rainy night in Washington, DC. Anni was put on the spot, yet rose to the occasion.

Serberus, on behalf of the organization, did not question Sonny's judgment to make the switch. However, following that appearance, Serberus railed into Anni for questioning the Producers's intent about the content of material and duplicity of interview. Anni had Little Miss' best interest at heart, to be sensitive to the time, her need to get some sleep and to get them to call a taxi for Little Miss' safe return to the hotel.

Also, Serberus accused Anni of drinking on the job and had her written-up for this and other infractions. The accusation of drinking was unwarranted, as Sonny Bergone, also had wine with dinner at the same USO gala and at other venues. Sonny was not judged, nor, were Cheryl's actions, who had purchased wine for herself and Anni at the Christmas luncheon, knowing she had to drive an hour away afterwards. She also had no issue with all the champagne on the table at the Sunday brunch.

When Anni had one cocktail on a travel day, Serberus was splitting hairs. They were not appearing that day, just merely traveling to another locale. Obviously, Little Miss provided information to Serberus, who attempted to build her unreasonable case against Anni.

In addition, Serberus used the pettiness of her pen to write that Anni showed a lack of initiative when she did not provide her undivided attention to the chaperones at the Homecoming Hospitality reception. Anni knows she is a consummate professional who has strong social and interpersonal skill. She made an effort to introduce herself and find out who the people are around her regardless of title, age or demographics. There certainly was no rule or guideline highlighting she can only associate with judges and chaperones when in those environments. Anni recognizes, the hotel reception was a laid-back after-hours get-together, not a scheduled appearance. Serberus does not care, rather intends to stir up dissension.

During the initial meeting with the Senior executives from "The Nation's Most Wanted," Anni wanted the team to look well-versed and well-intended, not a bunch of amateurs. Following the meeting, Anni approaches the CEO to reaffirm it was acceptable she made a few comments. The CEO nodded affirmatively that it worked out fine. He certainly did not refute her actions, when she questioned him directly about this. It was a non-issue at that point.

Anni could not believe how tongue-tied her own CEO was in getting his voice heard. The CEO sat in his own silo, unable to come-up with any response. The extreme, dead silence for long stretches of time was inappropriate, Anni took initiative by setting the tone of the meeting with examples and timelines after the TV Senior Producer, questioned the Miss Patriotic Organization team what the point of the meeting is anyway.

Cheryl exaggerated the situation to Serberus, that Anni overstepped her bounds. This gave Serberus more fuel to ignite her discord for Anni. Cheryl, verbally slapped Anni on the hands for taking the lead and Serberus' noted in her report…"Your role is to observe, record information…not to speak."

Anni could not believe that in hindsight the organization tells her to speak only when spoken to. This certainly is archaic and not a way to perpetuate the leadership ability of young, talented professional women!

* * * * * * *

Fast forward to June 28, Anni was working out at her hometown gym and doing her normal multi-tasking: doing the elliptical machine and reading the newspaper. She finds an intriguing story. The headline read: "Miss P Dumps AC"…Anni's former boss Cheryl Pearson noted as spokesperson, verifies the notion that the Miss Patriotic Organization is abandoning its roots in Atlantic City to down-size to the sleepy, inland town of Linwood. The report highlighted that the organization never rebounded from its lack of television partnership and is slipping into oblivion.

Miss Patriotic had been the pride of the Atlantic City boardwalk and a piece of Americana. First, the separation began when then pageant for more than 80 years was held by the seaside, then stripped away to appease the Hollywood moguls for the lavish flair that the West Coast has to offer. In the process the cable group with the "exclusive" four-year contract (transmitted on a cable system not accessible by the original core audience) abandoned them in South Jersey. These are the folks who supported and volunteered with the organization and pageant in the Delaware Valley and in the Atlantic City area especially.

Since the CEO's status changed at the organization from interim CEO to full-fledged what actions have been taken to move things forward? Tremendous reductions, Anni concludes.

Folks comment to Anni, following her job loss that Miss Patriotic is "past her prime." Her heyday was decades ago, somewhere in the 70's. The pageant is lost in time. The scholarship awards don't even fall in line with the current cost of education, Anni's neighbor states.

* * * * * * *

For months there were articles proclaiming some South Jersey Mayors were not open to considering alternate sources of material to renovate the aging boardwalks in their respective towns. The boardwalks need maintenance and innovation to literally support the many seasonal shore seekers. Innovate or lose opportunity.

Similarly, the Miss Patriotic Organization failed to innovate, let its foundation go-the volunteers and audience from the Atlantic City area by alienating them: moving the pageant out of town, then putting the show on a cable station they could not receive in their viewing area. Trying to regain a warm reception for the Miss Patriotic pageant has been overshadowed by the sandstorm they created. The Miss Patriotic Organization's original foundation: the Atlantic City boardwalk viewing the entire horizon with its pride and pagenatry faded, nearly into oblivion.

The headquarters of the Miss Patriotic Organization relies on Serberus' skewed observations of reality. In the meanwhile, she remains overwhelmed in the undertow of the waves, unable to adapt to trechnology and all things new, instead stuck in "back in the day" mentality.

Not only did Serberus lead the charge on usurping Anni's ability to operate efficiently, but she also tainted the perspectives of Cheryl Pearson and the CEO about Anni's contributions. Anni is an assertive, decisive maven and is adaptable to trying new environments and approaches to enhance business. She proves this when she finds a more effective way to instantly download the digital photo files to the network compressing the time span from a month to a matter of hours. Serberus clung to her old-style work habits. Sonny barely knew how to maneuver with the laptop and did not upload the photos, but relied on the PR coordinator to compile her information.

Anni realizes, the final communication from the Organization, was when the PR contact made Anni update her login for the network when she was in D.C.; the guise to update the passwords for security, the reality to lock Anni out of the system forever!

In life's encounters there are those along the way who are not interested in perpetuating the success of others. Serberus does not have a positive connection to the pageant system anymore and her personal life is fleeting too. She is a pathetic widow with no family and her life is decaying along side of an American institution in disrepair.

Serberus' only sense of control and recognition is at the expense of people. Through the Miss Patriotic Organization, Serberus became an effective manipulator, since others, like Pearson, relinquished their authority to focus on their personal matters. Little did Anni know Serberus' limited replies would come back to haunt her.

In the meantime Anni decides to move on and find ways to offer random acts of kindness and see beauty in simpler things. Anni reflects, it was a brief and fantastic voyage visiting various parts of the nation and meeting diverse people within it. Anni would not trade her experiences for the world!

Likewise, she appreciates Little Miss' closing remarks posted on her blog:

"I've experienced more ... than I ever dreamed possible, and I know that the memory of this amazing time and the people who were a part of it will live in my heart forever."

Anni is confident she is one of the people she is referring to who helped Little Miss evolve towards her next opportunity for greatness.